GIRL
IN
THE
DARK

GIRL IN THE DARK

A NOVEL

Marion Pauw

wm

WILLIAM MORROW
An Imprint of HarperCollins*Publishers*

This book is a work of fiction. The characters, incidents, and dialogue are drawn from the author's imagination and are not to be construed as real. Any resemblance to actual events or persons, living or dead, is entirely coincidental.

HarperCollins books may be purchased for educational, business, or sales promotional use. For information please e-mail the Special Markets Department at SPsales@harpercollins.com.

A version of this text was originally published in the Netherlands in 2009 under the title *Daglicht* by Ambos|Anthos *publishers,* Amsterdam.

This text was translated from Dutch to English by Hester Velmans.

Designed by Leah Carlson-Stanisic

Title page photograph by Glebstock/Shutterstock, Inc.

Library of Congress Cataloging-in-Publication Data has been applied for.

ISBN 978-0-06-242479-2

978-0-06-245869-8 (international edition)

16 17 18 19 20 OV/RRD 10 9 8 7 6 5 4 3 2 1

FOR NADJA AND JIRI

GIRL
IN
THE
DARK

CHAPTER 1

RAY

There's not much difference between transporting a prisoner and moving a load of hogs. They have to get to their destination in one piece. And that's all, really.

I was handcuffed. I felt uncomfortable and clumsy. It took all my concentration not to lose my balance as I climbed into the van. My escort, a guard with a square-shaped head, gave me a shove. It wasn't deliberately brutal, just rough indifference.

"Hurry up." The only words addressed to me directly. I staggered, regained my footing, and sat down on the leatherette seat.

Ostentatious jingling of keys. The scrape of metal on metal. The cage clanged shut; I was being moved inside a cage.

I'd been locked up for eight years. I had grown partial to the monotonous rhythm of my days, but I had never gotten used to the bars.

The van's windows were shaded. I was seeing the outside world again for the first time, only through a dark, gray film. Still, I'd been looking forward to the trip. To see cars driving along, and trees, and teenagers riding their bikes into the wind. Maybe even a train racing us alongside the highway. Or boys on top of the overpasses yelling at the cars whizzing by below. The kind of things you don't get to see on TV because they're too commonplace, but that make you even sicker with longing for the world outside.

The van set off. I was being transferred from the prison in Amersfoort to the Hopper Institute in Haarlem.

I hadn't quite figured out if my transfer to the forensic psychiatric unit was something to be happy about. I'd had far too much time to think about it, the same way I had far too much time to do everything. There were days when I felt optimistic. A less strict regimen. A cell all to myself. More diversity in the daily routine. One step closer to freedom.

And then there were days when I was so angry and frustrated that I couldn't see the plus side of anything anymore. When I just wanted to get home to my fish. I was very worried about my fish. At night I'd picture them floating belly-up. A stinking pile of *zebrasoma, holocanthus,* and *amphiprion.* I'd yell and scream until the entire cell block was awake.

"It's the nutcase again."

"Yo, freak, shut the fuck up!"

"I'll get you tomorrow—you better watch your back, motherfucker."

But in actuality, no one ever laid a finger on me, not once. It wasn't like on those TV shows. The prisoners spent the greater part of the day just bullshitting. Every now and then a scuffle would break out over something minor, like a missing pack of cigarettes. But rape wasn't their thing, and nobody knocked anybody's teeth out to get better blowjobs, either.

Instead they just made fun of me. Once, when I was in the shower, I had my clothes stolen. I sometimes had my mother's monthly letter ripped out of my hands and read out loud in the rec room. My food was spat on almost daily. But did they ever touch me? Never.

If I wouldn't stop screaming, the guards would make me swallow a pill to calm me down. And the next day everyone would act as if nothing had happened. Sometimes they simply ignored me. Months would go by when nobody would sit next to me at mealtimes. It didn't bother me. All I ever wanted was to be left alone.

The A28 and A1 highways hadn't changed much since 2003. I pressed my nose to the window and tried to take in as much as I could: the clouds (though in prison I'd seen plenty of those), the meadows, and the water especially.

"Hey! Stop sliming up the window," said the guard. He was sitting next to the driver in the passenger seat and had twisted around to look at me. "Sit up straight."

I wanted to look out. I wasn't about to let them take that away from me after all I'd been deprived of already.

"A bad attitude means leg irons." The guard turned to face the front again. "*Asshole.*" He said it under his breath, just a barely perceptible distortion of the mouth, but I heard it. Of course he wasn't allowed to say that sort of thing. I had read the rulebook. Too much time on your hands makes you do things like that. It said that a prisoner's escorts had to make sure that "the transport not heighten existing stress levels."

I was used to being cussed at; I'd been subjected to far worse. So you could argue that the word *asshole* didn't heighten my stress level, and so the guard hadn't done anything wrong. But it was certainly open to question. I thought about writing a complaint. Though in the institution I wasn't sure if I'd still have too much time on my hands. I was being sent there for court-ordered rehabilitation, after all—I'd be undergoing therapy so I could be reintegrated into society someday. Or so the pamphlet I'd received some weeks before my transfer said, anyway.

"Do you know who this is?" the guard asked the driver, with a jerk of the head in my direction.

I doubted they were allowed to talk about me in my presence.

"It was all over the papers, remember it? Freak here gets rejected by his pretty little neighbor and goes berserk. First he takes it out on the lady herself, then on her little girl, only four years old. Once he's done hacking and slicing, he lights up, cool as a cucumber. Stubs his cigarette out on the dead kid. Can you imagine?" The guard turned back toward me. "I bet you liked that, didn't you? Did it give you a hard-on?"

I pressed my nose against the window. There was an SUV driving alongside. Two little kids were belted into zebra-print car seats in the back. A boy and a girl, twins by the looks of them, about three years old. Both with curly blond hair, and the girl made me think of Anna, the little girl next door. I swallowed, to get rid of the metallic taste of blood in my mouth.

The driver said in a loud voice, "We *could* drive the car into a ditch, let the fucker drown in his cage."

"Accident—ooh, sorry!" The guard glanced over his shoulder to make sure I'd heard.

"And then we'll just sit there and have a smoke."

"A big fat joint, you mean."

I gazed at the little girl in the SUV. It felt as if we were making eye contact, but that was impossible, of course, since I was sitting behind dark glass. Her eyes were wide open and she had long lashes. Like one of those dolls. Eyes that just stare at you and only shut when you lay it down on its back.

We drove up to a high wall topped with metal spikes. A gate swung open and we entered some sort of dock. For a moment we were stopped inside a fluorescent-lit concrete enclosure. Cameras zoomed in from all sides.

"Smile for the camera!" said the driver. Snickering. The gate lifted and we were let through.

We arrived at a sand-colored, horseshoe-shaped building. The van stopped in front of the entrance. The guard-escort got out, rattling his bunch of keys until he found the right one. Finally, the cage clicked open.

"Get out."

I got to my feet with difficulty. The handcuffs were tight around my wrists; my hands tingled. I almost fell on my face getting out. The guard caught me, but let go again as soon as he could, like a garbage man handling trash.

He herded me ahead of him up some steps. I felt sick. Horribly sick.

Automatic doors slid open. We stepped inside a small hall; on one side was a reception desk attended by a woman with hair the color of a maraschino cherry. She glanced up, then went on with her phone call uninterrupted. Who was she talking to? Was she talking about me?

Another guard walked up to us and began searching me without saying a word. He frisked my body with his big hands. I tried to remain calm. Tried not to let him touch me, even though he was running his hands along my crotch and the inside of my thighs. Then I was led through a metal detector.

A man in a red T-shirt was waiting for me on the other side.

"Welcome, Ray," he said. "Welcome. I'm Mohammed de Vries, a social worker in the orientation unit. That's the unit you'll be in for the time being. You can call me Mo."

"Mo," I repeated. I knew his kind. The jolly ones. The ones who pretend to be your friend at first and then drop you without a word.

"First I'm taking you to the medical station for drug and alcohol evaluation. After that you'll be going on to the orientation unit."

"Can't the handcuffs come off?" I asked.

"Not yet."

"Why?"

No answer.

"Why not?" I asked again.

"Will you sign for him?" The guard shoved a clipboard under the nose of the man I was allowed to call Mo. Mo printed his name and then signed. "Just like taking delivery of a FedEx package, eh, Ray?" He winked.

"Okay, then, later." The guard left through the sliding doors.

"Walk with me?" asked Mo.

As if I had a choice.

CHAPTER 2

IRIS

I am a professional. Or, at least, I start each day resolving to be. Even when that includes having to represent middle-aged men who do nasty things to naive young women and fatten their wallets while doing so.

I had agreed to meet Peter van Benschop at one of those overpriced restaurants in the Financial District. He was seated by the window, tapping away on his smartphone. It must be said that Peter van Benschop was a lot less dignified than the rest of the Van Benschops. The only child not involved in the family's thriving shipbuilding business.

"Mrs. Kastelein, so nice to meet you." He rose to his feet and spoke so loudly that I wondered if he had a hearing problem. His handshake was, predictably, crushing.

We sat. I slung my handbag over the back of my chair, folded my hands, and said politely, "Mr. Van Benschop, what can I do for you?"

A waiter came and inquired what we would like to drink. I asked for a glass of fresh orange juice. Van Benschop ordered a double espresso.

"I take it you've had a look at the case?"

"I've read the letter from the plaintiff's lawyers, yes."

With a smirk: "And the DVDs?"

"I have received those, too."

"And?"

"It isn't my favorite form of entertainment, let's leave it at that. But from a legal point of view it's an interesting case."

"You think I'm a pervert, don't you? A dirty old man."

"Is that how you would describe yourself?"

"No, but that's how *you* see me."

I gave it some thought. He had a point. But then I smiled and said, "You're not that old, surely."

"Go on, admit it. You find me revolting. You think I like to hurt women. And yet I get stacks of fan mail from women. Highly educated, intelligent women like yourself."

The waiter brought us our drinks. "Have you had a chance to look at the menu?"

"I'd like a cup of tomato soup, please," I said.

"The club sandwich with fries. Ketchup, hold the mayo."

The waiter nodded pleasantly and left us.

"There are plenty of mixed-up people in the world. Even women. As your fan mail just goes to show." I took a slow sip of my OJ.

He laughed. "Do you have to be mixed-up to like sex, Iris?"

"No, but your sexual tastes are a bit more . . . extreme, wouldn't you say?"

"Well, guess what, Iris? Women like it. A lot."

"Some *deeply troubled* women, maybe," I said.

"Don't those women have a right to some fun, too, some pleasure in their lives?"

I couldn't help but speak my mind, although I would definitely hear about it later from Rence. "So now you're some sort of philanthropic do-gooder concerned with the psychological welfare of your fellow man?"

"Maybe."

"Let's talk about your case. Are you aware that using underage actors in X-rated films is illegal? It's child porn."

"Her ID said she was eighteen. And her cunt was definitely of age. No question about that."

I wished Van Benschop would keep the volume down a bit. "Do you mean to say she had a forged ID? Did you keep a copy of it?"

"Sure."

"I need to see it. As soon as possible."

"Tsk. That's a problem. My partner has it."

"In that case, could you ask *your partner* to produce it for me? If we can show that the girl—"

"*Girl,* my ass. Young woman. I insist that you call her a 'young woman.' "

I gave him what I hoped was a resolute smile. "If we can show that the *young woman* misled you with forged identity papers, that would seriously decrease the chance you'll be found guilty of producing child porn. And besides, it would prove the *young woman* had participated of her own free will."

"My partner disappeared—with the contracts and a portion of my investment." Van Benschop slurped his espresso and laughed. "But don't you worry, you'll get your money. And maybe I'll even throw in some extra for a little celebration afterward. Have you ever been to the Bahamas?"

I wondered again why I had been assigned this case. My boss had argued that assigning a female attorney to Van Benschop was a brilliant move. And Martha Peters, the other partner at the firm, just happened to be *too busy*, even though she was the one supposedly handling all the Van Benschop family's affairs, and making a big hoopla about it, too.

"To get back to your case: the fact that you don't have access to a copy of the ID does make it a bit harder. I take it that the"—I was going to say "victim" but managed to control myself—"the *young woman* signed a release, a quitclaim detailing the nature of her"—again I had to search for the right word—"work?"

My phone started buzzing in my pocket. I glanced under the table at the number on the screen. It was the one I dreaded more than any other number in the world: Aaron's day care.

"You really ought to go there sometime, the Bahamas. The ocean's simply glorious," Peter van Benschop continued.

"Excuse me. I have to take this." I stood up and walked outside. "Hello?"

"It's Mika." Her voice sounded hysterical. I knew exactly how she felt, even if all I could think was: *Please, not now. Just deal with it yourselves. Let me do my job. Please.*

"Aaron's gone ballistic. He was coloring, and when one of the younger kids snatched away his crayons he bit her hard. Broke the skin—she was bleeding and everything. Now he's bonking his head on the floor and won't stop. Petra says you've got to come pick him up. *Now.*"

It was clear there was no point trying to negotiate. Let alone say, "I spend a substantial portion of my after-tax income entrusting my child to your care three days a week. Can't you just see it through for once?"

"*Now,* Iris," she repeated. As if I hadn't heard. "Not in half an hour. Right now."

"I'll do my best."

The first person I called was the Procreator, even though I knew there wasn't much point. I'd heard from mutual acquaintances that he liked to complain tearfully about how little he saw of his son. But I got his voice mail, as usual. Next I called my mother. She was having a pedicure but promised to come pick up Aaron from my house as soon as her toenails were dry.

"Can't you come sooner than that? I'll treat you to another pedicure. I'll throw in champagne and a foot massage. Please?"

"Sorry, darling. I just can't."

I wished that I could say the same thing. How wonderful it would be to say, "I just can't"! "Mother, I'm with a client. Do you have any idea what it looks like if I just get up and leave?"

"You don't really expect me to drop everything, do you? I'm happy to help, and I do that often enough, in case you've forgotten. But Aaron is *your* responsibility. You *are* his mother, after all."

"No need to tell *me*," I snapped. I noticed Peter van Benschop observing me through the window with an amused expression on his face. He raised both hands as if to say, *What's keeping you?* I turned my back on him. At the same time I heard my mother snort, "Well?"

"Sorry." I hated having to apologize to her. Which happened all too frequently. "Okay, I'll pick him up and take him home, but please come get him as soon as you can. Please?"

"I'll do my best," she said loftily.

I hung up, and instead of screaming and hurling a brick through the window at Van Benschop's aggravating mug, I took a deep breath. I squared my shoulders and marched back inside.

"I started without you," said Van Benschop as he motioned to the food that had appeared while I was on the phone. "It was taking so long." His top lip had a piece of lettuce stuck to it.

"I'm so sorry, but you'll have to excuse me. It's an emergency."

"Your kid, I'll bet."

"I'll call you this afternoon to make another appointment. Again—so sorry."

"Single mother. It's easy to tell. I'm an expert at reading women. I can also tell that you prefer black underwear. And I bet you try reading at night before going to sleep but you always nod off with the book in your hands."

I suppressed a sigh of annoyance. "I'll pay the check."

He grabbed me by the wrist. "I've never let a woman pick up the check in my life. I'm not about to start."

"Company policy." I jerked my arm loose and took out my credit card. "I'll call you this afternoon."

I'd been told that a child enhances your emotional life. There was some kernel of truth in that. Ever since I'd had Aaron, I was often overtaken by a feeling of total incompetence.

It was the third time this month I'd had to pick up Aaron up early because he'd misbehaved. There had been other incidents as well, but my mother had been able to fill in.

I was thinking about the Procreator, who only had to worry about his son every other weekend but somehow still considered himself to be the perfect gentleman. After all, he had legally acknowledged the kid as his, and he did pay 250 euros a month in child support. It felt like hush money. We had contributed equally to Aaron's conception, yet my life had changed forever while he was able to go on just as before.

I could have spared myself a lot of misery if I hadn't had Aaron. But I was fourteen weeks along when I discovered I was pregnant. That's what you get when you work sixty hours a week. You don't have time to keep tabs on your menstrual cycle. Meetings, reports, lawsuits, deals all coming at you in such rapid succession that in the end you have no idea what you're doing, and yet somehow or other you manage to get it all done, and done damn well, too.

I had an ultrasound. On the monitor I saw little arms and legs waving. A heart beating. A real baby. How could I have that removed?

The Procreator hadn't been charmed, to put it mildly, by the prospect of fatherhood; he gave me hell for it, claiming the kid *probably wasn't his anyway,* since he certainly wasn't the only one I'd slept with. Didn't I want an abortion? he had asked. He had even offered to help pay for it, which was ridiculous, seeing that abortion is free in the Netherlands. He wrapped up his argument with the complaint that it had been the worst sex he'd ever had. My career, my figure, my entire life down the drain, and then to have to listen to that kind of crap . . . I didn't want to let it get to me, because it was so terribly childish. But it *did* get to me. So I told the Procreator he could go fuck himself.

Back in those days I still had some sort of survival instinct. I might be alone, but I was young, strong, and smart; I could handle it. I'd be the poster child for the tough, independent woman with a simply *adorable* child. I'd be mother and father, both caretaker and provider. I was proud of my swelling belly. Wept with joy when I first held Aaron in my arms. Wept with despair when a few days later I hadn't snatched more than two hours of sleep in a row.

One month after Aaron's birth I received a letter. The Procreator was indignantly demanding to have contact with his child. I didn't object.

He paid us a visit, with his mother. She had a grim, determined look in her eyes; the Procreator came trotting along behind. I wasn't in the mood to offer them baby-blue-and-white sugar sprinkles on toast to mark the happy arrival of a newborn.

Without asking, the Procreator's mother snatched Aaron out of the crib and shoved him into her son's arms. He just stood there. He had no idea what he was supposed to do with the baby, and I had no idea what to say. But his mother did. She had the whole scenario down pat. In a solemn voice she intoned, "This is your daddy, Aar*on*," pronouncing the name wrong, with the emphasis on the last syllable. I'd have giggled if I hadn't been so exhausted.

"It's *Aa*ron," I said.

"We'll need to get used to your name, of course," she cooed at the baby.

"Mother, please," said the Procreator. To me he said, "I like his name—*Aa*ron."

We smiled at each other cautiously.

Since then the Procreator and I had found a way to get along. As it turned out, we were quite capable of exchanging information in a normal conversational tone, along the lines of "Aaron's already had his bottle," or "He refused to go to sleep, and then he smeared poop all over the walls." Sometimes we'd even have a cup of coffee together, although the Procreator was determined not to give me *any hope*—as a mutual friend informed me.

I had been attracted to the Procreator only once in my life, and that was after the consumption of a fair number of cocktails at a New Year's Eve party four years earlier. The arrogance of the man, to assume I was just dying to have a relationship with him, irked the hell out of me. Still, I was glad he didn't want to give me *any hope*. The alternative, it seemed to me, would have been exhausting.

When I arrived at the day care center, Aaron was in a corner, playing with a stack of brightly colored blocks. When he caught sight of me, a big smile came over his face. "Mommy!" He ran clumsily up to me, the way three-year-olds do, and flung his arms around my neck. I picked him up and cuddled him. He smelled so good—I could have picked his smell out of millions.

"Hey, sweetie pie! Having fun?"

Aaron proceeded to demonstrate to me how a tower of blocks collapses if you pull out the bottom one.

"Clever boy!"

He was immediately so intent on his game that he didn't notice me walking away. Petra, Mika, and Emily were preparing fruit for snack time on the kitchen island in the center of the space.

"All appears to be well now," I said to Petra, the buxom mother superior of the team of twentysomething, pierced-navel day care workers, none of whom I could believe would actually want to spend their days doling out Play-Doh to a gaggle of three-year-olds.

"Yes, because he knew you were on your way," Petra replied in a withering tone.

I took a deep breath. "I realize Aaron sometimes gives you a hard time. I know you try your best, and I'm full of admiration for the way you run this day care. But I just cannot drop everything and come running for every little thing—today I was in a very important meeting with a client." I was trying to talk to her as pleasantly as I could manage. *We're both adults and can discuss this reasonably, can't we? Notwithstanding the fact that you consider me the worst mother you have ever encountered, with a child who's a little terror. And in spite of the fact that I suspect the only reason you've taken the job of running a day care center is that you can boss around not only the little kids but their parents as well.*

Petra put her hands on her hips. "Iris, biting isn't just a little thing. It's unacceptable behavior. If an adult did that, he'd be under arrest. You, of all people, ought to know that."

"But they *aren't* adults."

"Listen to me. I've been in charge here for twenty years, and I've seen quite a few children come and go. Aaron is an exceptional case. I think you should consider taking him to a child psychologist."

"I admit he can be difficult. And as you know, our pediatrician has already given us a referral and we're on a waiting list."

"It would make a big difference if he weren't able to get away with so much at home. If you'd discipline him a bit more."

Mika and Emily were setting out the fruit. I watched Aaron climb onto a chair and pick up a piece of apple from the plate. He began chewing, content.

"You have no idea what goes on at my house."

"You should be glad we're willing to keep him here. And speaking of waiting lists, I'm sure you're aware there's currently an eighteen-month wait for this day care center."

"Of course I am, of course. I'm very, very grateful. That's what you want me to say, isn't it, Petra? You want me to grovel at your feet and tell you what a true Mother Teresa you are, don't you?" As a lawyer, I was trained to negotiate, to come up with the best argument, to find the correct tone, to touch the right nerve. But when it came to my son's day care, I couldn't do it.

"I think it would be best if you took Aaron home and kept him home for the rest of the week. And then next week we'll just try again." Petra bared her teeth in the grimace of an aggressive ape. "Best of luck."

I had lost. I had lost well and good.

For some reason Aaron did know how to behave with my mother. Probably because, like the rest of the world, he was a little scared of her. Even I was never completely at ease around her. She was sphinxlike. As if there were a number of invisible lines around her that must not be crossed. Only you never knew what, how, or when.

My mother arrived, scarlet toenails peeking out of her white sandals. She listened to my story and then reminded me, in an irritated voice, that she was leaving for vacation in two days, so she couldn't watch him. "Besides, you were going to do something for *me* for once. You were going to watch my house, remember?"

She picked up Aaron and carried him to her car. "You've got this afternoon and tomorrow to arrange something for him. Otherwise you'll just have to take the rest of the week off. Or tell them you're sick."

She belted Aaron into the child seat. That's how you can tell if someone's a devoted grandmother. They have more elaborate equipment for your kid than you do yourself.

"Nobody's going to die from skipping work for a few days. Not even you."

CHAPTER 3

RAY

I was taken to a small room with a urinal and a large mirror next to it. A guard removed my handcuffs. I shook my arms to get the stiffness out.

A nurse without a white coat, or anything to show she was a medical professional, started giving me orders. She told me to drop my pants down to my knees, lift my shirt up to my chest, and then pee into a designated cup.

"Could you please give me some privacy?"

"No." No apology, no explanation, nothing.

I was used to peeing in the presence of other people, but not in the presence of a female.

"I know this isn't fun," said the man named Mo, "but all newcomers have to be tested for drugs and alcohol. There have been some drug-related incidents in here lately."

"I'm telling you again: drop your pants and pull up your shirt so that I can see your stomach." She wasn't wearing a white coat, but she certainly had a bossy voice.

I dropped my pants and underpants, and stood there with my limp white penis. It made me mad. Why did I have to pee in front of this horrible woman who didn't even have the decency to dress right? Why were they doing this to me?

"Easy," said Mo. "It'll be over soon."

"Now pee into the cup," she said again.

I tried to relax in spite of my anger, to let the pee come, but nothing was happening.

"Just take it easy," said Mo. "It'll come."

I felt panic rising in me. In the mirror I saw the nurse staring straight at my crotch.

"Can't she look the other way?"

"No, I can't."

"She has to make sure there's no cheating," Mo explained. "That you don't slip someone else's urine into the cup."

I had no idea how I'd have managed that, and anyway, I wanted nothing to do with anyone else's pee or other bodily fluids.

"It's not working. She's got to leave. Or at least look the other way. I can't do it."

"And everything was going so well—" Mo began, but the woman cut him off: "No more whining, only whizzing. *Now.*"

I saw that Mo was laughing. He was against me, too.

"If you can't pee, you'll be put in solitary until you can," she said.

We had a solitary unit in the prison, too. I'd been put in there once, when I was new and didn't yet know it was best to do what they tell you. They left me in there for three whole days until I couldn't remember who I was or where I was or if I even still existed.

I took a deep breath. Straining as hard as I could, I managed to squeeze out a few drops of urine.

"Just in time. Pull up your pants," the woman said.

Once I was dressed, I was able to think clearly again. It occurred to me that nurses probably don't have the power to decide who gets put into solitary. In prison they didn't, anyway. I decided to find out as soon as I had the chance.

I was assigned my own private cell. It wasn't very big, six by nine feet at most, but it had all I needed. A bed. A desk for writing, although I was hoping that, in here, I wouldn't be left with too much time on my hands. And a shower, sink, and toilet in a separate stall. It didn't have a regular door, just little swinging doors. I'd be allowed to shower, poop, and pee in private, then. It was a definite improvement.

Better than the dormitory in the Mason Home where I spent most of my youth, with its communal showers and toilet doors that were way too small, so you couldn't even take a dump without everyone knowing. There, if you sat on the toilet and farted, they'd all start cheering. They also applauded if you won the masturbation contests in the showers, though I could barely get my penis up when there were others around, and so I never won. But farting was my forte.

Then there was Harderwijk penitentiary, where for years I'd had to share a cell and toilet with another guy. He stunk to high heaven, even though his diet was the same as everyone else's. He'd go sit on that crapper twice a day, producing the worst stench you can ever imagine. You could close the door, but the stink somehow filtered out through every crack anyway. I often complained, even wrote letters about it. Addressed to him, but also to the warden, and the queen, who'd said on TV she wanted to be a queen for all people, and I was still a person, wasn't I?

But my cellmate Eddie just made fun of me. "That's just the way a *real* man craps, Raynus. Smell and learn." The more I complained, the worse it got, until he stopped closing the door altogether and the stink was completely unbearable. The warden sent someone to tell me to stop whining, and I never heard from the queen.

For a whole six months I was forced to inhale that smell two times every day, once in the morning and once at night. In the end my whole system shut down. I got more and more constipated. From an average of one crap a day, it turned into three times a week, and then I couldn't seem to go at all anymore. My stomach blew up like a balloon. I was in agony. I couldn't eat or drink; I didn't even want to move. I just lay there flat on my bed while Eddie kept doing his stinking business with the door wide open.

I was moved to the infirmary and they gave me an enema. It was humiliating and painful, but my bowels finally came loose. The foul smell wafting through the green-tiled bathroom of the sickbay was even worse than my cellmate's stench. That was kind of satisfying, in a way.

When I got back to my cell Eddie had gone, and I spent the last six months in relative peace, although with too much time on my hands, as always.

I had my own toilet once, years ago, when everything was still okay. I loved that toilet. Unlike the one in the boys home or the prison, that toilet was all my own.

"Your things are being delivered this afternoon," said Mo. Startled, I sat up; I'd completely forgotten he was still there.

"Then you can arrange your suite the way you want. Maybe you've got some personal items you'd like to display. Or hang on the wall. We do have a rather strict policy about smut. Tits, okay.

Ass, not okay. The other rules are: no alcohol, no drugs, no cell phones, and no Internet."

"What about my fish?"

"You have fish? What kind?" Mo sat down on the edge of my bed, like a mother getting ready to have a nice bedtime chat with her teenager; at least, that's what I'd seen on TV. My mother had visited me in prison pretty often but had always gone home before it was time for bed.

"I have a saltwater aquarium."

Mo whistled through his teeth. "Expensive hobby."

I didn't know what to say to that.

"What kind of fish do you have?"

"All sorts: surgeon, clownfish, angelfish, cowfish . . ."

"I'll mention it to the people upstairs, okay? As long as the aquarium isn't too big, they might allow it." Mo slapped himself on the thighs and stood up. "I'll leave you alone for twenty minutes. To let you recover from your journey and get used to this place a bit. Then I'll come pick you up for your intake with the psychiatrist."

"Okay."

"After that I'll give you a rundown on the daily routine. And tomorrow, if the psychiatrist says it's okay, I'll introduce you to the other inmates."

The steel door of my cell clanged shut. There was a small sliding hatch at eye level. That way they could spy on you whenever they liked.

I counted exactly five paces from the steel door to the wall. Normal walking steps. I paced back and forth a few times to make sure I'd measured right. Then I sat down on the bed and stared at the freshly painted white walls.

CHAPTER 4

IRIS

"Aaah, there she is, my own rising star!"

I was in the reception area of Bartels & Peters waiting for my mail as Lawrence Bartels made his entrance, in the swanky navy trench coat he'd had made to measure somewhere deep in the wilds of Italy. Where exactly was a closely guarded secret, as if the rest of the world would descend on this undiscovered gem en masse otherwise. He flounced up to me with outstretched arms, in the manner of a talk-show host. "Good afternoon, *cara amici.* Come into my office."

I wondered what I was in for; I was almost certain that Peter van Benschop had lodged a complaint about me. Walking out on a client was indefensible, and I had a feeling a trip to the day care wouldn't count as a worthy excuse.

There are few, if any, law firms that are in business to serve their fellow man out of the kindness of their hearts. Bartels & Peters certainly wasn't one of them. It was all about billable hours. Though working here was a great improvement over my previous place of employment, an international mergers and acquisitions firm. There I'd regularly been woken in the middle of the night on account of some foreign client needing to get something done before close of business in whatever time zone they were in. I slogged away many a night with a slice of congealed pizza on the mouse pad. Canceled many a vacation.

When Aaron was on the way, it became clear I'd have to dial it back a bit. Then, as if someone up in heaven had taken a personal interest in my situation, I was offered a job at Bartels & Peters. A stone's throw from my apartment, and I'd have to come in only three days a week, virtually unheard of in the legal profession. It should have made my life a lot easier. But all I can say is: the front lines of the law are a cakewalk compared with the demands of a three-year-old.

Lawrence had an office befitting a successful law partner. A desk the size of a pool table that made him look even smaller and chubbier dominated the room, and an antique Persian carpet covered the marble floor. A baffling but doubtlessly priceless work of art hung on the wall.

"Sit, sit!" Rence boomed, as if he were standing on a stage and had to muster the rapt attention of two hundred audience members.

"Are you going to chew me out?"

"What are you talking about? Peter van Benschop just called me, and he's wildly enthusiastic. He told me he's seldom encountered such a *tough female.* Which may not be all that surprising, considering the nature of his oeuvre, let's say. He's crazy about you."

"So he didn't mention the fact that I had to leave?"

Rence's face fell. He waved his hand, irked. "I don't want to know about it. Haven't I told you over and over again not to be so damn honest? Being *believable,* that's what it's about. Honesty's a bad trait in a lawyer. Don't you know that?"

"I'm sorry."

He burst out laughing. "And don't ever admit you're sorry either. Just don't do that. Ever!"

"If I'm not here to be raked over the coals and beg forgiveness, why am I here?"

"Because, dear Iris, I wanted to compliment you on your success today. That's the one and only reason for this little tête-à-tête—no need to get all anxious. All I wanted to say was: Well done. I don't care what it is that you did; whatever you did, it was a good job, and that's all that matters."

"In that case, thanks."

"Now. Peter van Benschop is coming to the office tomorrow to hear the strategy we're proposing. He'd like to get the whole business behind him by the end of the week."

"Impossible, I'm afraid."

"Excuse me?"

I considered telling him the truth, but decided to simply stick to the facts. "I can't come in Wednesday and Thursday, and Friday is my day off anyway. I can work from home. But I can get less done there than here."

"Had this been discussed?"

"No. Circumstances beyond my control, I'm afraid."

Rence silently shook his head of unruly gray curls, or what was left of them. He stubbornly refused to acknowledge that he was balding.

"I'm sorry," I added.

"I've already told you I don't want to hear any excuses!" he burst out. "Fuck it, Iris. Fuck it all." A ball of spittle was stuck to his bottom lip. With a theatrical flourish he got up, walked over to the window, and stood with his back to me. Eccentric. Flamboyant. Exhausting.

"Then I'm not sorry. Actually, I'm not sorry at all. Haven't you ever heard of emergency leave? Maternity leave? Or should I take all thirty of my outstanding vacation days in one go?"

Rence was speechless. "Okay, then," he finally said. "I've already told you I don't care what you do as long as you're doing a good job. So even if you have to do your work from the North Pole, just do what you have to. As long as Peter van Benschop is happy, and as long as I'm happy with the bill I can send him when it's done."

"Don't worry."

"You'll never guess who my latest client is . . ." It was evening, and since Aaron was sleeping over at my mother's, I was in a bar having a drink with a girlfriend. Like any normal lawyer.

"No idea. The Pope? Oh no, wait a minute." Binnie held her forefinger in the air. "Your mother is finally being charged with irreformable iciness toward others."

"Ha, ha." Binnie and I had known each other since elementary school. Ever since my mother had asked her to say "Good afternoon, Mrs. Kastelein" instead of her usual elated "Hellooooo!" those two had never gotten along. My mother was as prim and proper as Binnie was exuberant and messy. Binnie's real name was really Brigitte, but she hated that name. No one could remember how she'd first come up with "Binnie."

"Go on, tell me." Binnie took a big sip and placed her empty glass on the bar with a bang.

"Peter van Benschop."

"Who?"

"Peter van Benschop of the fabulously wealthy shipping family Van Benschop."

Binnie's eyes began to gleam. "Is he single?"

"No idea."

"But surely that's the first thing to find out when you get a man like that as a client. What's he look like? How old? How tall?"

"In his forties . . . around six feet . . . Now that I think of it, he may be your type. You like a man to be dominant, don't you?"

"Love it."

I almost lost my footing because some guy trying to order a drink at the bar jostled me. He struck me as the type who works in a realtor's office. Ugly suit and an insolent look on his face. White wine spilled out of his glass and onto my chest, right at nipple level. Whether he knew what had happened or not, he pretended to be unaware of what he'd done.

"Hey, watch it," Binnie snapped at him. "You've just splashed your wine all over her shirt."

Turning to face us, he inspected Binnie from head to toe. "Jesus, you're a tall one."

"No? Really?"

I rolled my eyes.

"Wow, are you ever tall," the guy repeated.

"Tall enough to notice you're already getting pretty thin on top. What do you think, Iris? Will he look good bald?"

"Oh, let it go." I took a napkin and started dabbing at the wet spot. I looked like someone who'd forgotten to stuff a bra pad into her nursing brassiere. Lovely.

"I don't think it'll suit him." Binnie put her finger to her chin and looked thoughtful. "He's got such a funny round little head. I'm sorry, but someone will have to tell him. Five years from now, I'm afraid you'll look like a little piglet."

I couldn't help laughing.

"If I were you I'd try to make the best of the few good years I still had. I'd start by trying to act a little less boorish. Watch where you go, and if by chance you should cause a little accident and spill some white wine on a lady, make sure you apologize."

He stared blankly at her for a few seconds. "Cunt."

"I, too, very much enjoyed making your acquaintance." Binnie turned toward me. "Peter van Benschop the millionaire. I can already picture it. I'm *so* ready for a rich man. Because being a journalist is great—it's all that I expected it to be. Yes, I *have* shaken Nelson Mandela's hand, and yes, George Clooney is gorgeous in real life, and yes, I've written exposés about fraud and written impressive articles about shar-pei amphetamine abuse. But I hadn't taken into account that I'd have to get my rocks off on the prestige and the top journalism awards that will undoubtedly be heaped upon me some day. Because the pay is a pittance. How long do I have to keep sharing an apartment with a roommate? And having to cope with tanning product smeared all over the sink or listening to Marie-Ellen screwing noisily at two in the afternoon while I'm trying to make a deadline? Oh, Iris, if Peter and I get married, you can be my bridesmaid."

"Are you also willing to get chained up in an S&M dungeon?"

"What?"

"And get a prick rammed down your throat until you choke, be forced to drink piss from the source, engage in strangle-sex . . ."

"What?"

I paused a moment, for the effect.

"Tell me! Tell! Tell!"

"Peter van Benschop makes very twisted movies. Try Googling the name 'Pissing Peter.' Can't tell you more than that—client-attorney confidentiality."

"Hmm. But is he good looking?"

"If you like a Geraldo Rivera type."

"To tell you the truth, I prefer Mediterranean men with fine, elegant hands. Only they never like me back and it isn't very sexy to feel their erection poking into your kneecaps while you're French-kissing. How's your love life, anyway?"

"The pits."

"Oh, come on. You, who are constantly meeting men in need? If you ask me, lawyer and dental hygienist are the best professions for snaring a man."

"Oh, come off it."

"Men who find themselves in a helpless situation and are completely dependent on you. Vulnerable and scared, they yearn for safety and warmth."

"I can assure you that they don't have romance in mind."

"No, darling, it's *you* who doesn't have romance in mind. Ever since you had a kid, you've decided you're permanently retired from the relationship scene. Wake up! You're young, pretty, independent, funny, and you don't have any obvious physical handicaps. In ten years' time, Aaron won't want to be mothered anymore; he'll be all consumed with motorbikes and girls, and then you'll think: 'What the hell did I *do* all those years?' Why not try online dating?"

"Oh, please."

"If you ask me, you're not at all happy."

I shrugged.

Binnie looked at me with concern. "Are you all right?"

I shrugged my shoulders again. "Problems with Aaron. I'm afraid he's going to get kicked out of day care."

"How come?"

"Never mind. I'm just glad not to have to think about that right now."

Binnie place her hand on my arm. "It's going to be okay."

"That's what I keep trying to tell myself." *Except that it's getting harder and harder to do.*

CHAPTER 5

RAY

I'd been to see shrinks before. Several times, in fact. They'd evaluated me at the Peter Baan Center for Behavioral Health. After days of interrogation by cops screaming their heads off at me, I'd been prepared for the worst. But these shrinks acted like I was their friend. They said they were trying to understand me. They'd nod at anything I said, or they'd make approving *mm hmm* noises.

Those conversations were nice. I'd never been much of a talker, but after everything that had happened, I liked getting it all out.

The report was read out at the trial. How could I have known they'd turn against me? The only shrink I'd ever seen before had been the one at the Mason Home. And that one had been real nice. He'd ask questions like "How are you?" Though I never knew how to answer that. I did feel pretty okay, generally. Sometimes I'd get angry or scared. But usually I felt fine. So that's what I'd tell him, and then we'd talk about the birds in the woods and which shark species was the most dangerous, the great white or the bull. But he never told people behind my back that I was crazy. Because they can come up with all the difficult words they like, but that's what it's about: Are you crazy or aren't you?

Dr. Römerman shook my hand and made me sit down on a

chair across from him. There was a pair of horn-rimmed reading glasses on his desk. And a thick file.

"You've been here for several hours, Mr. Boelens. What's your first impression?"

I had no idea what to say.

"Do you know why you are here?"

"Yes," I said.

"Can you explain it—in your own words?"

"Who else's words would I explain it in?"

He smiled. "Fair enough, Ray. In that case I'll ask you simply to tell me why you are here."

"Because I was sentenced by the judge. And because my prison term is based on me coming here."

"And what were you convicted of?"

"The murder of Rosita and Anna Angeli. On May 17, 2003. I don't know what time it happened."

He jotted something down on a piece of paper. I tried to read what he wrote so I wouldn't be unpleasantly surprised later by words like *psychotic, compulsive, obsessive,* or *dysfunctional.*

"Do you know today's date?

"Sure do."

"Can you tell me what it is?"

"June first." I glanced at my watch. "It's three P.M. or, to be precise, two minutes and twenty-three seconds past three. What else do you want to know?"

"You are very exact."

I nodded.

He wrote something down again. His handwriting was cramped and illegible. That in itself was worrying.

"Do you have any questions?"

I was briefly taken aback. It hadn't occurred to me that I might be allowed to ask questions, too. Once I got used to the idea, I could think of only one question.

"Is keeping fish allowed? I have a saltwater aquarium."

"I'll have to check on that. Do you like taking care of animals? Are you a caring sort of person?"

"I am."

"Are you good at taking care of people as well?"

It was a red-flag question. The kind of question the people at the Peter Baan Center had asked. An apparently casual question, but later they'd draw all kinds of terrible conclusions from your answer. I decided not to respond and focused instead on the horn-rimmed glasses.

"Whom have you taken care of in the past?" the doctor tried again.

"Dunno."

Dr. Römerman leaned back, arms crossed. "I see. Don't you know, or would you rather not answer the question?"

"All I want is my aquarium. That, or to get out of here as soon as possible."

"Of course you want to return to your normal life. And that certainly is a possibility, but in order for that to happen, quite a few things have to happen first."

"Quite a few things?"

"To start with, I need your full cooperation. So when I ask you a question, you must try to answer it."

"I've answered thousands of questions, but the answer stays the same: it isn't my fault Rosita and Anna are dead. And yet I'm still here."

"Mr. Boelens, I'm not here to play the judge. We could spend ages debating your guilt or innocence. However, we both know perfectly well that something's not quite right with you."

I shook my head. If I'd tried to make one thing clear since Anna's and Rosita's murders, it was that I was *normal.* Normal enough, anyway. "There's nothing the matter with me! When will you all finally get that through your heads!" I slammed my fist on the desk. Dr. Römerman's horn-rimmed glasses jumped in the air.

The doctor didn't move a muscle. "Again, we are not detectives. We aren't going to revisit the work of the police or the judge. So whether you are guilty or innocent is not pertinent. I will tell you, however, that it's not advisable to keep denying your offense. It might lengthen your stay here even more."

I tried to take in what he said.

"If you are convinced of your innocence, you can of course file an appeal with the Supreme Court. If there is reasonable doubt, the judge may find in your favor. But even in that case, good behavior will count. That means going to therapy, taking your medicine, and no aggressive outbursts, verbal or physical. And that applies doubly during our sessions. You don't want me to give you a negative write-up, do you?"

I had to go along with something I didn't agree with. But if I didn't go along with it, things would get even worse. It was always the same story.

"Your first evaluation hearing will take place in two years. And if indeed there is nothing wrong with you, as you claim, you will be allowed to leave the hospital."

Two years was a long time. But less time than eight years in prison. "What do I have to do to get out of here?"

"You'll have to follow the rules."

I could do that. I could do that no problem, in fact. "And what else?"

Dr. Römerman gave it some thought. "You like writing letters, don't you? I understand you are very good at it. Your first assignment, then, is to write a letter to your neighbor"—he rummaged through his papers a moment—"Rosita."

"She's dead. Why would I write a letter to someone who's dead?"

"Just pretend you're writing a letter to her in heaven."

"But she's dead."

He sighed. "Just pretend she's alive, then."

"What am I supposed to write?"

"That's your decision. Just write whatever comes to you. Tell her what you think about her. What you're feeling. How you are holding up. How you feel about . . . what *transpired*."

I nodded.

"You may hand in the letter the day after tomorrow, at our next session. But if you need more time, later in the week or next week is fine, too."

More time. The last thing I needed was more time. But I thought about the full cooperation I'd be showing him and said, "I'll get it done."

CHAPTER 6

IRIS

My meeting with Peter van Benschop was scheduled for ten thirty. He arrived right on time, dressed in jeans and an expensive-looking sky-blue jacket.

I had an intern bring him a coffee and took the seat across from him.

"Right, Mr. Van Benschop. I have gone over your case thoroughly."

"So? What did you think? Have you watched the DVDs finally? Can I interest you in a nice little part in my next production? MILFs are a hot seller these days."

"Actually, I was more interested in the legal aspect."

"I haven't told your boss you walked out on me yesterday. I told him we had a very fruitful conversation." He winked. "So now you're really going to take good care of me, aren't you?"

I swallowed my annoyance. "Yes, of course. Let's discuss the case, then?"

"All right, go ahead. So, how does it look?" He took out a notebook.

"To put it bluntly: not good." I gave a nice long pause, in the hope that it would alarm him and he'd stop acting like a clown.

"'The risks you're facing are serious enough to incline me to advise you to settle."

He was quiet for a moment. I was pleased to see his face fall. He started tapping the cap of his gold fountain pen nervously. "What does that entail?"

"You might have to take it down from the Internet. And pay Miss De Boer some kind of compensation."

"I've already paid her. Two thousand euro. Nothing to sneeze at, I'd say."

"Let's go over the case point by point, shall we?"

He tapped his pen again a few times. Then wrote the word *SETTLE* in block letters in the notebook in front of him.

"We are facing a number of possible grounds on which a judge could convict you. The first is the production and distribution of child porn." I saw him dutifully jot down *CHILD PORN.*

"Also sexual abuse, rape, and perhaps even attempted murder." I paused to give him time to write down those keywords, too.

"Miss De Boer will most likely accuse you of forcing her to participate. She'll claim that she was naive and that you twisted her arm."

"*She* was the one who came to *me,* actually."

"Can you prove it?"

He took time to consider this. "I don't know. Maybe."

"I'd be interested to find out. If you are unable to produce incontrovertible proof to that effect, a judge will be inclined to believe the plaintiff's story. After all, an eighteen-year-old girl tends to evoke more sympathy than a middle-aged man with a paunch in rather-too-tight leather pants, wouldn't you say?" I accompanied this with a friendly smile. Peter van Benschop didn't flinch.

"Let's first discuss the fact that Miss De Boer was a minor at the time of her employment. Filming sexual acts with a minor is a punishable offense. It is also a crime to *pay* a minor for performing sexual acts. Consensual sex with persons over the age of sixteen is legal. But paying for it, which puts it into the category of prostitution, is not."

"Ridiculous, isn't it?"

"Do you think so? Do you have children, Mr. Van Benschop?"

He shook his head. "Not as far as I know."

"I didn't think so. Anyway, the one advantage you do have is that the girl didn't look like a minor."

"*Young woman,* remember?" Peter van Benschop was sounding quite agitated. "Young woman. And she had a lot of street smarts, if you know what I mean."

I ignored his remark and went on drily, "Besides, the films you made weren't intended as child porn and weren't marketed as such."

"No, I don't do child porn. Never have, either." He smirked as if he deserved a Nobel Prize.

"That's good, Mr. Van Benschop."

Again he gave his pen a few taps.

"Producing child porn is a crime. The fact that Miss De Boer chose not to pursue criminal charges against you is not to her advantage. It will certainly raise questions in a judge's mind as to her motives."

Van Benschop was nodding enthusiastically. In the dumps one moment, cheerful the next. Just like a little kid.

"The question is, why did she lodge a civil complaint? Why didn't she go to the police? I think it can only mean one thing."

My client leaned forward in order not to miss one word.

"She wants money. A criminal case is one brought by the public prosecutor against the accused. A civil case is where one citizen sues another citizen. As is the case here."

Van Benschop wrote the words *CRIMINAL* and *CIVIL CASE*.

"Now, it is possible to have a civil case heard in criminal court. In that case, the judge's decision will include victim compensation. However, in those cases the compensation is usually not all that great. Leading me to conclude that Miss De Boer has chosen the civil court because she wants money—a lot of it."

"It's always the same story," Peter van Benschop said wearily.

"And you should thank your lucky stars. Because if Miss De Boer were to have you prosecuted, I'd have to wait on the judge. If the judge ruled that rape was involved, or sexual abuse, or one of the other punishable offenses I mentioned, then you could easily get four or more years in jail. And who knows what else might come out once the police start digging into your affairs."

"Such as?"

"You tell me. You mentioned yesterday that you like to go to the Bahamas. May I conclude from that that you keep your money in a foreign bank account?"

He didn't reply.

"*That's* what I mean."

Peter van Benschop tapped his fountain pen one more time and underlined the word *SETTLE* in his notebook.

CHAPTER 7

RAY

I wanted to please the doctor so I could go home. But I couldn't get any words on paper. That night in bed I felt as if I was back in Pain de Provence, the French bakery on Princess Irene Street where I used to work. In the seventies, the baker, Pierre Henri, had followed his summer-romance girlfriend Margaret home to the Netherlands and set up his patisserie in a blue-collar neighborhood. Back in those days, the locals had never tasted a croissant, baguette, or brioche before; they wouldn't even know how to find Provence on a map. But Pain de Provence became a big success anyway. There was an ever-growing line of patrons coming from the fancy neighborhoods on the other side of town.

When he couldn't manage the bakery by himself anymore, Pierre took me on as his apprentice. Margaret, now his wife, manned the store, and had such a loud voice that we could literally hear every single order. "Four plain and two chocolate croissants for the lady. Coming right up."

"Pff, croissants in the afternoon," Pierre would say. "You Dutch people are crazy! In France I sell maybe a hundred fifty croissants a day. Here, five, six hundred, and sometimes even a thousand on the weekend. You people are *vraiment* crazy about croissants."

Nothing I'd learned in baking school was useful, or even correct, according to Pierre. For example, at school we'd used yeast to get the bread to rise.

"Anyone, *tout le monde,* can work with yeast," said Pierre. "Yeast is for a baker who has no *personnalité.* Yeast is for the factory, for the robot, for the baker who'd just as soon have become a bricklayer. *C'est incroyable* that already at school, they teach you to be *mediocre. Incroyable*!"

Pierre used a bread starter his father had given him thirty years ago. For the first couple of years I wasn't allowed anywhere near La Souche, as Pierre called the mother dough. It was kept in a special temperature-controlled cupboard, far away from anything that could endanger it. Pierre would take out a piece of La Souche every day to make the dough for the bread, baguettes, or croissants. After that the mother had to be replenished again so we'd never run out.

La Souche had to be fed at set times and then brought back up to the right temperature. Pierre even talked to her. "How are you feeling today, my treasure? Are you comfortable enough?"

To me, he said, "It's like making wine, Ray. It's all in the timing and the temperature. Remember: time and temperature."

One day he called me over. "Smell." He held the earthenware vessel in which La Souche lived under my nose.

I leaned forward, shut my eyes, and sniffed cautiously.

"Do you smell how sweet she is? Fresh but not too sour? She is what *I* am, Ray. It's thanks to her that our bread is so crusty on the outside and so soft inside. She gives it that fresh, sweet taste. Without her, bread is just flour and water. Without her, it's nothing, *mon fils.*"

He taught me how to handle La Souche, because she was an exacting, fussy piece of dough, "more trouble than a woman," said

Pierre. He taught me exactly what she liked and exactly what she didn't like. What temperature worked best for her, at what time to feed her and how much.

A year later I was given full responsibility for La Souche. Pierre thought I was even better than he was at measuring her food exactly, or getting the temperature just right. He'd never met anyone as precise as me.

After five years I was able to handle the entire kitchen by myself. I started baking at three fifteen every morning. While the baguettes, the *pains aux noix,* the *pains aux céréales,* the *pains au chocolat,* the *chapatas,* the croissants, and the brioches were in the oven, I'd do the weighing. I'd get all the ingredients ready for that day, setting them out in little bowls: the flour, the chocolate, the raisins, the sunflower seeds, the cheese, the almond paste.

Margaret and Pierre would arrive at six thirty to start setting out the freshly baked goods in the store. When it opened at seven and the people from the fancy part of town began lining up, along with a few more sophisticated locals ("They're *crazy*!" Pierre would usually exclaim), Pierre and I would make the dough for the seven different kinds of bread, and we'd bake the *canelés* and *tartelettes.* The afternoon was devoted to the croissant dough. We'd keep folding the butter into the dough until there were hundreds of layers.

"Ah, perfection," Pierre would finally say. *Absolute perfection.*

After I'd been working there for years, Pierre and Margaret sold the business and moved to France. Pain de Provence was taken over by a man in flashy glasses who kept slapping me on the back. According to Margaret, he did that because he wanted to be my friend. After all, without me the bakery wasn't worth anything, *was it?* she said.

The day before they left, Pierre called me over. He was hugging the earthenware pot with the bread starter in his arms. "This is my most precious possession, *mon bébé.* It was given to me by my father when I started my first *boulangerie.* She's made me what I am. Since I don't have any sons, and Margaret is past childbearing age, I now give her to *you.*" There were tears rolling down his cheeks.

Salt is lethal to bread starter. I quickly took the earthenware pot from him to prevent his tears from falling into La Souche.

"Enjoy her. Employ her. I trust you, in turn, will find someone to pass her on to when the time comes. And if you don't, I expect you to destroy her. Will you promise me that, Ray? *Tu me le promets?*"

"*Oui,*" I replied.

After Pierre and Margaret left, the new owner of the bakery decided to renovate. Before, the preparation area and ovens had had their own separate space behind the store. The new owner had decided it would be fun if the clients could see me at work. So that they'd know that everything was fresh and made on the premises and didn't come from a factory. So the wall separating the store from the kitchen was removed and replaced with a glass partition.

Suddenly I had people watching me peeling apples for the *tartelettes* and looking on as I kneaded the dough with calm, deliberate movements. It made me shy. It made me lose my confidence.

Before, every *couronne* I made weighed exactly 525 grams. I made sure they did. It was just one of those things; it was important to me. After the glass window went in, a *couronne* sometimes wound up being close to 600 grams because my hands were shaking when I weighed the ingredients. Or sometimes I let the *canelés* burn. I hated being stared at. Until I met Rosita. From that moment on I constantly kept an eye on the glass wall so that when she came into the store I wouldn't miss a minute of her. Eventually I got used to the nosy glances, and then everything turned out exactly the right weight again.

I'd never had much to do with the people in the neighborhood. I didn't know what I was supposed to say to them. They'd sometimes say hello and then I'd say hello back. That was as far as it went. I was kept plenty busy with my daily routine. The bakery. My fish. Eating. Sleeping. Showering. Cleaning. Laundry. Ironing. Shopping. Breathing.

The day Rosita moved in next to me, the sun was shining. It was hot that day. She drove up in a rusty old delivery van, with a kid in a faded blue child seat and a man with greasy hair pulled back in a ponytail. Rosita and the man hauled a few pieces of furniture inside. A brown sofa set. A small table and two chairs. The biggest double bed I'd ever seen.

The man looked tired and old, even more worn and ragged than the mattress or the brown leather couch. Rosita, on the other hand, was all smiles. She wasn't wearing much in the way of clothes. A pair of very short shorts and a sleeveless T-shirt. Sweat dripped from her dark curls to form a big wet spot on her back. I didn't think she was wearing a bra.

I decided Rosita was the most beautiful woman I'd ever seen. Prettier even than the girls on television, much prettier than the other women I saw in the street. The women on the street all had yellow teeth, and didn't wear bras, either. Only their boobs weren't as perky as Rosita's. They always seemed to be yelling, too. At their husbands. At their kids. At the stray dogs that pooped in their front yards and were responsible for Queen Wilhelmina

Street's nasty smell, especially in the springtime, after the snow had melted.

And why couldn't they take care of their front yards? The neglected front yards really, really irked me. Sometimes at night, before starting my shift, I'd take a pair of hedge shears with me. I couldn't very well tackle other people's gardens, but at least all the hedges along Queen Wilhelmina Street were dead straight.

It was a relief that I hardly ever saw the old man with the weird hair who came that first day. I did regularly see Rosita, however. I liked watching her from behind the dark red curtains my mother had picked out for me. As soon as I came home from work, which was always 3:05 in the afternoon, I'd settle myself in a chair at the kitchen window and look out, hoping to see her.

When it wasn't raining she usually came outside for a walk with her stroller. From where I sat I could watch her walk all the way down the street until she turned the corner onto Princess Beatrix Street.

The way she walked mesmerized me—head held high, in heels that clacked loudly with every step she took. And then her hips. The way they swayed from side to side in silent rhythm. I sometimes counted along out loud: *One, two, three, four. One, two, three four.* She never fell out of step, not even the tiniest fraction of a second.

Sometimes she'd stop for a chat with a neighbor. Or she'd stuff the pacifier back into the baby's mouth. But most of the time she just walked straight down the street without stopping.

The first time I saw her turn that corner, I jumped up and ran over to her house to read the nameplate by the door. *Rosita and Anna Angeli,* it said. The letters were hacked into a piece of brown slate. I must have said her name aloud at least a hundred times: *Rosita, Rosita, Rosita.* It sounded like the name of a savory brioche. With Gouda and herbes de Provence.

My favorite times were when she came back from her walk. Then I could see her face, although I found the hollow between her two collarbones possibly even more attractive.

Sometimes she'd wave at me. Then I'd dive back behind the curtain. Just the idea that I might wave back made me nervous. There was no way that I could.

CHAPTER 8

IRIS

My mother still lived in the house in which I was born, quite a nice bungalow with a garden in a suburb of Amsterdam. My father had passed away ten years earlier, shortly after he'd retired. He had been looking forward to all the traveling he and my mother were going to do, the hours he was going to spend gardening, and the books he was going to read. He wasn't even halfway through *Anna Karenina* when he collapsed. Heart attack. Two days later he was dead.

My mother liked me to stay in her house when she was away on vacation. Since I'd have to stay home with Aaron for a few days anyway, and the weather happened to be good, I didn't mind this time. All I had at home was a six-by-ten-foot roof terrace. Not enough to keep a young child occupied. In my mother's garden there was room for a kiddie pool, in which Aaron could splash to his heart's content with his plastic whale collection while I tried to work under a parasol.

The garden was great, but the house made me nuts. My mother was terribly finicky about her things. She made me throw a big quilt over the sofa when Aaron was there. "I only buy the very best quality," she said. "As long as you take good care of it, it'll last you forever." Every item, therefore, had its own maintenance routine. There was a special soap for the kitchen floor, wax for the wooden dining table, cleaning product for the Swarovski collection, polish for the stainless steel stove, special conditioner for the sofa and chairs; the cleaning arsenal took up the entire hall closet. My mother had left five pages of instructions for me so that her precious things would receive the attention they deserved.

When the weather was nice, the garden outweighed all the trouble. Besides, Aaron loved the aquarium—the ridiculously outsize aquarium that had appeared in the bungalow's living room simply out of nowhere one day a few years ago. Aaron hadn't been born yet. I had just finished my studies and felt the world was my oyster.

"I didn't know you liked fish," I'd said to my mother.

"There's a lot you don't know," she'd answered.

And this wasn't even your ordinary aquarium; it was a saltwater setup with enough bells and whistles to rival the equipment in an intensive care unit. The fragile ecosystem of corals, tropical fish, and sea anemones had to be kept at a constant temperature, not to mention the need to control the salinity, the water's pH, the weekly water change, the special vitamins that had to be administered. My mother had a man come in, naturally, to do the lion's share of the work.

"What's wrong with a nice goldfish in a pretty bowl?" I'd asked.

"Oh, stop."

"Or a dog? One of those cute little dachshunds."

"Sure, and all the fussing and coddling that goes with it? To this day, I can't believe it when I hear adults yelling 'Good job, little poopie!' at their dog as it takes a shit in the middle of the street in broad daylight. Not for me, thank you very much."

I couldn't decide if the aquarium suited my mother. It seemed unnecessarily complicated, but so was the Swarovski collection, which had to be kept gleaming, and the wooden kitchen counter that needed to be oiled every month.

After Aaron was born I began to see the plus side of the colossal fish tank. Whenever Aaron wouldn't stop crying, which happened a lot, I'd drive to my mother's house and park him in front of the aquarium in his infant seat. It seemed to calm him down. The aquarium was his favorite "game"; he loved it even more than Tickle Me Elmo or his Playmobil airplane. He could sit for hours watching the waving coral and brightly colored fish.

For his third birthday, my mother had given him a saltwater fish encyclopedia. Ever since then I'd had to read that book to him every night. Aaron could point to any fish and declare with a delighted expression on his face: "Look, a sailfish blenny." Or: "Doctorfish!"

Sitting in my mother's backyard, I worked on Van Benschop's case. I'd been shocked by "Pissing Peter's" hard-core images. I had scanned the DVDs and then tried to forget them as quickly as I could. Especially since it was clear from the film that the "young woman" was at first hysterical and later completely apathetic. But a contract is a contract, even if Van Benschop didn't seem able to produce it. I did my best to concentrate on creating sound and fluent legalese.

I was just writing the conclusion, in which I invited the plaintiff's attorney to come in for a settlement discussion, when I heard Aaron calling me.

"Mommy! Mommy!"

I realized I had stopped watching him and that he must have gone inside. His voice sounded distressed. I ran inside, anticipating a shattered display cabinet or an enormous stain on the carpet that no cleaning product in the hall closet could ever remove. I found Aaron sitting in front of the aquarium. Where else?

"What's the matter, love?"

"Kee-Kon is dead. Kee-Kon is deh-he-d."

King Kong was Aaron's favorite fish. A large, dark blue doctorfish with a bright yellow tail. It was floating at the surface on its side, its mouth hanging open, as if it were still trying to get one last gasp of oxygen.

A dead fish was a disaster. It meant the entire tank would have to be tested and cleaned. It had happened a month ago. It was the only time I'd ever heard my mother complain about the aquarium.

"Deh-he-e-ad," Aaron wailed again.

"I know, darling. That's so sad."

"I wanna hold Kee-Kon."

"No, we're not going to do that." I decided I'd better call the aquarium guy, who went by the name Maurice. Maurice was an ace *seaquarian,* as he termed his profession. I'd met him on two occasions while visiting my mother. He wasn't exactly the chummy type, but he'd surely know what to do. I found his number written down in waterproof marker on a piece of tape affixed to the top of the aquarium.

Maurice's voice mail picked up. I tried calling my mother but couldn't reach her, either. Every year she and her friend Lina tootled off to some Slovenian health resort, where she had her bowels cleansed, her blackheads squeezed, and her eyebrows plucked, and was expected to swim one kilometer a day. I pictured a stern Eastern European lifeguard standing at the edge of a swimming pool with a pole in her hand, shouting at my mother to keep swimming. Even though my mother hated the spa, she went back every year.

It appeared I'd have to figure it out myself. I lifted the aquarium's heavy lid and used a net to scoop King Kong out of the water. It was looking a bit mottled, its color rather more faded than the deep blue it had been when I'd last seen it swimming around.

"I wanna!" yelled Aaron. "I wanna hold him!"

"Sweetie, fish aren't supposed to be held. Especially not when they're dead."

I carried King Kong into the kitchen, wrapped it in some paper towels decorated with little kittens, and stowed it in the fridge. My mother had sent the last fish that died, Hannibal, to the veterinary department at Utrecht University. I couldn't remember if it had produced any results, but no doubt King Kong, too, would have to be autopsied.

"See him! I wanna see him!"

"He's in the fridge, Aaron," I said. "Let's go do a puzzle, okay?"

"I want Kee-Kon!"

"Remember that shark puzzle? The one with the big scary shark with its mouth wide open so you can see all its teeth?"

"Kee-Kon." But luckily he accepted my hand and walked with me into the living room.

Attention. I had to give him more attention. One of the day care mothers had once said to me that the reason I had problems with him was because I was trying to do too many things at once. "If you just accept the fact that you can't do anything else except play with him, not even read the newspaper, nothing, you'll see that it gets a lot easier." But who in the world had time for that? Besides, the same woman had also told me that when her son had a temper tantrum she parked him under a cold shower. She said it as if she was proud of it.

Still, I decided to follow her advice. For the next two hours.

Both Van Benschop's legal case and the dead fish in the refrigerator could wait.

Aaron and I were just putting together the shark puzzle for the third time—seventy-five pieces that had to be arranged in a special sequence according to Aaron's directions, when the phone rang.

"Hey. I'm on a camping trip," a male voice said without further introduction. I assumed it must be Maurice.

"That's too bad," I said. "What should I do?"

"What should you do? Don't ask me. I told your mother I'd be away this week. Call an aquarium dealer."

"Can you recommend one?"

"Call Sea Water World Van de Akker, in Amersfoort. That's where your mother's aquarium came from."

Mr. Van de Akker turned out to be most helpful. He immediately offered to come over after he closed the shop.

"You'll come all the way from Amersfoort?"

"Sea aquaria are serious business. Can you make sure to have the logbook ready at hand?"

"Logbook?"

"If it's still being kept, that is."

"I'll look for it."

I tried my mother again, this time to ask her how to find the logbook. This time she did answer. After she'd said hello, I heard a loud crackling noise.

"Mother?" I tried. "Can you hear me? Could you please tell me where I can find the logbook for the aquarium?"

I heard my mother saying something, but it was totally inaudible.

"Mother?"

There was a loud buzz, and then the call was lost. I tried her again but got her voice mail.

I'd have to find the logbook myself.

Apart from her phobia regarding permanent stains, cracks, dents, and scratches, my mother hated it if you touched her things. As far back as I could remember, she had a room in her house designated as her study, although I could never work out what exactly it was that she was studying, and the room was always under lock and key. Not even my father was allowed inside.

Once, when I was a kid, in an unguarded moment—I think my mother was in the bathroom—I stuck my head around the door of her Fort Knox. What I'd seen had been disappointing. A desk, a chair, and an enormous armoire. The armoire was crammed with big file boxes. I stepped inside and wondered about their content. I tried to picture my mother as the head of an international crime syndicate, though it was hard to reconcile that with her immaculate perm and her shiny polished shoes. When my mother had caught me in there, she'd been livid. She'd even given me a spanking.

"What are you hiding in that room? What's so terrible about the child wanting to peek inside?" my father asked her. It was one of the only times I remember him actually arguing with my mother.

"You have your office. Iris has her school. Is it so much to ask, for me to want a place of my own, too?" She retreated to her room and we heard her lock the door.

"Let her go," my father said to me. "We'll break in at night sometime, while she's asleep." But of course we never did.

From that day on I kept a watchful eye on my mother, but I never caught her red-handed. I had resigned myself to the idea that the time she spent in that room was for bookkeeping or embroidery. If I wanted an exciting life, I'd have to make one for myself.

The logical place for anything to do with the aquarium would be somewhere in its own vicinity, it seemed to me. I opened the cupboard that held the fish food and pH-testing strips, as well as the replacement filters, the trace minerals, and the brush for cleaning algae. No logbook. I did find the manual for the protein skimmer. On the cover, in neat handwriting, it was marked *R. Boelens.*

Boelens was my mother's maiden name. But her first name was Agatha and her middle name Antonia. A. A. Boelens. Not R. Boelens. My grandfather's and grandmother's names were Truus and Jan, but they had passed away a long time ago.

"No logbook," I said to Aaron. Not that he understood what I meant. "Let's have a look in the bookcase? And in the hall closet? Or, what do you think of looking in the kitchen cabinets? And then, if we can't find it, you know what we'll do?" I picked Aaron up and pressed my nose to his. "Then we'll go have a look in Grandma's secret room. What do you think of that?"

"Kee-Kon. I wanna see Kee-Kon."

"Maybe we'll find stuff that's even more exciting than a dead fish."

I found the logbook in the back of a drawer under the aquarium. This, too, was marked with the name *R. Boelens,* in the same handwriting. I leafed through it quickly. The logbook had been kept since 1990. For thirteen years R. Boelens had kept meticulous track of everything to do with the aquarium. What fish had been purchased, what fish had died, the water's salt content, the temperature. But halfway through 2003 the handwriting changed. Wasn't that the year the aquarium had appeared in my mother's house? Even in the new handwriting, the acquisition of fish and their demise continued to be calmly recorded, as were the water test and temperature notations. The handwriting was a bit sloppier, however.

I had never heard of an R. Boelens. I thought he might be an uncle who had gone into a nursing home. Or perhaps my mother had taken over the aquarium from someone with the same last name. But in any case, it was weird.

It was six thirty—I was just feeding Aaron his dinner of mashed potatoes and pureed green beans—when Mr. Van de Akker arrived.

"Ah, lovely," he said in a reverential voice, as if he were in church. "Truly one of the country's most impressive sea aquaria in private hands. Tsk. I recall that it won the Netherlands Society of Seawater Aquarians' first prize in 2001. I have to say, the aquarium was stunning back then. But it still is pretty spectacular."

"Wasn't it purchased at your store?"

"Yes," he said proudly. "He was one of my most loyal customers back then. You look like him. But your son even more so."

"Kee-Kon," said Aaron, who had toddled up behind me. "Kee-Kon deaaaad."

"Like who? R. Boelens?"

"Of course." Van de Akker stared off into space. "Terrible, what happened. Truly terrible." He took a step closer to the tank and peered at one of the sea anemones. "May I have the logbook, please?"

I handed him the notebook with the cardboard cover. Of course

I was dying to ask him what, exactly, had happened, but it didn't seem like the right moment.

Van de Akker scrutinized the last page. "The numbers are good; I can see that some fresh live rock was added six weeks ago. Another of our little friends died not long after. That could mean the water was contaminated. But in that case it should have affected the other fish, too."

He took out a thermometer, or something that looked like one, and lowered it into the water. He read out the results. "The water's salt content is fine. So that's not it, either."

"Would you like to see King Kong?"

"See Kee-Kon," Aaron emphasized.

"Yes, you can see King Kong, too. Once you've eaten your dinner. So go sit down and finish it."

"No."

"Yes."

"No!"

I grabbed him by the arm and lifted him into his chair. "First you eat, then you can see King Kong." I said it in a calm and friendly voice, the way a good mother should.

The telephone rang. I picked it up but could hear nothing but crackling on the other end. It had to be my mother. "Hello?" I said a few times. The reply was a high-pitched tone. I put the receiver back on the cradle.

In the meantime Aaron had climbed out of his chair and walked back to the aquarium. "No!" I said sternly. "Finish your dinner first." I picked him up and firmly put him back in his chair.

Aaron started bawling. I immediately regretted not letting him have his way. But I had to be consistent. Once you've laid down the law, it's important to stick with it. Every book on child-rearing tells you the same thing.

"Stay in your chair. Do you hear me? You stay there until your plate is empty." I could hardly hear myself speak over Aaron's yammering. I wished I had a remote control to switch it off.

I walked to the fridge and took out the paper towel bundle containing King Kong.

"Here you are," I said to Mr. Van de Akker, loud enough to be heard over the racket Aaron was making.

He put on a pair of reading glasses and examined the fish.

"Sorry about the noise."

"No worries," he said, at an equally amplified volume. But I noticed his neck was starting to show red patches. He didn't seem the type who could tolerate much noise. He surely hadn't chosen to work with fish for nothing.

The telephone rang again, adding to the pandemonium. I picked up the receiver and immediately hung up. Aaron was howling even louder. I went up to him and tried to say in as dignified and stern a voice as possible, although I really wanted to scream, "You really must stop. If you don't stop, I'll make you stay in your room and then you'll never get to see King Kong again. Do you hear me? Stop it!"

He just stared at me, glassy-eyed, and went on shrieking. Like a machine.

I grabbed his arm—a bit roughly, I have to admit. "Stop it! For God's sake, stop it!"

His eyes still had the same glazed look, without a trace of fear or anything even resembling awe. That made me even more furious.

"Okay, then. You're going to your bedroom!" I lifted him out of his chair. He began flailing his arms around wildly. First he swept his plate of food onto the floor, and then he started hitting and kicking me.

"Sorry!" I yelled at Van de Akker. "I'll just be a minute!"

Aaron kicked my hips black and blue and bit into my right

shoulder. But I wouldn't let go. I threw him into his room and slammed the door shut. Unfortunately my mother hadn't provided this door with a key, or I'd have locked him in. I heard him throwing stuff around.

I opened the door. "Enough! Stop it! Don't touch anything!" We had come to the point where I was no longer able to control myself. I stood, yelling at my child hysterically, even with Mr. Van de Akker in the next room.

I slammed the door shut again, pressed my hands to my temples, and took a deep breath. I was being consistent, for Chrissakes. And it *still* wasn't working. Why didn't it work for me? What was I doing wrong? And then I thought the thought no mother was ever supposed to have: What if Aaron simply didn't exist? What if I had just gone home the night he was conceived, what if I had had that abortion anyway, what if another sperm had been just a little bit quicker and I had had an easy child?

On the other side of the door I could hear Aaron raging on unabated, in a frenzy of paper-ripping, head-banging, and shrieking. As if there was a wild baboon in that room. *Too late,* I said to myself. I squared my shoulders and walked back into the living room.

"Well," I said to Van de Akker, who was kind enough to pretend nothing was the matter. We could still hear Aaron howling, but were able to conduct a conversation at a normal volume. I forced myself not to burst into tears of fury and humiliation and asked, "Were you able to discover anything?"

"I'm not completely sure. It could be due to a bacterial infection. If you have no objection, I'd like to take a sample of the water and send this one"—he nodded at King Kong—"to the lab for examination."

"Fine," I said. "That sounds like an excellent idea."

The shrieking stopped abruptly, as if someone had finally found the off switch. I found myself able to breathe again.

"Okay, then."

"About R. Boelens," I said. "Who is that, and what happened to him?"

"Don't you know?" Van de Akker took off his glasses and peered at me quizzically.

I shook my head.

He hesitated. "I don't think I'm the right person to tell you. I, ah . . ."

"Why not?"

"I'm sorry," he said firmly. "I can't talk about it."

"I don't understand. The guy is clearly related to us. My son looks like him, you just told me."

"I suggest that you discuss this with your mother." He ran a hand through his hair nervously. "As far as the aquarium goes, it's probably best to replace twenty-five percent of the water and filter the rest of the contents a few times. I'll call you as soon as I have the test results." He suddenly seemed to be in a hurry to leave.

"Is R. Boelens dead?" I tried one last time.

Van de Akker did not reply.

Aaron's bedroom was a battlefield. He was lying down in a corner with his thumb in his mouth. He looked very vulnerable. Just minutes ago I could have murdered him, but at that moment I felt nothing but that treacherous maternal love.

"Hey." I stretched out next to him and pulled him close. "What was that all about, little man?"

He did not respond, but it was good to feel him close to me, to sniff his deep-caramel smell, and to listen to his breathing. He fell asleep in fifteen minutes. I decided to let it go. Carefully I lifted him into his bed and stroked his tousled brown head.

"I love you so much," I whispered, hoping that he'd hear it and know it was the truth. "More than anyone else in the world. You do know that, don't you?"

I cleaned up the remnants of yet another failed meal and searched the hall closet for the appropriate carpet-cleaning product to remove the vegetable stains from the rug. I found one, too. While the smelly foam was doing its work, I pondered the mysterious R. Boelens. I knew just a few things. That he'd purchased the aquarium in 1990 from Van de Akker in Amersfoort. That the aquarium had been consigned to my mother in 2003. That there was something terribly wrong with him. Something that apparently had to be kept hidden, like a spot that won't come out of the carpet and you cover up with a piece of furniture. *Who was R. Boelens?* I stood still outside the door of the study, which was still under lock and key, and wondered if I should try to open it. I knew, of course, that I didn't have any right to poke my nose in my mother's hidden things. I also had to ask myself if it was a good idea to risk a war with the only dependable babysitter I was able to count on. Once upon a time I had managed to wrestle myself free of her. But that freedom was long gone. I needed her, dammit; I needed her a whole lot.

I stood there for a while with my hand on the doorknob. I could try jimmying the lock with a piece of wire. I could call a locksmith and pretend I'd lost my key. Then it suddenly hit me. Hadn't Van de Akker said that the aquarium had won some sort of award from the Netherlands Society of Seawater Aquarians in 2001? I turned on my laptop and Googled it, together with the name Boelens. I got two hits. The first was a list of the society's members. R. Boelens's name was somewhere halfway down the page. Ray Boelens, name and address. He lived in a small village near Amersfoort. I knew where it was but didn't remember ever having been there.

The second hit was an address list for the Maastricht Soccer boys' youth team. That Boelens was only eleven years old. Him I could cross off.

I said the name out loud a few times. "Ray, Ray Boelens. Ray." The name sounded familiar, although I had no idea why.

CHAPTER 9

RAY

The Hopper Institute was made up of several units, Mo explained. We were on our way from the medical unit, where a doctor had listened to my heart and taken blood for an HIV test, to the orientation unit.

There were two social workers in charge during the daytime; Mo was one of them. Besides hanging out in the ward—Skip-Bo was a favorite game in here, Mo said—you were expected to spend a certain number of hours a day working a job and going to therapy. You were also allowed to work out in a gym and sign up for different activities, such as the theater club or the gardening committee.

At the start, though, I'd be staying mostly in the orientation unit, where I could get used to the place gradually, and where they could observe me and examine me. And then from here they'd figure out which unit I was most suited for. "The institution is divided into units for the various disorders; for instance, people with autism have different needs than people who are psychotic," said Mo.

The institution's corridors were painted in muted colors. Back at Mason, we often played with color. A shrink would show me a color and then I'd have to name it. It could be a real, actual name, like brick red, but it could also be a made-up name, like hubba-hubba, which turned out to be the only pretend name I could ever think of. If you asked me, the walls in here were like the tail fin of an *Arothon hispidus.*

"You'll be taking your meals in here for now. Usually a sandwich or soup and salad for lunch, hot meals at night. Tuesday is french fry day."

Mo took out an ID pass and waved it at a gray plastic sensor. There was an electronic whine and then the doors swung open. "Here's the ward," said Mo. "Think you can handle it?"

The patients, or the *criminally insane,* were sitting at a long table eating their lunch. They ate neatly, with fork and knife, and passed one another the cheese or butter or mustard. All of them looked up when I walked in.

"Boys," said Mo, "say hello to Ray Boelens, the new resident."

I looked down at my shoes. Worn, brown lace-ups my mother had bought for me at the start of my prison sentence, eight years ago.

"Ray-nus," said a familiar voice. "That's our *Raynus.*"

I felt my face getting hot.

"You know each other?" asked Mo.

"Sure do. Raynus with the bunged-up anus," said my former cellmate Eddie. "I'll tell you all about it sometime, boys." I heard laughter. It alarmed me.

"Ray." Mo said my name the right way with extra emphasis. "Would you like to shake hands all around, or rather not?"

"Come on, man, sit down." A heavyset guy with a silver lightning bolt stud in his ear pulled out the chair next to him.

"That's nice of you, Hank," said Mo.

I sat down and Mo took an empty chair across from me.

"Brown or white?" The lightning bolt guy waved the bread basket under my nose. It held tasteless, industrial sliced bread. "The crust and the inside, they're almost the same. *Dégoutant,*" Pierre would have said.

"Brown."

"White bread's so constipating, right, Raynus?" asked Eddie.

"So, Raynus," said a young man with gaping upturned nostrils you could easily push a marble into if you were so inclined. I hated that my old nickname was already catching on. His eyes bulged so wide that the whites showed all around the irises. "Let me guess: you couldn't keep your paws off the little girls."

"I believe that isn't one of your strongest points, either, Melvin," said Mo. "Now, why don't we all let *Ray* here eat in peace?"

I made myself a peanut butter sandwich. Not because I was in the mood for peanut butter, but because the peanut butter was the only thing within reach. I tried to get my knife to spread the stuff smoothly on the bread, but my hand was shaking. They'd all see it and then they'd know I was scared.

"Did you guys watch *America's Next Top Model* last night?" asked a man with a small mustache.

Then to my great relief they all started talking. There were two opposing camps. One side was rooting for Erica, the other for some girl named Beverly. I ate my sandwich and then made myself another one with liverwurst, because that plate had come to rest close to me. The peanut butter jar had flown.

"Which one's your favorite, Ray?" asked Hank, the lightning bolt guy.

"I've never watched that show," I said. "I'm more interested in Animal Planet or the Discovery Channel."

"Let me give you a little tip." Hank leaned his colossal body closer. He stank of stale tobacco and had a fine scar running from the middle of his top lip to the bottom of his nose. He whispered, "You're for Beverly, get it? That would be best, at least for now."

After lunch Hank said he was going to a social skills training session, but was first going to have a smoke in the yard. "Wanna come?" he asked.

I looked at Mo questioningly. He said that was fine. "But after that you may want to go back to your suite for a rest."

The yard was a cheerless gravel patch running parallel to the common room. You could see inside through the glass. Two men were clearing the lunch dishes. In the middle of the yard was a big bucket overflowing with cigarette butts. Hank offered to roll me one, but I declined. The smell of smoke was already horrifying; I couldn't imagine how disgusting actual smoking one would be.

A camera clicked around at us. I looked up and heard it zooming in on us.

"Listen, Ray," said Hank. Now that I was standing next to him, it was even more noticeable how big the guy was. He could easily make mincemeat of me with a well-aimed fist.

"I've been here awhile, so I'm going to help you a bit with the unwritten rules. You'll be taught the official rules by Mo and the other goons who run this place. But I'll tell you what really counts if you want to have a nice time in here—who to stay away from and what to say and what not to say, what you have to do in order to get a leave, or permission to have visitors, especially a certain *kind* of visit, if you know what I mean. You're lucky you have me to guide you. "

I nodded.

"As far as what you've done, I don't give a shit. We've all had our moments of weakness, but you seem like a nice boy." He tossed his cigarette butt in the pail and emphasized, "*Real nice.*"

At that point Mo stuck his head outside. "Coming?"

Hank put his big hand on my shoulder. "Remember what I told you. I'm one of the only ones you can trust in here."

Mo said, "I really appreciate your offering to show Ray the ropes, Hank." But not even a minute later, as we were walking back to my room, he said, "Watch out for that guy."

That confused me. How was I to size up Hank? There was no scale on which to weigh him, so I could decide: too much or too little. Or: just right.

My mother sometimes said, "You're a good sort, Ray." But most of the time she'd yell at me. "Don't be such a sucker, Ray. Can't you see that your friends are using you? They make the trouble, and you get stuck with the blame. Or they'll needle you until you snap and then they can laugh their heads off. You're like a bad TV show. A runaway train. You're always just steamrolling ahead, you don't seem to have any brakes, no inner warning system, nothing. You do such dumb things that to this day I can't figure out what the hell is wrong with you."

Thinking of my mother yelling at me made me have bad memories. Some people down the street had a dog. It was a mean little pest that growled at you and would go for your ankles if you got within its reach. They let that dog roam free and sometimes it even came into our backyard.

I was scared of it. My friends said, "Bet you can't hit that dog with this rock, Ray. Wanna bet? Bet on your momma?"

"What about her?" I asked.

"We're going to pull your momma's pants down so she'll be standing in the middle of the street with a naked cootie. Unless you hit that dog."

I was very sure that I didn't want my friends to see my mother naked. I took the rock from them. It was round and smooth; it felt good in my hand.

"Throw it! Throw it!" they shrieked in my ear. There were at least seven kids crowding me. I couldn't think clearly.

The dog was trotting along a grassy patch about fifteen yards from where we were standing. It was sniffing at a Popsicle wrapper on the ground, still on its leash.

"Throw! Throw it!"

I raised my arm. The rock fit perfectly in my hand. I bent my wrist back slightly.

"Throw! Throw!"

I hurled the rock forward as if my hand wasn't a hand but a catapult. It was my best throw ever. The rock sailed through the air and hit the dog right between the eyes.

The little dog didn't make a sound. It took a few wobbly steps and then its legs gave way. There was a moment of silence.

"Run!" yelled one of my buddies. "Ray killed Bonnie!"

Within seconds they'd all scattered, and I was alone with the dog. I didn't know what to do. The sun was shining and the dog looked like it could jump up and nip at my ankles any moment, but five minutes later it was still lying in the grass, not moving, next to the Popsicle wrapper. It wasn't such a big deal. I decided to go home and play with my Lego Technic.

That night the neighbor came to our door. I was already in bed, but the yelling woke me up. Then I heard my mother's footsteps on the stairs. She flung open the door to my bedroom and screeched, "Is it true you threw a rock at that dog's head?"

"Yes, Mom."

She stormed up to my bed and started shaking me. "Have you lost your goddamn mind? How the hell did you get it in your moronic head to do such a thing? Not a day goes by that you don't manage to do s*omething* incredibly stupid. What am I going to do with you?" She collapsed on the edge of my bed and began to cry. I started patting her hair; I didn't know what else to do. She had very soft hair, the color of the sand on the North Sea Beach, my mom.

But she slapped my hand away and stomped out of the room. I listened to her angry footsteps on the stairs and then heard her talking to the neighbor. I stared at the poster of the universe pinned to the wall above my bed and recited, "Mercury is closest to the sun, then Venus, then Earth," but I knew something was terribly wrong.

Two days later my mom told me that I'd be living at the Mason Home, that it would be good for me. They would be able to give me the help I needed.

"But I don't want to be away from you, Mom."

"You'll thank me for this someday. Trust me." Since she said it with a smile, I assumed that she was right.

But after all the time that had passed, I still wasn't grateful. I asked myself how long it would take before I was finally able to thank her.

"I want to go to my cell," I said. "I'm tired. And sad. But mostly tired."

"Fine," said Mo. "You can stay there until dinner."

CHAPTER 10

IRIS

The street where Ray Boelens lived, or used to live, was lined with dismal fifties-era row houses. After the war, the town planners' focus had not been on aesthetics; everything was squalid and gray. Shabby and nondescript. I parked my car in front of number 13.

"What we doing?" asked Aaron from the backseat.

"We're looking for Ray. Ray is the owner of the fishies."

"Kee-Kon?"

I kicked myself, realizing it wasn't smart of me to have broached the subject. Aaron hadn't asked for King Kong all morning; he had even been behaving unusually sweetly, and I wanted to keep it that way. I sometimes thought Aaron was a bit like a radiator that needs the excess air let out from time to time. After a big blowup he was always remarkably calm and good.

Before he could give King Kong too much thought, I said quickly, "Let's go get an ice cream after this, okay? What would you like? A cone with candy topping or a Popsicle?"

"Candy!"

"Right. That's what we'll do." I lifted him out of his car seat and put him down on the sidewalk. "First you're coming with me like a good boy, to see if Ray is home."

We walked hand in hand to the front door of number 13. The house looked seriously neglected. The front yard was untended, although you could tell that in some distant past it had been lovingly maintained. Someone had once planted lilacs here, hydrangea and delphinium. But the flowers had not been deadheaded; there were weeds everywhere and the overgrown hedge looked as if it might explode.

A worn burgundy curtain hung at the window. It was drawn, although it was nearly noon.

I felt uneasy, but rang the doorbell anyway. Nothing happened. After half a minute I decided to try again. I heard the bell ringing somewhere inside. After what seemed like hours I saw a shadow lumbering into the hallway.

At least four locks were turned. The door opened.

"Yes?" Facing me was a man of around forty in a dirty pair of jeans and no shirt. A pile of mail lay at his feet, shoppers' guides and flyers. A musty smell assaulted me. I had to repress the urge to pinch my nose.

"Ray?"

He didn't respond and went on staring at me aggressively from beneath his greasy hair.

"Are you Ray Boelens?" I tried again.

"He doesn't live here anymore." The man was about to slam the door shut.

"Do you happen to know where he lives?" Aaron had crouched down and started playing with the envelopes on the mat.

The man began to laugh. A loud, unpleasant sound. He struck me as the type who only laughs about unpleasant things. "Hey, there's a good one. Where oh where might Ray Boelens be? Try jail, I'd say. And if he ain't there, you could try hell."

I wanted to say something, but the guy was already shutting

the door. "And tell Mr. Smartypants here to keep his fingers off my mail."

I picked Aaron up and mouthed *asshole* at the door as it was slammed in my face.

As we walked back to my car, I heard all four locks being turned again. "Asshole," I said again, this time out loud.

"Asshole," Aaron repeated, and began to shout with laughter.

"You think that's funny, don't you? And now we're going to get an ice cream."

I belted Aaron into his car seat again and kissed him on the forehead. "What a good boy you are today. Good for you!"

Around the corner was a bakery that also sold ice cream. While waiting in line I watched the baker at work behind a glass wall.

"It isn't as good as it used to be," confided an old lady standing next to me. "The baker they used to have, *he* was great. This one's just so-so."

Aaron and I took our ice cream cones and sat down on a bench across from the store. If Ray really was behind bars somewhere, it should be possible to find out. I could check the aquarium's logbook for the date Ray had stopped looking after the fish. Then I could try Googling again. I realized that I should probably try *Ray B.,* as last names of convicts were always initialized because of privacy reasons.

I took out my iPhone and typed his name. *Slaughtered,* I read. And *Ray B., the Monster Next Door.* In the *Daily Record* I read that Ray had become obsessed with his neighbor, and had murdered her and her daughter because she hadn't returned his love.

I felt sick to my stomach. What was my mother doing with an aquarium belonging to a murderer with the same last name as hers?

The chocolate ice cream was dripping onto Aaron's shirt. I took a wipe out of my bag and dabbed him clean. "You have to lick quickly, sweetie, before it all melts."

The two bodies had been found in the front hall, bathed in blood. The woman had been stabbed fourteen times with some sharp implement, the little girl five times. An innocent little kid. But the most gruesome detail of all was the one about the cigarette stubbed out on the little girl's body. After his savage rampage, Ray sat there puffing on a cigarette. How could *anyone* be so utterly depraved?

The rest of Aaron's ice cream dropped onto my shoe.

I pressed the off button on my phone, produced the last wipe from my bag, and dabbed at the blob on my shoe. It left an unsightly stain. Only then did it occur to me that I should have saved the wipe for Aaron's face.

CHAPTER 11

RAY

I'd been weighing the raisins for *pains aux raisins.* It was a Monday, close to noontime. I was so involved in what I was doing that she made me jump. "May I come in?"

I knew that voice, though she'd never spoken to me before. Rosita was standing in the opening in the glass wall dividing the kitchen from the shop, with Anna in her stroller.

I dropped the bag I was holding. Raisins rolled all over the floor.

"Did I scare you?" She quickly bent down and started picking up the raisins. I got a glimpse of her underwear sticking out of the top of her jeans, a tiny sliver of red.

"Leave it," I said quickly, trying to tear my eyes away from that protruding backside and the dizzying slip of fabric. "Not that I'd leave spilled raisins on the floor, of course. We can't have that, no way. But just leave it and I'll pick it up later. Once you're gone. Not that I want you to go, of course. But you'll want to go home *eventually,* I should think, and *that's* when I'll clean it all up." I couldn't believe how many words had come out of my mouth.

She stood up again and smiled at me broadly. "Sure, hon."

I looked at Anna. She must have been three or four years old.

She was staring at me with big, clear eyes. There was a little snot under her nose. "Would she like a treat?"

"Ask her."

I crouched down by the stroller, and it occurred to me that it was the first time I'd spoken to a child since I'd become a grown-up. "Would you like a croissant? Or maybe a nice *pain aux amandes,* brioche, *tartelette* . . ."

She just stared at me.

"I think she'd like a little bun," said Rosita. "A soft roll. Do you have any?"

"The only rolls I've got have a crust, they're called *petits pains,* that's the way they're supposed to be. But tomorrow I'll bake one especially for her. All right?"

"In that case I'm sure she'd like a little croissant for now."

"A croissant? Would you like that?" I was still on my haunches in front of the stroller and talking in a squeakier voice than normal, the way I'd heard people talking to little children.

"Croissant," Anna repeated. She really was a smart little kid.

I hurried to the rack of croissants I'd just taken out of the oven. One thing I was really good at was making all my croissants come out the exact same size. As if they'd come out of a croissant mold, even though I'd rolled each one by hand. Before the glass wall my boss had even said to me, "Ray, those croissants look *too* perfect. They're so perfect, they don't look as if they were made by hand here on the premises." But once the glass went up, people could see with their own two eyes how I turned the soft, fluffy dough into perfectly sized croissants, and then my boss didn't have to complain anymore.

Even so, I did my best to pick out the best croissant from the tray of identical croissants for Anna, and gave it to her.

She bit into it right away.

"Yummy, isn't it, sweetie?" said Rosita. "And what do you say to our neighbor?"

"Thank you," the child said contentedly.

"I've seen you in here before," said Rosita. "But you never look up from your work. Did you know that people come here from far and wide for your bread?"

I felt myself get hot in the face.

"Aren't you proud?"

"Yeah?"

She burst out laughing. "You're a funny one, but I like you." She extended her hand. "Rosita."

"Uh. . . Ray."

"And this is Anna."

I wondered if I should shake her kid's hand, too, but she was busy with her croissant. The floor was covered in crumbs as well as the raisins. But I didn't care. Not *really*.

Rosita started to laugh. I'd never met anyone who laughed as much as she did. It was infectious. I started laughing, too. At first I was just chuckling along a bit, cautiously, more to please her than because I really had to laugh; after all, there wasn't anything that funny about it, but then it turned into real guffaws. So much so that my boss stuck his head around the corner. "Hey, pipe down in there!"

That seemed to strike Rosita as funny, too.

We went on laughing and laughing until Rosita had to wipe the tears from her cheeks. "I have to go, Ray. And next time I wave at you, you have to wave back at me from behind your curtain. Deal?"

The next day I brought Anna a madeleine. It wasn't a soft roll, because soft rolls just aren't part of a French baker's repertoire, and that's that. Pierre had a horror of soft rolls. "Tasteless, soggy industrial pap. It's a crime that people have to eat that junk. *C'est abominable!*"

I rang Rosita and Anna's doorbell. I was scared, but also excited.

Rosita opened the door. She was wearing sweatpants and a skimpy top that showed the hollow at the base of her neck very clearly. I couldn't keep my eyes off it. She took my chin in her hand and lifted my face up. "I'm up here."

"Uh, yeah." I held out the madeleine. I'd wrapped it in a napkin, then slipped it into one of the bakery's paper bags.

She took it from me. "What is it?"

"It's for Anna. It's a madeleine. It tastes better than a soft roll. At least, that's what you said yesterday. That she likes soft rolls. Madeleines are soft and sweet. I thought she'd like one."

"How very kind of you. Why don't you give it to her yourself?"

She pressed the paper bag back into my hands and walked down the hall into the living room. It was the same kind of hallway as mine. Except that mine didn't have a stroller, and mine had carpeting. She had nothing on the floor. You just walked on the cement. When she got halfway to the living room she turned. "Come on." There wasn't any carpeting in the living room, either. Just the rug I'd seen the old man with the long hair and her dragging inside that time. I also recognized the leather sofa set, the wooden table, and the plastic chairs. There was a photo on the wall of Rosita when she was pregnant. She wasn't wearing any clothes and her belly was enormous. She was covering her boobs with her hands and she'd been photographed from the side so that you couldn't see her privates. But still, she was completely naked. The photo was wonderful and scary at the same time.

"Look who's here! Uncle Ray, our neighbor."

I tore my eyes away from Rosita's naked body and turned to Anna, who was sitting on the couch watching TV. "I am not really your uncle," I said. But she was completely engrossed in four brightly colored puppets that kept saying "Uh-oh." *Teletubbies,* I found out later.

"Anna? Look here?" asked Rosita.

I pressed the paper bag into her hands. "For *you*."

She opened it and unrolled the madeleine from the napkin.

"What do you say?" asked Rosita sternly.

"Thank you." The girl bit into the cake without taking her eyes off the TV.

I watched her little teeth tear off tiny bites of the not-too-sticky, not-too-dry, just-right cake, her eyes still glued to the screen.

"It's perfection," I said. "You won't get a better pastry anywhere. Not even in France."

"Little kids don't understand that sort of thing," said Rosita. "And you can't blame them for it."

I had been thinking so much about Rosita that I hadn't noticed that the social worker with the glasses was standing in my cell, staring at me. It made me feel very uncomfortable.

"I've come to get you for dinner," he said.

I stood up and expected him to leave my cell with me. But he just kept standing there.

"You better hurry up," he said, still not moving, as if he was planning to stay.

I did not want to leave him alone in my cell, but I also did not want to get in any trouble. So I passed him and walked out into the corridor that led to the communal space. I kept looking behind to see if he would follow, but he didn't.

"Come sit next to me, little Raynus." Hank pulled back the chair beside him.

I looked around uncertainly. Perhaps the woman called Jeannie would come to my rescue, but she didn't. She was talking with another social worker.

"What are you waiting for?" Hank was impatiently patting the chair's plastic seat.

I couldn't think of what else to do, so I sat down.

"So, are they not bothering you too much?"

"I've been mainly staying in my cell."

"Your *suite,*" said Jeannie. She came and sat down on my other side. She smelled of lilies of the valley. I wondered if female attendants were allowed to wear perfume in here. I thought probably not.

"You just call it whatever you want, boy." Hank winked. The social worker with the glasses walked into the room and sat across the table. I wished he would not have been in my cell. Even after all those years in prison, I still was not used to the lack of privacy.

Two carts were wheeled in. I could smell overcooked vegetables and burnt meat.

"Shit, are we ever going to get some decent chow in here?" someone across the table complained.

"As if that curry and rice you lot go for is any improvement," said Eddie. "At least this is honest Dutch grub. Which is what you eat if you live in the Netherlands."

"Let's keep it civilized," said Jeannie. "It may not be haute cuisine, but there's no need to argue about it."

"What else should we argue about?" Eddie asked loudly. "About the fact that every day when I go to the library I'm told that the *Seventeen* is out on loan? Again? Who's hogging it?"

"Eddie . . ." is all Jeannie said.

"Yes, my darling?"

"I realize you may get a bit stroppy once in a while. But remember that if you keep this up, there will be consequences."

The food was dished out and passed around.

"There's nothing better than a nice piece of beef." Hank started sawing at his piece of meat. The lightning bolt in his ear quivered along. "Right, Ray?"

I took a bite of potato. Utterly bland, tasteless. *Abominable.*

Hank sent Jeannie a probing look, but she was talking to the guy seated on her other side. Then he turned to me and asked, "Are you expecting any visitors?"

"Not really," I said. "Maybe."

"Oh. Well, if you do expect a visitor, just let me know, won't you?"

"Why?"

He glanced at Jeannie and began to whisper. "Because there are some things you can't get in here. Things you do need, if you get my meaning."

I cut off a piece of meat and stuck it in my mouth. It didn't taste that bad.

"I'll tell you exactly how to smuggle the stuff you need in here. The stuff to make you feel a little better, if you know what I'm saying. But the advice comes at a price. You understand, don't you? Tit for tat, right?"

The vegetables were string beans with the strings still on.

"Hey, Ray." Jeannie turned to me. "Is it true you used to be a baker?"

I glanced around. I preferred that nobody know anything about me. "Yes," I whispered.

"So, tell me. I have a bread machine at home. I follow the recipe exactly, but the bread comes out sticky every time."

"Are you using yeast?"

"Yes."

"You have to use a bread starter."

"Really?" She had pretty eyes, which were gazing at me in a

way that was making me hot all over. It had been a long time since I'd had that feeling. What did she want?

"I can give you the recipe. It's easy to make yourself." I was stuttering a bit.

"Raynus is showing off for the ladies," Eddie yelled across the table, loud enough for everyone to hear. Guys started laughing.

"Eddie, this is your last warning," said Jeannie. "One more violation and you're spending communal time in your suite for the rest of the week."

"Watch out with that one." Hank leaned forward to whisper in my ear. I wished that he wouldn't. His teeth were brown, and I preferred to keep that sort of decay at a distance. "She's the sneakiest one of the lot. But she gets horny as hell working in here. You can tell."

CHAPTER 12

IRIS

"Excuse me? *What* did you say?"

"You know perfectly well what I'm talking about, Mother. *Who is* Ray Boelens to us?" Aaron was in bed, and Slovenia's telephone network was finally granting us a connection.

There was a pause on the other end of the line. An indignant pause, giving her the time to formulate the torrent of words that followed. "Jesus, Iris. I thought something serious had happened. I've tried calling you dozens of times. Don't you know I'm on vacation? And to find it's just some nonsense about some Ray Boelens? Did you really have to bother me for that?"

"Who is he, then?"

"That's completely irrelevant."

"Aha! You won't tell me. That only makes it more interesting."

"Iris, stop it. Don't you have more important things to worry about? Your own son, for instance."

I wasn't going to let her off that easy, even though her comment about Aaron made me seethe. "I can't *tell* if it's important or not, as long as I don't know why you have been taking care of his aquarium for all these years."

"I'm telling you, loud and clear, it's got nothing to do with you.

And if you persist in sticking your nose into my affairs, you'd better just run along home. I'll ask my neighbor to water the plants and take care of the aquarium."

"So—Ray Boelens is your affair, then. In what way?"

"Save your legal tricks for the courtroom."

"What are you getting so mad about?"

"Nothing," she said firmly, and just a bit too quickly.

"Come on. Why can't you just tell me? Is he your brother?"

She hung up. Or else the Slovenian operators had decided it was time to end our conversation.

I tried calling back but got her voice mail. "We weren't done, *Mother dear.* Call me back" was the message I left her, knowing she wouldn't.

If I had to rate her as a mother, I'd say she had been adequate. Not that good, not that bad, not very human, either. My mother had done everything by the book. The cup of tea when I got home from school, nutritious meals, sensible footwear, the right kind of after-school activities, and a nice sum to furnish my room when I left home for the first time. With a mother like that, I had no right to complain.

When we were fifteen or so, Binnie's older brother gave her a joint. She showed it to me in between French and Economics. We used to smoke the occasional cigarette behind the bicycle shed, but we'd never tried a joint before. According to Binnie, her brother smoked practically every day, and it made you mellow.

I looked at the cone-shaped thing. "Where do you want to smoke it? And when?"

"After school, in the park," said Binnie. She made it sound as if it were the most ordinary thing in the world.

"Okay," I said. "Let's do it."

The stuff didn't have much of an effect on me. We passed

the joint back and forth, as we did when we shared a cigarette, sucked at it thoughtfully, and then stared up at the sky, waiting for whatever was supposed to happen. We lay on the grass, each with one of my Walkman ear buds in an ear, listening to Womack & Womack.

"I feel very relaxed," said Binnie. "Do you feel anything yet?"

"I think so."

"Did you know smoking a joint can give you the giggles?" She started chortling experimentally.

"Really?"

"Yeah. This stuff especially, my brother says."

"That would be fun."

Then we started singing along with the music. *"Next time I'll be true. I'll be true. I'll be true."*

I had a slight headache when I got home, and felt sleepy.

"You're late." My mother looked at me with a frown. "Are you feeling okay?"

I muttered something about homework and was going to disappear into my room, but she stopped me. "Where were you?"

She sniffed, widening her nostrils. "Iris, have you been doing drugs?"

I felt myself getting red and knew that there was no point trying to lie.

She stared at me, a shocked expression on her face. I was expecting a sermon, a tirade and being grounded for at least a week. But instead she said, "You and I are going for a little drive this evening. Go freshen up. You stink."

That night we drove into Amsterdam. I hadn't the faintest idea where she was taking me. A shrink, I guessed, or maybe a mental health clinic. But she drove on into the town center and parked the car along the Prince Hendrik Quay. "Get out."

I followed her into the warren of streets and canals of the red-light district, which at the time wasn't the relatively safe tourist trap it is now. There were pockets where even the police feared to go.

The sun set as we walked along the illuminated red windows. I had heard of the red-light district, but I'd never been there before. My mother was coolly strolling along as if she were shopping in the supermarket on a Saturday morning. I peeked at the girls in the windows as discreetly as possible, and had to run to keep up with my mother.

There weren't many people in the street. Just a man here or there slinking out of a curtained berth and vanishing into the night. Junkies begging for change. Chinese men roaming the streets in long leather coats.

We turned into an alleyway and stopped in front of a dilapidated house. The windows were nailed shut with wooden boards and the front door's glass pane was smashed.

"Here we are. Go on in."

I hesitated, scared. I wondered what my mother was up to. She prodded me in the back. "Hurry up."

We stepped into a concrete hallway reeking of mold and sweat. There were slogans painted all over the walls. *Fighting for peace is like fucking for virginity.*

"What are we doing here?" I asked, my voice shaking.

My mother did not reply, but pushed me inside a dark room. It took a few seconds for my eyes to get used to the gloom. I saw someone lighting up. Then I realized that there were human shapes all over the floor. Stretched out on worn mattresses, with very little clothing to cover up their emaciated bodies. A shudder went up my spine.

A walking skeleton approached us. His eyes bulged out of their sockets. "Got some for me?" He stuck out his hand.

My mother shoved me forward. "Ask her."

I was deeply shocked. My mother, who always worried about whether I'd washed my hands before a meal, was pushing me into the arms of a junkie.

The druggie came even closer. He stank.

"What you got? Give me what you got."

I thought, *What if he has a knife on him? What if my mother intends to leave me here?*

"Mother," I pleaded. She was holding me fast. She wasn't leaving me any room to step back or turn around. I was fifteen, but my mother was still much stronger than me.

The junkie stretched out a hand toward me. To touch me or to dig into my pockets, I'm not sure which. I just saw that hand coming at me in slow motion. A vulture's claw. "Mommy, please."

When the skinny yellow hand was about to graze my face, my mother yanked me backward. She rummaged through her handbag and took out a twenty-five-guilder bill, which she tossed to the ground. "Here," she said. "Have yourself a party. Shoot yourself up until you drop dead."

The junkie dove after the money. My mother and I left the building.

"That was it," she said as we walked back to the car, ogled by pimps, dealers, and the prostitutes at their windows. "That's all I wished to say to you."

I stared at the aquarium. At the coral that had been lovingly and patiently nurtured. It grew just a few millimeters a year, depending on the water quality. Ray had created a magnificent habitat for his fish. And then he had gone off and murdered his neighbor and her young daughter. It seemed a strange combination.

I picked up the logbook and started leafing through it. It had been kept meticulously. Ray never skipped a day. The ink was never smudged, and there were no food crumbs or spills. Until the year 2003, no one else had ever recorded anything in that book, but that year someone had written *King Kong* in a childish hand. *King Kong,* and then in Ray's writing, *January 25.* The words took up three whole lines, as opposed to Ray's own neat handwriting. A child. Ray had been with a child.

The letters the child had written were shaky, as if the child wasn't yet able to hold a pen properly. How old? Four? Five? Six? I wondered if the handwriting had belonged to the neighbor's little girl. The thought alone made me shudder.

CHAPTER 13

RAY

From that day on I brought Anna a madeleine every day. I was usually invited to come in. Then Rosita would make me a cup of coffee, and we'd talk for a while until she said I had to go. On other days Rosita would only open the door a crack to take the offering from me. "Not today, Ray."

I asked my mother for advice. She explained that it was quite understandable that Rosita wouldn't let me in every day. People don't always have the time. It wasn't anything personal. After all, my mother also had very little time for me these days. She came by once every other month. She'd always bring me something. A tablecloth and a stripy red duvet cover. Tall drinking glasses and a picture of a boat to hang on the wall. She thought it was important for my house to look nice.

I couldn't think why. Apart from her, nobody ever visited me.

Rosita didn't have visitors very often, either, but she did have them more frequently than me. The old man who'd helped her with the move came at least once a month. Rosita told me he was her stepfather.

"Where's your mother, then?" I asked.

She told me her mother was dead. She had died of cancer

shortly after marrying her second husband. Rosita said her stepfather had taken good care of her mother and so she'd always be grateful to him.

"Why does he come here?" I asked.

"He comes to talk. To fix things in my house. To see Anna."

"Do you like that?"

"I like it better when you're here; it's more fun. He's nice and all, and he's a very good handyman, and that's nothing to turn your nose up at if you're a single mother like me. But do I enjoy his company? Not really. To be honest I think he mainly comes and helps me because he's so lonely himself. Otherwise he's just hanging around at home. He used to be very rich. He had a successful tulip-growing business, but he lost it all. Couldn't stop drinking." Rosita lit a cigarette and went on, "When he met my mother, he was sober. He said he had finally found happiness. But then my mother got sick. So he never really got what he wanted."

The stepfather didn't bother me. As far as I was concerned he could come as often as he wanted, and unclog the drain or paint the woodwork. It was the other visitor who bothered me: Anna's father. He was married to another woman and refused to get divorced. That was why he couldn't live with Rosita and Anna. But he did come by. Not on a regular schedule, like my mother's visits to me, but at random.

"Only when it suits *him,*" Rosita had said, with an expression I couldn't place. Angry? Sad?

"But what about Anna? He's got to look after her, doesn't he?"

"He has *three* kids with the other woman, and they're married."

"But doesn't he want to live with you?"

"He'd like to, but he can't. Want to know why?" Rosita sucked deeply at her cigarette and puffed out the smoke again almost immediately.

I really couldn't think of a reason why anyone wouldn't want to be with Rosita, no matter what it took.

"Because she was first. So here I am. In a house without carpeting on the floor, with *his* kid. While she lives with him in a fancy townhouse and can do as she pleases. Not because she's better than me, or prettier, or smarter. And definitely not because she's skinnier." Rosita smiled with her mouth, but not with her eyes. "Not even because he loves her more than he loves me. But because she was first."

"You need someone else," I said. What I meant was: *You need me.* But of course she didn't, really.

"You're not cut out for having a relationship," my mother always said to me. "No woman will ever stick it out with you, so you better stay away from them, before you get into trouble."

"Of course I ought to end it," Rosita replied. "But the problem is that I love him. There's nobody else who even comes close. I want no one but him. Does that make sense?"

Anna's father usually came in the middle of the night. But he was sometimes there when I brought Anna her madeleine. Then Rosita would ask me to watch the kid for a bit.

"We get so little time to be together, me and Victor."

One time Victor came and stood next to her in the hall. He wrapped his arms around her from behind and gazed at me with his head on her shoulder. She looked so happy that it turned my stomach. As far as I could tell, Victor was nothing special. Maybe he was smart. And he drove the kind of fancy car we hardly ever saw on Queen Wilhelmina Street. But I looked right through him. He might act as if he had a right to be there, but I saw a man who was making the mother of his child live in a house without carpeting. That's what *I* saw.

As Rosita went to fetch Anna from the living room, he tried to start a conversation with me. "So, you're a baker."

I did not respond.

"It's nice to know someone's looking after my girls when I'm not around."

I looked down at my feet until Rosita and Anna stepped back into the corridor.

I took Anna home with me to look at the fish. She was the first person to ever come visit, apart from my mom. I told her their names, and she repeated them after me. "Hannibal, François, Maria . . ."

As she sat there next to me in the blue light of the aquarium, I tried not to think of Victor pulling off Rosita's clothes. Caressing the hollow between her collarbones. Taking her boobs in his hands and kissing them. Lying on top of her and pumping away. Touching her naked privates and making them filthy.

"Chili, Saturn, Venus . . ." I went on, repeating the names of the fish to calm myself down.

Sometimes Anna and I would sit there looking at the aquarium until it got dark outside, the bed stopped creaking, and Victor's car disappeared down the street.

I sat at the desk in my cell staring at an empty sheet of paper. Dr. Römerman had ordered me to write a letter to Rosita, but I had only one thing to say to her.

I'm still really angry at you.

CHAPTER 14

IRIS

"Lovely fellow," said Binnie after I had told her the whole Ray situation. "Have you figured out yet how you're related?"

We were sitting at the dining table. A mahogany antique that had been passed down in my father's family for generations. Six months after he died, his sister had asked my mother for it. It was one of her family's only surviving heirlooms, apparently. She even offered to buy my mother a new table. "Over my dead body," my mother had snapped. There hadn't been much contact with my father's side of the family since then. Although the aunt in question *had* sent a teddy bear when Aaron was born.

"Maybe he's your brother," said Binnie.

"No way." But at the same time I realized how little I knew of my mother's life before she'd met my father. All I really knew was that she'd had me early in their marriage.

"Try and think. Your grandpa and grandma, let's say. Could *they* have had another child late in life?"

I tried to calculate. My grandparents had died when I was still very young.

"Write it down," said Binnie, thorough as always.

I picked up a pen and a blank sheet of paper. "My grandma's

year of birth, I'm guessing, anywhere between 1920 and 1930. My mother was born in '48. Ray in '70 and me in '85."

"If Ray is your uncle, your grandma would have been well in her forties when she had him. It's possible."

"But pretty late."

"But within the bounds of possibility, although of course we don't know the exact year your grandmother was born, so we may be barking up the wrong tree."

"If he's my brother, my mother could have had him when she was twenty-two."

"Totally possible."

"He would have been around fifteen when my mother had me. Where would she have kept him all those years? Maybe he was my mother's cousin or something."

"*I* think he's your brother," Binnie said decidedly. She took a big gulp of wine. "Why else would your mother go to so much trouble to keep it a secret? And why be so touchy about it? Your grandparents died ages ago. Surely there must be a statute of limitations on the obligation to preserve family secrets?"

I topped off our wineglasses and took a long drink. "True, Ray could be my older brother." I felt myself grow dizzy at the prospect.

"Let's go and look around the study."

I giggled, the wine starting to take hold. "We can't."

"If you have a brother, Iris, your mother has been keeping your own flesh and blood from you. You've told me often enough you were lonely growing up. I think you have every right to know the truth."

"I don't know."

Binnie was already on her feet. "Oh, stop acting all scared of your mother."

"You're right," I said.

"Do you know how to jimmy a lock?"

"Of course not."

"Come on, you're a lawyer, aren't you?"

"And you're a journalist. So?"

"Don't tell me you've never had to break into a locked office or hidden library in order to get your hands on some secret file."

"That only happens in the movies. Besides, I'm the most law-abiding girl in the world. Don't you know that?"

Binnie took out a hairpin and began fiddling with the lock.

"As if you'll get it open that way."

"Do you have a better idea?"

"Let's find the key," I said, finishing off the last of my wine.

My mother hadn't hidden the key to the study as thoroughly as I'd expected—probably because, living alone, she no longer had to guard against a nosy daughter or curious spouse. It was in one of the kitchen drawers, with the rubber bands, tweezers, and paper clips. It was that simple.

I turned the key in the lock and pushed the door open. My heart was pounding. I had been conditioned all my life to stay out of this room.

Her study looked exactly as it had on my first and last foray some twenty years ago. The same cherrywood desk. The large armoire, which was shut. The black desk chair.

"Go on in," whispered Binnie.

"What are you whispering for?" I stepped inside the Holy of Holies. Cautiously, as if my mother might jump out from behind the door at any moment. It smelled a bit musty, as the windows were probably seldom opened.

Binnie flung open the armoire. The shelves were groaning with files, stacks of magazines, and boxes. I pulled out a file at random and found a pile of telephone bills from 2000. "Who the hell *saves* all this stuff?"

After half an hour of snooping, we hadn't made much headway, other than finding eight years' worth of women's magazines, two decades of household accounts, and a stack of yellowed crossword puzzle booklets.

"Doesn't your mother have any hobbies?" asked Binnie.

"Can't you see? She collects paper." I pulled a faded blue pocket folder out from beneath a box of recipe clippings.

"Should I start on the desk?"

"Go ahead." The folder was labeled *Ray*. I stared at the three letters for a few seconds, to make sure I wasn't seeing things. "Jesus, Binnie, take a look at this." I opened the folder. There was nothing inside. "Oh," I said, disappointed.

"Give it to me," said Binnie, so I handed it to her. Opening it, she started waving it around. A photo fell out of one pocket.

I picked it up from the floor. My hands were shaking. The photo showed a boy of around five with tousled brown hair. He was sitting on a little red bike, smiling faintly.

Binnie put a hand on my shoulder. "Are you okay?"

"It's the spitting image of . . ." I began.

"Aaron!" Bennie exclaimed. "That hair, that look in his eyes, and just look at those legs!"

We both stared at the boy's skinny legs emerging from a brown pair of shorts.

"I bet he's your brother."

I shook my head. If Ray was my brother, why had my mother kept me in the dark about him? Where had he been all those years? It just couldn't be true.

"What are you going to do?" asked Binnie. "Go visit him? He'll no longer be this young, of course, and definitely not this cute."

"Ray B., the Monster Next Door," I said, more to myself than to

her. I looked at the boy in the picture again. His knee had a big bandage on it. "When or where did it all go wrong? What do you think happened?"

"I'm doing my best not to make any *unpleasant* observations about your mother right now."

"Totally." I stared at the photo, hoping to find some clue. But the sidewalk behind Ray's bike could have been any place. There was a bush of rose hips in the background, but that didn't tell me much more.

"It doesn't help a child's development, of course, to be abandoned. How old did you say he was by the time you were born?"

"Fifteen, I think."

"Do you think your father knew about him?"

"No," I said firmly, though I had no idea where that certainty came from.

"Your mother must have kicked that boy out when he was very young. There's no other explanation."

"Maybe he was violent and unmanageable."

"But why the secrecy? Why keep him hidden?"

"I don't know," I said. "But I do know that I want to meet him."

CHAPTER 15

RAY

I was starting to get used to the rhythm of my new surroundings. Wake up at seven. Shower, get dressed. Breakfast, therapy, lunch, work, dinner. Lockup and lights-out at eight. I tried to be as invisible as possible. The other patients scared me. They were loud. They were nosy. They bragged about their crimes. The less attention they paid to me, the better.

The only person who really bothered me was a guy named Rembrandt. He was a short little black fellow who'd been there only three weeks, but for some reason had everyone at his beck and call in just a few days.

Whenever he walked into a room, they'd all turn around and yell out in unison, "*What's up, bro?*" With anyone else, it was just "Hey, you."

Then he'd strut into the room, chewing gum or dangling a cigarette at the corner of his mouth. Like some cowboy sauntering into a Wild West saloon.

"What a shithole, man," he'd say.

Even the social workers tended to leave him alone. I saw that Mo was keeping an eye on him, but he didn't say anything to me.

"So I was just talking to that fat-ass shrink, and she asks me what I'm *feeling* when I'm offing someone."

Rembrandt flopped down on the couch. All the others crowded around him, except for Ricky and me. Ricky was sitting on the floor talking to the television, and I was standing by the window staring at the gray brick wall, my back to the others. In the window's reflection I could see what was happening in the room without having to be a part of it.

"So I say, 'What do *you* feel when you boil an egg for breakfast?' She just looks at me like the stupid bitch she is. 'Sugar baby,' I say, 'that's the way to look at it. For me, wasting someone is easy, like farting or watering the plants.' "

The other patients started to laugh, as usual.

"Me, I get horny as hell," growled Eddie. "Nothing gives me a hard-on like putting my hands around someone's neck and giving him a good squeeze. Squeeze, squeeze, squeeze until the body goes limp." Eddie gave a little mock demonstration.

"That's enough," said Mo. "Save it for the next time you see the shrink."

"Sure, man, whatever you say," said Rembrandt. "You just doing your job. Same way I used to do mine, nice and cool. You know all about that, don't you, Mo."

The others started laughing again.

According to Hank, Rembrandt had been a hit man. He'd worked with all the top crime bosses. "He's got connections; we got to stay on his good side," Hank had told me in the smokers' yard. Hank always asked me to go with him even though I didn't smoke. Out there, he told me what the other guys were in for. Hank himself was in for a series of aggravated assaults, Ricky had gone after his mother with an ax, and my former cellmate Eddie had a habit of raping and killing women. I had to listen to Hank's stories because I didn't have the guts to tell him he smelled bad and that I hated how he blew smoke in my face and that I was freezing in the windy courtyard.

"Yeah, you're real tough, Rembrandt," Mo said. "But you'll learn soon enough it won't do you much good in here."

"Is that right? Ooh, now I'm scared." Rembrandt got up from the couch and walked slowly up to Mo until there was hardly any space between them.

I felt the hair on the nape of my neck stand on end. Even Ricky realized something was up. He stopped talking to the TV. The only sound left in the room was coming from the television set.

"You're breaking the rules," said Mo, not twitching a muscle. "I've given you a warning. You've ignored it. So you're confined to your suite for the next forty-eight hours."

Rembrandt stood his ground. "What rules you talking about, Mohammed? Rules that say we're just supposed to do like we're told, like a bunch of sheep? That all we can talk about is the weather, because anything else is *out of line*? That we're not even allowed any fucking porn in here, so that all of us is walking around with a full load? *That* what you getting at?" Rembrandt's arms were hanging loosely by his side. But you could tell he could lash out at any moment.

"Got *that* right," Eddie chimed in, but no one was listening to him.

"Okay, Rembrandt, now you've gone too far. Forty-eight hours have just become seventy-two." Jeannie must have heard the commotion, because she had come over and was standing next to Mo. She was wearing a flimsy blouse; you could see her bra. I didn't think it was the right kind of thing to wear in a place full of sex offenders.

Rembrandt turned his attention to Jeannie. "Has anyone given you a good banging lately, girl? 'Cause the way you dressing, you need it bad."

"That's enough," said Jeannie. "I'm calling security."

"You do that, sugar, be my guest. Think I give a flying fuck about spending some time in my room? Why don't you take me there yourself?"

Mo made a show of pressing the beeper attached to his belt. I heard a loud buzz and doors locking automatically.

"Shit, man!" Rembrandt grabbed Mo by the collar. "I was just messing is all. What a pussy you are." He shook Mo from side to side with each word. The chain holding Mo's ID badge snapped and fell to the floor.

"Hey, *cool* it," said Jeannie. She didn't sound cool at all. Her boobs were heaving up and down under her white blouse. I couldn't keep my eyes off them. "Let go of him, or you're in serious trouble."

"Stay out of it, bitch." He let go of Mo and it looked as if Jeannie was next. I turned around. If I'd had the guts, I would have rushed to Jeannie's aid.

At that moment the doors opened and six guards stormed inside, brandishing clubs.

Ricky began wailing loudly. "They've come for me! Don't take me! Don't take me!"

"They ain't after *you,* stupid," snarled Eddie.

Rembrandt was seized and handcuffed by two of the guards. The whole time he was yelling terrible stuff. About God and Mo's mother's cunt and how "You're all getting it in the ass."

The guards dragged him away. Just before they pushed Rembrandt violently out through the doors, he suddenly glared at me. I looked around. I was the only one standing on the far side of the room.

"I'm going to get you! I'm going to get you!" He was screaming so loud that his voice cracked. I'm not even sure if he was really looking at me or at the gray brick wall. All I know is it scared the shit out of me.

"There goes our great connection." Hank walked up to me. "He'll be in the cooler for a nice long time."

I didn't answer him. Why did Rembrandt have it in for me, the way everyone always seemed to have it in for me in the end? I couldn't think of a reason. Had I missed the signals, as usual?

I had discussed this with the shrink back at the Mason Home. He had shown me pictures of faces. I had to tell him if the people in the pictures were happy, angry, or frightened. Later on he'd added startled, relieved, sarcastic, and incredulous. The last three were hard. I still wasn't very good at telling which was which. You can never be totally sure. You can't just ask someone, "Is the emotion you are feeling right now relief?"

Mo rearranged his collar and Jeannie had tears in her eyes. She was sad, that was easy to tell. Everyone was just standing around. What were we supposed to do? Should we just go back to our usual activities?

"Back to your suites," said Mo. "We're all going to cool off for a while."

We walked to our cells. Nobody was joking. There wasn't even any grumbling. There was a buzzing sound and the doors locked. I stood in my empty cell and thought about how good it would have felt if the fish had been there waiting for me.

"Hey, Raynus," I heard Eddie shout. "Your little girlfriend, the bitch you're so sweet on, she almost got it good, didn't she."

I walked into the shower stall, sat down on the closed toilet seat, and put my hands over my ears. "Saturn, Maria, Hannibal, François, Margie, Peanut, Venus, and Raisin. And King Kong. We mustn't ever forget King Kong."

CHAPTER 16

IRIS

Kim de Boer's attorney sent us a proposal. Van Benschop was to take the film off the Internet, pay six months of Kim's salary, since she had been unable to work, plus another six thousand euro in compensation—around twenty thousand euro total.

The proposal was delivered to me by courier. Aaron was splashing around in a half-filled inflatable kiddie pool, playing with his plastic whales. I read it while tanning on a lounge chair in the sun.

"I'm just going inside, okay?" I told Aaron. "Mommy has to make a phone call."

He barely reacted, intent on his new favorite game, which involved reciting whole passages from *Finding Nemo.*

Wrapped in a towel, I sat down at my mother's desk and called Peter van Benschop.

He wasn't happy. "I already *paid* her. I paid her the agreed-upon amount. She signed on the dotted line. She didn't seem to have any problem with it during the shoot . . ."

"Maybe because she was in shock?" I regretted saying it before the words were out of my mouth. I looked out the window. Aaron still didn't seem to notice that I'd gone inside.

"Very funny," said Van Benschop.

"I'm sorry. I'll stop with the sarcastic remarks. Now, as far as . . ."

"What good is it to me to have a lawyer who's constantly disparaging me?"

"I'm not disparaging you."

"You are."

I sighed and gazed out the window again. Aaron was throwing his whales up in the air to watch them land in the pool with a big splash. It was too nice outside to prolong quibbling.

"Getting back to the business at hand—I think I have a pretty good sense of Miss De Boer's state of mind during the shoot." In the video she'd looked quite cheerful—at first. Wearing hot pants and a transparent T-shirt, she'd sat giggling on a leather couch. But less than three minutes later, you can see fear and disgust in her face. At the end of the film she was apathetic, almost like a zombie. I'd had trouble making myself watch to the end. "But could you please tell me how she was after the shoot? Did she go straight home?"

"She went and took a shower, then had a Coke . . ."

"With you?"

"Shower, you mean?" he said eagerly.

"I was referring to the Coke."

"We all sat around having a drink afterward, the whole crew."

It seemed strange to me that after having been pissed on and subjected to all sorts of other nasty stuff, you'd still feel like sitting around with the crew sipping a soda. But I decided not to say anything that would prolong the conversation unnecessarily. "So we can conclude that after the shoot, Miss De Boer was by all indications . . . *in good form,*" I continued.

"Absolutely."

"Something else. You told me over lunch that *she'd* approached *you*. Can you tell me how that came about?"

"Her boyfriend called me. He said his girlfriend wanted to make some extra bucks."

I had to suppress my exasperation. "That's not the same thing as someone approaching you on her own initiative, is it."

"Well, the two of them came to see me in any case, and we made a deal."

"With whom did you make the deal? The friend, or Miss De Boer?"

"Well, she signed it."

"Who did the negotiating?"

"Her friend."

"With friends like that, you don't need enemies." I *had* to learn to control myself better.

"What are you getting at?"

"Didn't it occur to you that the girl herself had very little say in the matter? Are you really sure you did right by her?"

"There you go again, pointing the finger. And didn't we agree to call her a young woman?"

I sighed. "I'm just appealing to your common sense. Again, it is not my place to judge you. That's the judge's job. All I'm trying to do is make you see what it looks like from the other side."

"You don't get it, do you, and you don't want to understand. All you have done is point fingers. Why have you never asked what's motivating me?"

Aaron was still stolidly playing with his whales out in the yard and I was starting to get a chill sitting inside.

Van Benschop didn't wait for my reply. "It may be called 'hard-core,' but it's just another way of making love. That's the way you ought to look at it. By going to extremes, a person can reach a kind of ecstasy. You have to view my film work as an ode to the human body's surrender."

I wondered if Van Benschop had taken an adult-ed philosophy course at the local community college. "Of course. As I said before, acting in good faith, I'll do everything I can in your best interest. I'll contend in your defense that Miss De Boer knew exactly what she was in for and had signed a contract. That she was so eager to participate that she even forged her date of birth. I'll also inform them that she joined you in a drink with the crew afterward. We'll leave the boyfriend out of it."

"What do you see happening?"

"How hard is it to take the video down?"

"If it gets out that I'm being sued, it could get very hot."

"In that case we'll have to offer her a considerable sum. Enough for her not to turn it down. But not *too* much. That would look like an admission of guilt."

Aaron had clambered out of the pool and was on his way to the back door, naked and dripping. "Mr. Van Benschop, I'll get on it right away and e-mail you the proposed counteroffer in the morning."

CHAPTER 17

RAY

"There's someone coming to see you today," said Mo.

For as long as I've been in prison, my mother has come and visited me just a couple of times. Margaret and Pierre had also visited once. They used to come back to the Netherlands every summer, when it got too hot in France. When they heard I wasn't on Queen Wilhelmina Street anymore, they came and looked me up in prison. Although Margaret said it would be the last time, because Pierre was getting too old to travel.

He'd changed, Pierre. He walked more slowly and had to stop to catch his breath every few steps. It was only ten steps from the door to the visiting room table and four chairs.

"All those years in the bakery have worn him out," Margaret told me. She still talked just as loud as before. "He just doesn't feel like doing anything anymore, do you, Pierre?"

The whole time, the twenty minutes they were with me, it was Margaret who did the talking. Pierre didn't say a word; he didn't even look at me. I didn't say very much, either. I think all three of us were happy to have Margaret fill up the silence by describing the farmers' market in Grasse.

Rosita was never mentioned. The mother dough wasn't, either.

"My mother's coming *here*?" I didn't think she would come; she'd been pretty firm about that, actually. Not even for a chat with Dr. Römerman, at least that's what he'd told me. But Dr. Römerman also said it was time for me to face up to what I'd done, even though I hadn't done anything.

"No. Another lady is coming to see you." Mo glanced at a list. "Iris Kastelein."

"Who's that?"

"Don't you know her?"

"No."

"Strange. She says she's related to you."

Hank came and sat next to me at lunch. He'd been avoiding me for the past few days. I didn't know why and I didn't feel like asking him, either.

It was fish cakes day. They were on a plate at the far end of the table, but I could smell them. I was in the mood for a fish cake.

"You and me, we're buddies. Right, Ray?"

The plate was coming this way, but it wasn't close enough for me to take one.

"I'm the only one you talk to, right? The only one looking out for you?" Hank turned and yelled, "Hey, pass those fish cakes!"

A new inmate, his name was Jamal, tossed a fish cake at him. The plate stayed where it was.

"Jamal. I know you still have to get used to the rules in here. But one rule is that we don't throw our food," said the social worker with the glasses—I could never remember his name.

"Rude behavior at mealtimes means confinement to your suite for two days, okay, we all know," said Hank. He wasn't scared of this one. I'd heard that the social worker with the glasses sometimes smuggled in cocaine. You could buy it from him at fifty euro a gram. And the quality was excellent, I'd overheard Eddie tell Rembrandt.

Hank was yakking on and on. But my attention was elsewhere. On the fish cakes that were making a tour of the table but never seemed to land close to me, but also on the news about the visitor coming to see me. I didn't know if it was good news or bad news. My mother was the only family I had. And her name wasn't Iris Kastelein.

"Are you listening to me?" Hank was breathing right in my face. Reeking of fish cake and tobacco.

I nodded.

"You are such a smart guy. I'll show you the ropes. Since we're buddies and all. Understood?"

"Yeah, sure," I said quickly.

"The way you could . . ." Hank stopped because the social worker was looking at him pointedly. "Hey, don't you want a fish cake?"

"Yes, please."

"Dammit, Deepak, pass those fish cakes over here, will you?"

Hank passed me the fish cake platter. There was only one left. It was a bit squished and split open, with the white spilling out. I picked it up and bit off one end. It tasted good. I loved the crusty exterior combined with the gooey warm insides, and the little flecks of fish in it.

"Just look at the kid sucking on that thing!" yelled Eddie. "Hey, Raynus, it's goo-food, isn't it?"

All the other guys started whistling and cheering.

"Okay, enough," said the social worker with the glasses.

"They're coming for me!" wailed Ricky. "I know it."

"Oh, Ricky-dick, shouldn't they be upping your dosage?" asked Eddie.

Everyone thought that was very funny.

They had already settled me at the visitors' table when the woman whose name was Iris Kastelein came in. Mo came in behind her and sat down on a chair by the door next to the guard.

He nodded at me. "All right, Ray?"

Iris Kastelein was a pretty young woman. Like the ones from the neighborhood with the big houses that would come to the bakery specially and stand in a long line to buy croissants.

"Oh, that's funny," was the first thing she said. "My son looks exactly like you."

She'd only just arrived and already she was making fun of me. I didn't reply and concentrated on keeping my hands in check.

I felt myself getting mad. She was making me all confused. *What did she want?*

She sat down on the plastic chair opposite me and looked at me the way the Mason Home shrink had sometimes looked at me. As if by staring into my eyes she thought she could see into my brain. I didn't like it.

"You must be wondering who I am and what I'm doing here." She had a nice, calm voice, I had to admit. She talked the way the anchorwomen on TV talk, not like the people who live on Queen Wilhelmina Street. And not at all like the guys in here. "Or were you aware of my existence? Have you known all this time?"

I glanced at her face. She had dark eyebrows and eyelashes caked with black mascara. Like Rosita used to.

"I think I'm your sister." Her voice was shaking.

It took a while for me to find my voice. This didn't make sense. It couldn't be. This woman was crazy, obviously.

"Could you say something, please?"

"I don't have a sister."

"So tell me, what's your mother's name?"

"Agatha Antonia Boelens," I recited.

"Well, Agatha Antonia Boelens is *my* mother, too. I was born in 1985. But then where were *you*?"

It was too much for me. My hands started whipping around in all directions.

She grabbed them and held them, the way Rosita used to.

I quickly jerked free.

"Sorry," said this woman whose name was Iris Kastelein and who said she was my sister. "Do you want a glass of water or something? Can he have one?" she asked the guard.

The answer was no. Not during the visit.

Iris Kastelein who said she was my sister looked at me. She did look a lot like my mother. She had the same eyes. I was surprised I hadn't noticed it before. I quickly looked away.

"You're allowed to look at me, you know. I realize this must come as a shock. And I'm sorry to spring it on you like this. But . . ."

I looked at her face again and saw her eyes were wet. Why was she crying? And what did she expect of me?

"What happened to you, Ray? Where have you been all this time?"

I forced my hands down and sat on them. That helped.

"You're better off asking him more straightforward questions," said Mo from his corner.

"Okay," said Iris Kastelein who said she was my sister. "How old were you when you stopped living with Mother?" She was speaking very slowly, as if to an idiot, but I answered her anyway.

"Nine."

"Where . . . did . . . you . . . go . . . live . . . after that?"

"You can talk to me normally."

"Sorry. Of course. Where did you live after that?"

It was all getting too much for me. This female person coming in here just like that, asking all kinds of questions. How could I know she really was my sister? My mother had never mentioned she had another child. Let alone a brand-new, better child instead of me. A lady, no less, in a fancy suit. Why would my mother have wanted another child once she got rid of me?

"Ray finds emotions hard to deal with," Mo explained. "And I must say it's a bit much to take in."

"Yes, I understand it's a lot. Is it okay with you if I continue a bit, Ray? Or is this too much?"

I didn't say anything.

"Where did you live after you were nine? When you left home?"

"Mason."

"What is that?"

"A home for boys."

"Ray was at a boarding school for troubled kids," Mo explained. I very much doubted he was allowed to give out confidential information about me. Whose side was he on, anyway? Mine or hers?

"How awful," said Iris Kastelein who said she was my sister, and whose eyes were still wet. "I just don't know what to say. I can't *believe* Mother never told me about you. Incredible. Did she ever visit you at the school? Do you still ever see her?"

This conversation was exhausting and confusing. Especially when she called my mother "Mother." I just didn't have the energy to answer her questions. I caught sight of a *Pholcus phalangioides,* a common skull spider, moseying up the wall.

"Should I come back another time? To give you a little time to let it sink in?"

The spider was going to spin her web up against the ceiling. Then she'd wait for another spider or insect to get trapped and use more thread to reel it in. I'd seen it plenty of times on the Discovery Channel.

"Ray?" said Mo. "Iris was asking you a question."

"Sorry." Iris Kastelein who said she was my sister was staring at me with my mother's face, which didn't scare me, but did make me nervous.

"I'm tired. I want to go back to my room." I got to my feet.

"Wait." She rummaged in her bag and took out a stack of photos. "I brought you something."

"You're not allowed to hand things over like that," said the guard. "Please give them here. We're here to see to it that the resident receives them."

"Oh."

"Sorry," said Mo. "But rules are rules. We're having a problem with drug use among the patients."

"I understand." She turned to me. "I took some pictures of your aquarium, Ray. I thought you might like to see them."

King Kong, Hannibal, Saturn, and Maria! Peanut and François! I sat back down.

"The aquarium is fine. Mother has a guy, Maurice, who comes and takes care of it once a week. The coral has grown quite a bit. And Mr. Van de Akker also came by recently."

"Van de Akker?"

"Yes." Her face took on an expression I couldn't place. Was it fear, worry? "He said the aquarium wasn't quite as magnificent as when you took care of it, but that it's still in great shape."

"And the fish. Tell me about my fish." I leaned forward so as not to miss a word.

"What can I tell you? Saturn and Venus spend most of the day hiding in the sea anemones and . . ."

"Yeah?" Just to hear their names from someone else's lips filled me with joy.

"And Margie. She swims round and round in circles all day long. Has she always done that?"

"Always."

"Well, she's still doing it. She fights with François from time to time. I think it's because their territories overlap."

I shut my eyes and listened to the stories. Like when I was little and my mother read to me at bedtime. When everything was still fine.

". . . Aaron, my little boy, just loves the aquarium. He's nearly four and likes nothing better than to watch the fish all day long. He knows the names of all the species by heart. The doctorfish are his favorites." She paused. "You must miss them."

"Who?"

"The fish."

"I think about them every day. Every day I say their names out loud."

"I'm sure they're thinking of you, too."

"Fish don't think. Not the way we do, anyway. They can't even tell one person from another, so how can you expect them to think about people?"

"I think your sister meant it kindly," said Mo. "I think she meant to say that you did a great job taking care of your fish, and there's no one to take your place."

"You like to be very accurate, don't you?" said Iris Kastelein who said she was my sister.

But I couldn't think of her as my sister. I'd always thought of sisters as little girls, like Anna.

The guard handed me the bundle of photos. "Here you go."

I took them and hugged them to my chest.

"Don't you want to look at them?"

"When I'm alone."

"Can I do anything else for you? Do you need anything? Money? Food? Clothes?"

"The only thing I want is to go home. To my fish."

She looked sad. "Sorry. I don't think I can help you there."

"I didn't do it. They're keeping me locked up; they just won't let me go. While I'm innocent."

She was silent a long time, gazing at me with another of those weird looks on her face. "I could review your case. If you want."

I didn't understand what she meant.

"I'm a lawyer. I'll have a look at it and see if there's something I can do for you. But I can't promise anything, of course."

"I didn't do it." It was the only thing I could think of saying.

"No?"

"No. I didn't do it."

CHAPTER 18

IRIS

Mo walked with me to the institute's exit. It was a labyrinth of corridors, bolted doors that had to be unlocked, and security cameras.

"How do you think it went?" asked Mo. There was something about him that made me feel at ease. A certain vibration in his voice, the reassuring look in his gentle brown eyes, the confident way he held his body; it was hard to pinpoint what it was, but it worked. I could imagine that Mo would have the same effect on the patients in here.

"It was hard. Although I should have expected that." We crossed a courtyard with a little commissary. It was swarming with men, all leering at me. It was a strange thing to think that all of them had committed some serious offense.

"You did great, though. The photos in particular. A brilliant move, bringing those along."

"You think?"

"Didn't you notice? He was wary at first, as he is generally, but when you started talking about his fish I could just see him relax. Good for you. There are therapists in here who've been working with him for months, and they haven't achieved as much as you did in just half an hour."

I felt myself blush. "It must have been the blood connection."

"How can it be that you never knew he existed?"

"My mother just never told me she had an older child. Can you imagine?"

"You do have to remember that back in the seventies there was a different attitude to so-called 'difficult' children. Back then it was something to be ashamed of—people would think it was all the mother's fault."

"Still, I think it's pretty absurd that my mother never breathed a word about him. I wonder what would have become of him if he'd had a normal youth. If he had grown up in a normal family."

We had arrived at the exit. Mo waved his pass at a sensor. The doors swung open.

"That's always the tragic thing about people like Ray," said Mo. "He's actually a really sweet guy."

"He is, isn't he?"

"Absolutely."

I handed in my visitor's pass and shook Mo's hand. "Thank you."

He smiled. "You're welcome."

"Uh, Mo?"

"Yes?"

"Do *you* believe Ray—that he didn't do it?"

He started to laugh.

"Never mind."

I didn't have much time to think about my encounter with Ray, my *brother,* Ray, because the entire drive home was taken up with a phone call from Rence. Aaron had been allowed to return to the day care, so for as long as that lasted, I was back working in the office.

"Peter van Benschop complained about you."

I turned up the volume on my phone's speaker. "Oh?"

"I want you to think. What might Peter have complained about?"

"Surely you don't expect me to fall for that. If you're trying to catch me out with a loaded question, you'll have to come up with something better."

"Not bad, nice and sharp. That's what I like to hear."

"I'll be there in a minute. Do you want to meet?"

"I can't. Our good Werner B. is expecting me in half an hour."

Werner B. was a rather incompetent burglar and therefore one of our most loyal clients. "Is he still in custody?"

"They're keeping him another two weeks. I'm afraid that our friend won't be getting off so easy this time. Nice distraction, though, Iris. It's Van Benschop we were talking about."

I groaned. I'd been hoping to wrap up the Van Benschop case quickly and smoothly, but it seemed to have the same drawbacks as an X-rated film: lots and lots of the same action, over and over again, while taking much too long to come to a climax.

"Let me reformulate the question: Are you sure you've been handling Peter van Benschop's case to the best of your ability?"

"If I'd been handling the matter to the best of my ability, I'd have locked Peter van Benschop in a dungeon with a couple of premenstrual dominatrices."

"Be serious."

"Dear Lawrence, cross my heart, I swear that I have given Mr. Van Benschop's matter my full attention and will continue to do so." I hoped it sounded convincing.

"Peter van Benschop thinks you were too hasty in proposing a settlement. What do you say?"

"Need I remind you that according to the Bar Association's rules of professional conduct, settling a case out of court is always preferable to taking it to trial? Besides, I think a trial is risky."

I took the exit into the south part of Amsterdam and headed for the office. "We don't have much choice. I think Mr. Van Benschop should be glad the plaintiff has chosen to pursue the civil course. I'd hate to think what might have happened if the girl . . . *young woman* had gone to the police."

There was silence on the other end of the line. Then: "Where have you been, anyway? There's nothing on your schedule."

"I was meeting a potential client."

"And who might that be?" There was suspicion in Rence's voice.

"I'd rather keep that under my hat for a while longer."

"Or was it your kid's day care again?"

I felt the urge to scream but instead said as coolly as I could, "The client is incarcerated in the Hopper Institute. He was convicted of the murder of his neighbor and her little girl. He may be interested in an appeal."

"Hmm."

"An appeal would be prestigious for the firm, Lawrence." I knew that would sway him.

"Well, now. Little Iris wants to play detective."

"Are you trying to insult me?"

"Of course not, honey pie. But you know what's involved in an appeal. Before you know it, you've got the entire office working on it and we have to let more lucrative pieces of business slide. Not to mention the eventual costs of the forensic research, digging up new witnesses and so on."

"Pres-*tige,* Lawrence."

He sighed. "You know I can't resist."

"Exactly." I parked my car in front of the entrance of the eighteenth-century canal house.

"Look, I have to go. Take the next couple of weeks to do a little research. But not before you've applied for a subsidy from Legal Aid, naturally." Rence himself was just walking out the door as I was going in. We lowered our cell phones.

"If there's sufficient grounds for an appeal, we'll put together a team. Okay?"

"Great."

"Be good, now." Rence flounced off to his SUV.

I waved at him and then walked into the office.

"Brilliant move," I said to myself out loud.

Now I didn't have a choice; I'd *have* to start digging into Ray's case. The good news: It would give me the opportunity to get to know him, and get paid for it, too. The bad news: Bartels & Peters had a strict rule against representing family members. But Ray was really a stranger, I decided. I wouldn't let my emotions get in the way.

Ray, the *Monster Next Door*. I'd never have expected it, but I had wanted to throw my arms around him and tell him, "Come, we're going home." It must have been because he looked like Aaron. That must be it. After all, who was Ray to me?

Or was it the blissful look on his face when I'd started telling him about the fish? Like a child being read to before going to sleep. Had my mother ever read to him? Had he snuggled against her in the evening, in his pajamas, with freshly washed hair? Had she loved him? Had anyone ever loved him? Ever?

CHAPTER 19

RAY

Rosita was cheerful most of the time. But she could also be sad. That's when she'd open the door and trudge back into the living room without saying a word. I never knew what else to do but follow her, clutching the paper bag with the madeleine. Then she'd plop down on the couch and sit with her head in her hands.

"Ray!" Anna said happily. Her lips went up at the corners and her eyes were wide. The first thing she always did was to grab the madeleine. She didn't take the trouble to peel the paper off neatly, no—she'd tear the bag open and stuff the whole cake into her mouth.

"You have to take your time and enjoy it," I said. "You have to take a bite and then chew it slowly so that you can appreciate the taste and the texture. Can you taste the way it's a bit crusty on the outside and fluffy and sweet on the inside, a bit moist and yet airy?"

Anna usually sat on the couch watching TV. I didn't think it was a very good pastime for a child and my mother didn't think so, either. So I decided to buy a big box of Lego Duplo blocks for Anna. From then on, whenever I visited, I'd build something and she'd join in. We built castles, farms, and mansions. Anna said that we'd live in one of those for real someday. I did try and explain to her, over and over, that you can't really live in a toy house.

Rosita would sit on the couch, sometimes with her head in her hands, sometimes watching us, sometimes watching the TV, and sometimes, but not often, she'd come over and help.

One day she said, "You never ask me how I am."

"I didn't know I was supposed to," I said. "Sorry. Do you want me to?"

"Yes. Isn't that the normal thing to do? *Normal* people ask each other how they are."

That hurt me. I'd thought I was doing everything right. I stopped by every day, I always brought a treat, and the week before I'd done her gardening.

"You don't like it that I said that."

"No." I was nervous and didn't know what else to say.

"Why not? Come on, admit it, you aren't really normal, are you? Like the way you always seem to be sitting at home by yourself staring at your fish. Or the way you're so worried about time, bringing her one madeleine every afternoon at three fifteen on the dot. That isn't *exactly* normal, is it?"

I shrugged my shoulders. I couldn't look at her.

"And stop moving your hands around like that. You're not kneading bread in the bakery here." She grabbed hold of my hands and made them stay in my lap. Her hands were warm. Soft and warm.

"Or—take your mother. Talk about abnormal! Is it normal you hardly ever see her or speak to her?"

"She's busy," I mumbled.

"Bullshit. Want to know what *I* think? I think that mother of yours should be proud of you. Does she even know there're lines of people who come to the bakery just to buy your croissants?"

"Probably not."

"I'd like to give her a piece of my mind, that mother of yours. You have her phone number?"

I hardly dared say it. "No."

"You don't even know your own mother's phone number? Why the hell not?"

"I write her letters. And she writes me back. She always writes back."

"*Write*? What the hell? Does she ever phone you?" Rosita sounded really angry.

"Sometimes. If she has to come on a different day than the appointed date."

"What do you mean?"

"The appointed date. The third Saturday every other month."

Rosita rolled her eyes. "Okay. Give me her name and address, and we'll look up her phone number. She's got it coming, the old witch." She was talking very loud, much louder than usual.

"Are you mad at me?" I didn't understand what had her so upset. And I really didn't like the way she spoke about my mother.

She laughed. "Of course not, silly. I'm mad at your mother. How *dare* she ditch you like that?" She leaned closer. The hollow between her collarbones came closer, too, so close I could hardly breathe. She took my hand in hers.

"Ray, she's your *mother*. Suppose I sent Anna away. What would you think of that?"

I looked at Anna, who had stopped building castles and was watching TV.

"Exactly. People just don't *do* that."

I only had my mother's PO box number. That made Rosita even more livid. She called information, but they told her there were at least forty Boelenses in Amsterdam. "You have to ask her for her phone number, hear me? The next time you write. And then get her to give you her street address as well. I'd like to see how she weasels out of *that*."

Of course I never did dare to ask my mother. Although Rosita kept asking me.

The next time I found Rosita sitting with her head in her hands, I remembered what to do and asked her, "How are you?"

She raised her head a bit and stared at me under a lock of dark curly hair. Her eyes were red, but she smiled faintly. "How sweet of you to ask, Ray."

"How are you?" I said again, because I wasn't sure what I was supposed to say.

"Come sit next to me." She patted the spot beside her on the couch. "Put your arm around me."

I went and sat on the couch, and since I couldn't move, she took my arm and pulled it across her shoulders. We were sitting closer than ever before.

"Not so stiff, Ray, just hold me."

I wrapped my arm tighter around her. I wanted to do a good job.

"Not that hard to start with. Just gently. Shake your arm to relax it, and then put it around my shoulder. *That's* right. Very good."

We sat there like that for a bit. Rosita was making snuffling sounds and I waited for what came next.

"I just can't do this anymore," she said after a while. "It's driving me crazy, living like this."

She was quiet, and then she said, "Now you have to ask me why."

I cleared my throat. "Okay. Why? Why is it . . . uh, driving you crazy, living like this?"

"Can't you see? Here I am with a kid, no job, and no husband. I barely get by. Look around. Is this what you call a proper home?"

I looked around, and my eyes got stuck on the photograph on the wall of the naked, pregnant Rosita. I felt my penis get stiff.

"I can't even afford fucking carpeting. I was young and pretty once. I could have had any man I wanted. Men with good incomes, nice things. But I had to go and choose that fucking prick."

Rosita began to cry. My arm jogged up and down on her shoulders. Cautiously I stretched out my hand and caressed her hair. She didn't slap it away. She let me. Her hair was just as soft as my mother's when I was little. Only Rosita had more curls, and they were darker.

"But you know what? One day I will be rich. *Very* rich. I have this rich great-uncle in England, you know. But what good is that for now? As long as he doesn't die, I'm stuck in this dump. What should I do? You've got to help me, Ray."

I felt a slight panic rising in me. What did she expect of me? Did she want me to *kill* the great-uncle?

"I can't stand living like this anymore. Not just for my own sake, but also for Anna's."

I didn't know what to say. Then I had an inspiration. "Tomorrow we'll go buy carpeting for you. The best you can find."

"But I can't afford it."

"I'll pay for it. Wall-to-wall carpeting. Because I want you to have a proper home."

She looked at me. "Would you really do that for me?"

I nodded. I felt warm inside.

She threw her arms around me and gave me a kiss on my cheek. I sniffed her sweet smell and felt her breasts pressed against me. My penis nearly exploded.

"Oh, Ray." Rosita slapped her hand to her mouth. "You're not used to people touching you, are you?"

She laughed, and I laughed with her. We laughed a long time.

CHAPTER 20

IRIS

"The plaintiff is already seated in the conference room," whispered Claire, the receptionist. "We've parked Mr. Van Benschop in your office for the time being."

I tried not to show my annoyance. "Next time I'd appreciate it if you could find another solution. I prefer not to have clients wait in my office when I'm not there."

"On Lawrence's orders."

I rolled my eyes. "Of course."

There was a small conference table in my office. But that wasn't where Peter van Benschop was sitting. He was standing by my desk, studying a photo of Aaron and me at the zoo.

"Single mother, isn't that what I said?"

"Good afternoon, Mr. Van Benschop."

"When it comes to women I'm always right. They may think of themselves as complicated creatures, but to me they're an open book."

If you knew what I was thinking right now, you'd run back to your mama, howling, I thought. "Would you mind taking a seat?" I asked politely, pointing at one of the chairs at the conference table. "I'd like to go over what's going to happen in the upcoming conference."

He complied, even took out his notepad.

"Since the plaintiff's legal team has chosen to resolve this matter with both parties present, it probably means they want to make an issue of Miss De Boer's emotional state."

"How do you mean?" asked Van Benschop, an aggressive tone creeping into his voice.

"It's easier, naturally, not to have to face up to the fact that Kim de Boer is just a young girl . . . excuse me, young woman, when she exists only on paper. I have the feeling they'll want to play up her age and vulnerability, use it as their trump card."

"You mean she'll start sobbing or something?"

"She may. Things will be said that will seem unfair to you. Demands will be made you won't agree with. But I want you to refrain from speaking unless I ask you. Is that clear?"

"What do you mean, I can't speak? *I'm* the one being sued, aren't I?"

"True. But you have retained me as your attorney. So please let me do my job."

"But I *know* Kim."

"And isn't that where all the trouble started? More than anything, it's so you won't say anything ill-advised from a legal standpoint."

"Okay." He made a show of writing *KEEP TRAP SHUT* on his notepad.

I couldn't help laughing. "Are you ready for this?"

"I hope so."

Waiting for us in the conference room were a stony-faced Kim de Boer, her parents, and her attorney. This wasn't going to be a walk in the park.

"No need for introductions on my part, is there?" said Van Benschop.

"We know who *you* are," said the mother.

I had pictured a dysfunctional family. Indifferent parents who were too busy getting drunk to care and only willing to get involved if there was money in it. But Mr. and Mrs. De Boer sat in neatly pressed outfits, giving the impression of decent, steady people. It struck me what a painful mess it was for them.

Kim de Boer sat between her parents, with no makeup on. Her hair drooped in greasy strands down along her oval face. I tried to read her expression, but it was completely blank.

"We all know why we're here," I opened the discussion. "Miss De Boer holds my client, Mr. Van Benschop, accountable for damages arising from lost income and emotional distress."

"Correct," said Adrian de Leeuw, the plaintiff's attorney. I had met him once, at a Junior Bar Association cocktail hour, a million years ago.

"We believe that this is about something more than money damages or legal conditions. What we would like to discuss is that my client"—De Leeuw nodded at Kim de Boer, as if we didn't know who she was—"is a young girl traumatized for life."

Kim de Boer was staring straight ahead with the same blank expression on her face.

"You have already described your client's state of mind rather extensively in your letter," I said drily. "May I have your reply to the counteroffer?"

"When I look at your proposal, I don't get the feeling that you are conscious of the gravity of the situation. My client has suffered severe emotional distress and will need *years* of therapy."

"Your client knew what she was getting into. I'd like to remind you that it was she who contacted Mr. Van Benschop in the first place. She was thoroughly informed as to the nature of the production and signed a contract."

"And we did go over everything first, didn't we, hey, Kim?" Peter van Benschop jumped in. "We even had a Coke together afterward." I gave Van Benschop a vicious kick under the table.

"The real question here is to what extent a minor can be held responsible," said De Leeuw.

"She was so eager that she presented a fake ID. My client had no clue as to her actual age. You could also have read *that* in my counteroffer."

Kim's mother looked as if she might burst into tears at any moment. I suspected her husband was just raring to lunge across the table and make mincemeat of Pissing Peter. Go ahead, I thought. I'd gladly push my chair aside and give him all the room he needed.

"I don't know a thing about that," said De Leeuw.

"Then you ought to read more closely."

"Is that true?" Mr. De Boer asked his daughter. "Did you use a fake ID to take part in this disgusting . . . spectacle?"

Kim's expression did not change.

"We need an answer," I said.

She shrugged.

"Silence implies consent, I believe." I hated myself for saying that. This had nothing to do with consent. Let alone my own conscience.

"I *should* like to hear my client's own answer," said De Leeuw.

"Do you think I'm *crazy* or something?" yelled Van Benschop indignantly. As if he was the one who'd been traumatized. "I'd *never* allow a minor to act in my films. Do you have any idea how eager women are to do this? I've got them knocking on my door . . ."

"What Mr. Van Benschop is trying to say is that there was no need for him to permit a minor to participate in his production. There is a reason all actresses are obligated to give proof of their age." Request a copy of the fake ID, I tried silently signaling to De Leeuw. *Ask* for it. But telepathy was evidently not his strong suit.

"Without that fake ID your client would never have been given the role." I couldn't have given him a more explicit hint.

But instead of asking to be shown the evidence, De Leeuw turned to his client. "Kim, did you falsify your ID?"

The girl stirred herself at last. She squirmed in her chair and her mouth wavered. She was going to break.

Everyone stared at her expectantly. She seemed to shrivel in her chair.

"It was Rick—he's the one who did it," she finally said. The voice of a little girl.

"Did what?" asked De Leeuw.

Please put an end to this farce, I prayed silently. I decided right then and there that this was the last time I'd ever take this kind of case. I'd rather do nuptials.

"Rick did something to the copy of my . . ."

"What the . . . ?" said Mr. De Boer. "Damn it, Kim. We *told* you that you were not to see him!"

Mrs. De Boer's neatly painted mouth had become a thin straight line. A flat line on an ICU heart monitor. The only thing missing was the high-pitched alarm.

"I hope you'll sleep well tonight," Mr. De Boer said to me before leaving the conference room. "Congratulations."

We had gone over the numbers and arrived at a total just slightly under the original counteroffer.

I couldn't think of an appropriate rejoinder. No excuse, no protest, no retort. Normally I'd have said something like "Bye now." Or "Drive safe." But neither seemed fitting. I watched the girl, supported by her parents, led out of the conference room. De Leeuw gave a curt nod and followed them out. The door slammed shut.

"Well, that was easy." Van Benschop rubbed his hands together. "Let me buy you a drink? Champagne?"

"Easy? It was *easy*?" I asked.

"Yeah. I have to tell you, I didn't have much confidence, but the way you handled it . . . you were great. I told you, didn't I, that it was all just a bunch of malarkey on that Kim's part?"

I turned and stared at him, incredulous. "If you really think it was easy because you had the law on your side, you're totally mistaken. It's just your dumb luck the plaintiff's attorney was asleep at the wheel."

"It's the outcome that counts, I say."

"The outcome?" It took me all I had not to start screaming at him. "The outcome is that you've ruined her and her entire family, not to mention what you've done to all the other morons—the men who think it's okay to abuse their wives because your films show them how it's done. You have no idea how much damage you're doing."

"Excuse me? What a prissy, pompous bitch you are."

"And *you* are a narcissistic, opportunistic, immoral bastard."

As I said it, the door swung open. "Didn't it go well?" asked Rence with a frown, charging into the room. "How do you feel, Mr. Van Benschop?"

God, the icing on the cake. "We did extremely well," I said. "Mr. Van Benschop was just about to pop the champagne. Weren't you?"

"Oh. It didn't sound that positive," said Rence. He put his hand on Van Benschop's shoulder. "Is Ms. Kastelein behaving herself?"

I didn't give Van Benschop a chance to answer. "Did you think

I was being unkind? On the contrary, you could see it as an ode to the submission of . . . what was it you called it again, Mr. Van Benschop?"

Pissing Peter didn't answer, but he was looking pretty hot under the collar.

"I'll get the documents ready by the end of today. I'll send them over for you to sign off on?"

"Excellent," Rence said quickly. "I'm glad you were able to get this matter resolved quickly, Iris. Well done. And perhaps you'll give Mr. Van Benschop and myself the chance to talk it over."

I strode out of the room without a backward glance.

CHAPTER 21

RAY

It was in the yard that I saw Rembrandt again. I'd recently been allowed to do yard work. Some of the patients had their own vegetable plots. Or they grew flowers. I clipped the hedges.

There were lots of hedges in the central courtyard. People sometimes called it Little Versailles. The hedges were planted in a square. The corners were cut off by diagonal lines making a smaller inner square. Inside that square stood a statue of a naked man. Though he did wear a stone loincloth. The restriction on naked bottoms obviously applied to the statues in the yard as well.

They let me clip all the hedges once every other week. Not without someone to keep an eye on me, though. Because patients with hedge shears had to be closely watched.

I looked forward to the day I trimmed the hedges. It reminded me of when I lived on Queen Wilhelmina Street. When I still had my job. When I still had Rosita and Anna. When I was often alone, sure, but not nearly as lonely as I was now.

I was halfway done with the second hedge when I saw Rembrandt wander into the courtyard. He'd been sprung from solitary a few days before, and I had managed to avoid him.

"Hey, Ray," he said, tossing a cigarette butt on the lawn. I made a note to myself to pick it up and throw it away the moment Rembrandt was out of sight.

"Rainman. Word is you got a crush on the blond cunt, what's-her-name-Jeannie?"

I didn't say anything back but went on clipping. Snippets of boxwood rained rhythmically down. *One, two, three.* On *three* my blades would lop off the next twig.

"You think she's hot, don't you?"

One, two, three. One, two, three.

"Know what you should do? You should just grab her. She wants it *bad*. It's obvious, the way she's acting."

One, two, three. One, two, three.

"You can do that, can't you? You *are* a real man, aren't you?"

I stopped clipping and looked around to see where the guard was. He was having a conversation with a colleague. I hoped he'd look up and tell Rembrandt to get lost. Didn't he know patients with shears needed to be closely watched?

Rembrandt took another step closer. "Sneak up behind her and tweak her nice fat ass." I was worried he was going to pinch my bum. His hand was coming closer. I tightened my grip on the hedge shears.

At last the guard turned around. "How's it going?" he asked.

"Great," said Rembrandt. "Little Rainman and I were having a nice little chat."

"Stop distracting him."

Rembrandt waved his hand in the air. "Fine, fine. See, I'm walking away. We're cool."

I went on snipping at the hedge. But I couldn't find the right rhythm anymore.

"If you don't do it, I will," Rembrandt called over his shoulders.

"What's *he* on about?" The guard had come up next to me. I saw Rembrandt watching us from a distance and tried to concentrate on the hedge.

"Nothing," I mumbled. My head felt hot, as if I had a fever. I didn't think I had a crush on Jeannie. Although she was very nice and she'd brought me a slice of her homemade bread. I'd tasted it and said, "Needs more sugar."

I had to admit that I did sometimes think of her when I jerked off. But she didn't even come close to Rosita. No one could hold a candle to Rosita. I thought about Rosita's white teeth, her dimple, and her nails, which were much too long, and I was sad.

"I don't feel like doing this anymore," I told the guard. "Can I come back and finish tomorrow?"

"Sure, Ray. No problem."

Back on the floor I sat staring at the photos. Peanut, Saturn, Venus. I held them up to my face and studied them. The fish were looking good. And Iris Kastelein who said she was my sister was right: the coral had grown. My . . . *our* mother had obviously taken very good care of the aquarium, but there were a few fish missing. Where was King Kong? And where was Hannibal? I also saw a dwarf angelfish I'd never seen before. I'd ask about it when Iris Kastelein who said she was my sister visited me again.

Mother had never been good at answering questions. I don't remember exactly when, but at some point I just stopped asking. Whenever she visited me before I went to jail, she did ask me some questions. How my work was going. If I was eating enough. What the story was with Rosita. At first she'd been glad to hear I'd made friends with my next-door neighbor. She'd even said, "Maybe you'll turn out okay after all."

But then Rosita and Anna had come walking by one time when my mother and I were standing out in front of my house.

Rosita waved at me and I waved back.

"Is that her?" my mother had asked. "Well, that won't do, then."

"Why not?"

"Just look at that skirt, it's much too short. It's indecent. How old does she think she is—sixteen?"

I looked at Rosita's skirt. It barely covered her buttocks. I felt a stabbing ache in my stomach. "She's always too warm. And I don't know if she thinks she's sixteen. I thought she was almost thirty. But I'll ask her."

My mother looked at me, shaking her head. "I wish I could see the humor in it—you being the way you are."

My mother didn't care for Rosita, and Rosita didn't have many good things to say about her, either. I was always caught in the middle.

"So where's your father, then?" Rosita liked to bring up difficult subjects. She'd come and sit next to me on the new couch with an ashtray on her lap, hugging her knees so that her skirt rode up and I could see her brown legs. I had used a good part of my savings to buy that couch.

"He left," I said. "He wasn't in the mood for a child."

"What do you mean, he left? Haven't you ever known him, then?"

"No. He left when my mother knew she was having me."

"*Men.* They're all the same."

I'd never leave. I'd never leave Rosita. I wish she would have seen that. But instead of seeing it, she allowed Anna's father to disappoint her time and again.

"Hasn't he ever tried to contact you?"

"No."

"Why not?"

I shrugged my shoulders. I didn't want to answer her questions, even if I'd known the answers. But I did my best anyway. It was important to Rosita.

"You've got to find out who he is. Don't you want to know where you came from? You have a right to know, don't you? Take Anna's dad. He's a fucking bastard, but at least Anna *knows* him. Have you asked your mother who he was?"

I wavered. "No," I said in the end.

"Aha. You don't want to tell me, do you! That's it." She put a hand on my cheek and moved her face close to mine. I smelled her sweet perfume mingled with cigarette smoke. It was nice, and also scary.

"We're friends. You know that, don't you? I'm on your side. Look at me."

I took my eyes off the hollow between her collarbones and tried looking her straight in the eye for as long as I could keep it up.

"That's better. You don't have to be afraid. I'm not going to *eat* you, you idiot."

"I'm not an idiot."

She let go of my face. "Of course not, sweetie. You're not an idiot. Far from it. You're the nicest person I've ever met, actually. You hear me?"

I nodded.

"You can trust me, Ray. Why are you keeping all the bad stuff inside? Just tell me. What happened with your father?"

"He left."

"We know that. Do you know where he went?"

"It was just as well my father left, because I was a terrible cry-baby, my mother said."

"Babies cry, what do you expect? You should have seen Anna—she howled and howled, day and night. It drove me up the wall! Believe me, Ray, all babies cry their heads off and it drives every mother crazy, even the hoity-toity ones who think they're perfect."

I looked at Anna. She was watching a cartoon.

"If your father abandoned you because he couldn't take the noise, he's just a wimp. It's got nothing to do with you."

"I want to buy Anna a fish," I said. "I want to give Anna a nice big fish, because she likes looking at fish, and then she'll have one of her own."

"That's so sweet of you. But you won't get out of it that easy. Come on, who's your dad? What has your mom told you about him?"

I had asked my mother about my dad a few times. At some point it had struck me that most of the boys in the neighborhood, as well as the kids at school, had dads who played soccer with them and punished them if they did something bad. One time at dinner I asked, "How come I don't have a dad?"

My mother's mouth froze for a second, and then went on chewing again. "You don't have one, that's all."

"Why not?" I'd asked. I didn't usually push my mother.

"Because. But don't be sad about it, Ray. Just be happy he isn't here. What do you think your father would say if he could see you banging your head against the wall the way you do? Or when you start screeching in the supermarket because you're scared to walk past the meat, even though you're a big boy of seven? Or what do you think your father would think about you smearing poop all over the walls? Do you think your father would enjoy seeing that?"

This was stuff I couldn't possibly have told Rosita. So I answered, "I don't know."

She scrunched up her eyes. "You *do* know," she said. "But if you don't trust me, that's your problem."

I didn't want her to be mad at me. I tried as hard as I could to think of something that would satisfy her. But I didn't have much imagination. "My mother was very young. Just twenty-two years old. And my father . . . he's just never been around."

Rosita lit another cigarette and smoked it with big sweeps of her arm. "I'm sick and tired of men who walk out on their women. All they think about is fucking, and a condom spoils it, they'll tell you. 'It doesn't feel as good.' Want to know what doesn't feel so good? Squeezing a baby out of your body. But that's not their problem. *Oh, no.* The kid isn't their problem."

I nodded, to make her happy.

"You'd never do that, would you? You're such a sweet guy."

I got a bit embarrassed and tried not to look at her or at the photograph on the wall. So I stared at Anna's cartoon on the TV.

"Have you ever had a girlfriend?"

"Um, no."

She laughed. "I should have known. A sweet guy like you. And you're quite good-looking, in your own way. How's it possible you've never had a girlfriend?"

I felt uncomfortable. "Tomorrow we're going to go buy a fish, me and Anna. We'll take the bus to Amersfoort and go to the fish store."

Rosita laughed. Was she laughing at me? "Don't change the subject. You've never *been* with a woman, have you?"

"I've got to get home," I said. "I have to feed the fish and check on the levels. I have to prepare a quarantine tank for the new fish."

She put a hand on my knee and leaned closer. "Or do you sometimes visit the whores?"

Now she was making fun of me. I was sure of it. I got up and walked out of the room.

"Sorry!" she called out after me. "I didn't mean to offend you." But she was still laughing.

We didn't go to Amersfoort the next day, nor the day after. I couldn't face Rosita, not after the things she had said to me. I did leave the paper bag with the madeleine at their door. I wasn't sure about it—should I or shouldn't I? But I just couldn't *not* do it.

I missed Rosita. I missed our afternoons together. I missed it when we'd both start laughing for no reason and then couldn't stop. I even missed the tough questions she always had for me.

After two days without her, I saw Anna's father park his car in front of her house. I had been sitting at the window, behind my curtain, hoping to catch a glimpse of Rosita. I felt sick. So bad I thought I was going to throw up.

He got out. I thought about him being allowed to see Rosita's privates, even though Rosita had called him a fucking bastard. She called me sweetie pie, she told me I was different than the other men. But *he* was allowed to touch her breasts, be the father of her child, even if he was a very bad one, who only came over whenever he felt like it.

I thought of all the times I'd babysat Anna because *he* needed alone time with Rosita, the times he'd talked to me with a smarmy smile on his face. As if he was better than me, when *I* was the one who'd bought the wall-to-wall carpeting, the new couch, and a new stroller for Anna. Which I'd done even though my mother had said that a four-year-old was too old for a stroller. But then she thought everything Rosita did was wrong or ridiculous. I did really want to please my mother. But more than anything in the world I wanted to please Rosita.

Anna's father strutted up to her front door. I don't know why, but he turned his head and waved at me. With that grin on his face. As if I was his friend. But I wasn't his friend. No, I was definitely *not* his friend.

He disappeared from view. Rosita probably opened the door in her white bathrobe with nothing on underneath. I stared at his ridiculously big blue car. And I thought, *I'll fix it so you can't drive anymore. If you can't drive anymore, you won't be coming over anymore, either, and then Rosita will see she's better off with me.*

I rummaged through the kitchen drawer and found a big knife. It was the carving knife my mother had bought me. Part of a so-called starter set, which also included pots and pans, plastic containers, plates, and cutlery.

I didn't really know what I was supposed to do with a starter set, since I'd already been living by myself for quite a few years. Besides, I didn't like the knife; it was too dull and didn't have a nice grip. I had much better knives at the bakery to slice the apples and chop nuts. But for this job it was perfect.

I marched outside with the knife in my hand. Just then the woman across the street came strolling by. She greeted me. Naturally, I didn't greet her back, since hers was the messiest front yard on the block. Then she caught sight of the knife in my hand. Her face tightened.

"What are you going to do?" she asked in a high squeaky voice.

I'd never noticed before that she had such a funny voice. It was as if she had to force the words out by squeezing them up out of her throat. I walked to his car without answering her question.

The navy blue car stood there gleaming and the sun wasn't even shining. I glanced around. Rosita's front door was shut. I could picture Rosita taking Anna's father's hand and dragging him up the staircase to the second floor, into her bedroom. He'd make her take off her white robe. And she would let him touch her privates.

I raised my arm and punctured the car's right front tire. There was a feeble *pffff.* That was all.

I slashed all four tires and kept hacking at them until the woman across the street was screaming so loudly Rosita *had* to hear it.

I wasn't done yet. I suddenly noticed the silver jaguar on the hood of his car. I thought of it pouncing on some innocent prey. A helpless animal, whose jugular he'd ruthlessly sink his teeth into. I'd seen them do it on the Discovery Channel.

I started trying to pry the jaguar off the car's hood. It wasn't easy; it was screwed on tight. But I was mad. As I was tugging on the jaguar, I heard sounds coming out of my mouth I'd never heard before. I couldn't help it. I roared, the way a jaguar roars maybe, and yanked the silver beast off the hood.

I used the jaguar to smash the car's windshield. That wasn't easy to do, either. The windshield resisted. It wasn't until the fourth wallop—the glass was already webbed with cracks—that the jaguar finally shattered it. The neighbor screamed, the breaking glass clattered, and I was roaring again. Finally Rosita's door opened.

"Holy shit!" Anna's father came scampering outside wearing only his blue-and-white-striped boxers. "Have you totally lost your mind?" His voice cracked. He ran up to his car. He wasn't smiling anymore. He darted around the car, taking stock of the damage, wailing, complaining, and swearing.

Rosita came running out after him in her white bathrobe. She stopped a little ways off and watched. I couldn't make out her expression. Was it anger, disgust, shame, pride, humiliation, or triumph?

"I think maybe you'd better not come here anymore," I told Anna's father. Loud and clear.

I turned and went back into my house. I put the big knife back in the kitchen drawer and washed my hands. I felt calm. I had done good. I had done a very good thing.

CHAPTER 22

IRIS

"How did it go here today?" I couldn't help asking.

"Well, okay," said Petra. "It's clear that he's getting along much better since he's had a bit more attention from you."

I pasted a smile on my face. If she thought I'd let her provoke me again, she had another thing coming. "Well, then, see you tomorrow."

I helped Aaron into his jacket and walked him to the car. It was cold out. We'd had a few weeks of warm weather, but there'd been a cold snap and everybody was waiting for summer to show itself again.

"I'm hungry, Mommy."

"We're going to eat in the restaurant, sweetie." I hadn't had time to do the shopping for a change. I often made a foray to the supermarket at lunchtime but hadn't had the time.

"Don't wanna."

"Pizza. You like pizza, don't you? We'll have a yummy slice of pizza, and that nice man always gives you a lollipop at the end, remember?"

I buckled him into his car seat and tried to make him look me in the eye. He was gazing vaguely in my direction, but that was it.

I drove to the pizzeria around the corner from my mother's house. The food wasn't great, but they had a liberal children's policy, meaning that all kids under the age of fifteen were lavished with lollipops.

We went into the pizzeria. Our coats were taken from us and we were shown to a table in the back, by the window.

"I wanna go home," Aaron whined.

I sighed, annoyed. "I'm sorry, but we're here now. Tomorrow I'll cook at home. But I didn't have time for shopping. And anyway, you love pizza, don't you?"

The waiter came to our table. I ordered a glass of white wine and a lemonade.

"I wanna go home," he persisted.

"Tell you what. I'll ask if we can have it wrapped up for takeout. But first we have to have a little patience." That seemed to do the trick; as long as I could keep him occupied for the next ten minutes, disaster averted.

"Tell me. What did you do today in nursery school? Did you draw me another beautiful picture?"

Aaron slipped off his chair.

"What are you doing?"

"Going home." Aaron started plodding toward the door.

I got up and set him back on his chair. "Sit down. We'll go home soon. As soon as we have our food."

He started wailing. Of course.

"Shhh," I said, not very quietly. It was early, fortunately; the restaurant still pretty empty. But the few patrons who were there started shooting me annoyed looks.

The waiter came back with our drinks.

"There's your lemonade," he said. "Drink up, *ragazzo*."

"I don't want," Aaron screamed. "Go *way*!"

"I'm sorry," I said to the waiter. "He's not having a very good day."

"Would he like a lollipop?"

"He doesn't deserve one. Just give me the check, then we can leave before this gets out of hand."

"I wanna lollipop! I wanna go home!"

"Sit down," I hissed. To no effect. Aaron, flailing his arms around, spilled the glass of lemonade in front of him.

"Not to worry," said the waiter, hurrying off to get a towel.

"Look what you did!" I grabbed Aaron by the arm. "And now you're going to behave yourself."

I caught an elderly couple sitting a couple of tables away, staring at me. "In *our* day we handled things differently," the woman said, loud enough for me to hear.

"Bitch," I muttered.

Aaron wouldn't stop howling, not even when the waiter pushed a lollipop into his hand, not even after the table was wiped clean and a fresh glass of lemonade was set in front of him.

"We really have to go," I said to the waiter. "Do you have the check for me?"

"On the house," he said. "It's not your fault."

I felt myself on the verge of tears.

He put his hand on my shoulder. "Don't worry. We've seen everything in here."

I then had to carry a thrashing, kicking, and screaming child out of the restaurant. I tried to hold my head high, to preserve some small shred of dignity. But it was thoroughly humiliating. Another public disgrace, starring me as Incompetent Mother.

Wrestling Aaron into his car seat was another struggle. "What's your damn *problem*?" I had lost all self-control. I was yelling hysterically. "Why can't you just be normal?"

I was this close to slapping him in the face. Or just tossing him out of the car and gunning it. Instead, I slammed my fist into the backrest just inches from Aaron's head.

He immediately piped down, staring at me wide-eyed. I took a deep breath and clicked his seat belt into place.

"But I don't know *how,* Mommy," he said when I had climbed into the driver's seat and started the car.

I turned around. Seeing the drawn little face with those grave, big eyes, I almost burst into tears. Because I realized he was right.

That night Aaron and I watched the aquarium, completed the shark puzzle, and read the fish encyclopedia. Once Aaron was in bed, I thought back on our vacation in Tenerife, a year ago. We had played all day in the surf. We'd hunted for shells and built sand castles. We'd let ourselves get dragged into the sea by the tide. And then at the end of the day when Aaron had started screeching because he didn't want to go back to our hotel room, I'd tickle him and say, "Hey, silly boy, I'm glad you had *such* a good time today that you're mad we have to go. But know what? Tomorrow we'll do it all over again."

I had been truly happy then. I'd felt I was a good mother, even. I'd resolved we'd take another vacation soon.

I started to wonder what had been my mother's state of mind when she drove Ray to the home for boys? Even though motherhood wasn't particularly easy for me, I could never bear to send Aaron away. Because I loved him, of course I did, but if I were honest, the main reason was I could never live with the guilt. Wasn't maternal love just another name for Stockholm syndrome?

Maybe I was jealous of the layer of Teflon coating my mother's soul.

I went over the clippings about Ray again. There was very little background information on him, except that he was reclusive and withdrawn according to those who knew him. And he used to work in a bakery.

"Most of the time he'd walk right by you," a neighbor had told the *Telegraph* in an interview. "Even if you said hello."

Rosita was the only person he seemed to have had any contact with. I examined a photo of her. A Mediterranean-looking woman with a wide mouth and unruly curls. She wasn't beautiful in the classical sense, but she was definitely sexy. And then there was her daughter. Where the mother was dark, the little girl was fair. Where Rosita laughed provocatively into the lens, Anna seemed rather introverted.

I reread the account of the murders. Ray had slaughtered his next-door neighbor and her daughter with some sharp implement and had then, it seemed, sat down and smoked a cigarette. Cigarette ash had been found on the bodies, and the burn mark of a butt stubbed out on the little girl's arm. What did it all mean? The savage explosion of violence, followed by the cool enjoyment of a cigarette. I conjured up Ray's face and tried to imagine him doing such a thing. The Ray who kept such a meticulous logbook and who closed his eyes when you mentioned his fish. Ray couldn't have done it. It simply didn't fit the picture.

I started fantasizing about unmasking the real culprit, and freeing Ray from the mental institution. Maybe one day we'd all be living happily ever after.

CHAPTER 23

RAY

"Drug testing at eleven," said the social worker with the glasses at breakfast. I had found out his name was André.

I was spreading honey on the slice of pulpy factory bread, longing for a *pain de Boulogne* with a crispy crust and light, tender crumb with a sourdough touch. I would spread it with fresh dairy butter; that's all it would need.

He sighed, annoyed. "Will you please look at me, and at least give a sign you heard what I just said?"

I lifted my head up. "Yes."

"Yes, what?"

"I heard."

"I'll come for you at five of eleven. Then I'll walk you over to the medical wing to give your urine sample."

I dropped my knife. I'd have to pee in front of that woman again. The woman with the prying eyes who had nothing better to do than stare at my penis. Women always let you down. I suddenly lost my appetite.

"Nervous?" asked Hank. He glanced over his shoulder and then went on in a whisper, "Drink lots of water. At least three liters. That way your urine will be useless, and they won't be able to pin anything on you."

"What?"

"You're not very bright, are you? Let me explain it to you. You have to drink lots of water, to dilute your piss. That way they can't trace the dope. Get it?"

"I don't use drugs."

He laughed. "Everyone in here uses drugs. It's how we get through the day."

"What are you two whispering about?" asked André. "I think it's best if you two didn't sit next to each other at mealtimes. Deepak, would you please switch places with Hank?"

I wasn't very fond of Hank. But at least I *knew* him. I had grown used to the smell of tobacco and the patches of sweat under his armpits. Deepak hadn't been in here that long.

"You can't trust those gooks," Hank had said. "They'll fuck your wife and then shoot you dead for ten euros."

Deepak plopped down next to me. "Why do *I* have to sit next to the retard?" he said in a loud voice. I heard sniggers.

He was an adulterer and a poorly paid hit man. And yet *he* had the gall to call *me* a retard. Why couldn't he just mind his own business? It made me mad. I didn't want to be in here, I didn't want people to talk to me or say stuff about me, and I *certainly* didn't want to be called a retard.

"I AM NOT A RETARD." I had never spoken that loudly in the common room. In my cell I'd sometimes talk out loud; I even yelled sometimes, the way I used to do when I was in jail. But here, in broad daylight, surrounded by all the loudmouths, the freaks, and the con men, I tried to keep my mouth shut as much as I could.

"*Go* for it, little Raynus!" said Eddie, whistling through his teeth. "Get it out of your system."

Everyone laughed. Deepak loudest of all.

I was shaking. I picked up the knife lying beside my plate and brandished it in the air.

André jumped up. "Okay, calm down. Put the knife down and finish your sandwich."

"The sandwich is *gross.*" I waved the knife around to emphasize what I was saying. "You people have no idea what *good* bread tastes like! No idea! So *you're* the ones who are retards." I felt spit fizzling on my lips. Little drops of spittle fell on the gross bread, the plate, and the table.

"Put it down, Ray. Or your aggressive behavior means a stint in solitary," warned the social worker.

"Come on, sit down," said Rembrandt. They all turned to look at him. It was suddenly quiet in the room. "Rainman doesn't mean it, do you, hey, Rainman? We're all good."

I wanted to announce that my name wasn't Rainman and that we weren't *all good.* But the word *solitary* stopped me.

"*You're* not the one calling the shots in here, Rembrandt," said André. But I sat down anyway.

"I don't want any trouble," said André as we walked down the corridors to the medical unit. A guard came with us. "You don't do any drugs, do you?"

"Of course not," I said.

We walked through the yard with the store where once a week we were allowed to shop under supervision. We could buy stuff like canned beans, cigarettes, and shaving needs. Things were much more expensive there than in a normal supermarket on the outside. There was lots of complaining about that. One of the inmates even proposed a hunger strike, but he didn't get much support.

The nurse who didn't wear a white coat was waiting for me in the medical wing. Dr. Römerman had explained to me why the staff didn't wear white coats: it was deliberate; they didn't want to emphasize the difference between them and us. The guards were the only ones who wore uniforms. It was confusing. Sometimes I couldn't tell who was a patient and who was a doctor, social worker, or nurse. I learned you could spot them by the pagers they wore clipped to their belts and the name tags around their necks. The string would break if you tugged on it. I heard that was so we wouldn't be able to strangle them with it.

"You know what you have to do," said the nurse. "Pants down to your knees, shirt up, and pee in the cup."

I didn't move. Just looked at the cup and the mirror next to it.

"Inmate is a bit stressed today," said André. "There was a little friction at breakfast."

I shuffled slowly over to the urinal and halted in front of it.

"Pants down."

I fumbled with the button of my jeans. My hands shook so bad that I had trouble undoing it. "I can't."

"Here we go again," said the nurse.

The button popped open and the zipper slid down.

"Pants down."

It was cold in the tiled space. I thought of my fish swimming around in filtered, pH-neutral water that was always a constant temperature of seventy-eight degrees.

"Hey, I haven't got all day!"

I pulled down my pants and then my underpants, too. In the mirror I saw my penis dangling helplessly. I grasped it and shuffled closer to the receptacle.

"Shirt up," the nurse snapped.

I let go of my penis and wedged my shirt up under my armpits.

"Pee into the cup."

My penis didn't want to. I could tell it wouldn't. But I still kept trying. With all my might I tried to make the pee come out.

"Always the same story," said the nurse. "Has he been drinking enough fluids today?"

"I think so," said André. "Have you, Ray?"

A few drops dribbled out of my penis. And then a very thin stream.

"Okay, you can get dressed."

Pulling up my jeans and my underpants, I felt like crying. "Saturn, Maria, Hannibal and King Kong," I said out loud. "Margie and Peanut. Venus and Raisin. And François."

"What's he going on about now?" asked the guard.

Walking back to the unit, I repeated the names of my fish. Over and over again.

"I think it's best if you spent the rest of the day in your suite," said André.

But they didn't let me stay in my suite. Instead of having the rest of the day off to look at the photos and arranging them in order, I had to go to the therapy room.

Jeannie was waiting there for me. I hadn't seen her for a couple of days. I missed our talks about the mother dough she was growing according to my directions. She didn't have the equipment to keep her dough at a constant temperature, of course, but it sounded like she was on the right track.

I liked talking with Jeannie, as long as there weren't too many people around. She made me feel like someone who knows stuff. But on the other hand, she also made me nervous. Especially after Rembrandt told me I should tweak her ass, because she wanted *it.*

Maybe she was even expecting me to do it. I tried to work out if it was true, and if so, when was the right time to do it.

One time she'd called me over. She was standing at the unit's kitchenette counter making a sandwich and called to me over her shoulder. She was wearing a tight pair of jeans. Her bum was bigger than Rosita's, but maybe just as nice.

I walked up to her, unable to take my eyes off her behind. My heart started beating faster. I could hardly breathe because of the weight on my chest. This could be the moment. I stopped right behind her and was about to put out my hand, like Rembrandt had told me to. She turned around. "Could you please unscrew this lid for me? I can't do it."

"Sit down, Ray." Jeannie's voice sounded different than when she talked to me about her amateur bread making. Not friendly. Her voice was cold. I wondered why. Had I done something wrong? *Had the mother dough died?*

The guard stayed by the door. I was usually left alone with the therapist. What was he doing in here? What was going on?

Jeannie put her elbows on the desk, folded her hands, and took a deep breath. "While you were taken for drug testing, we searched your suite. It's standard procedure. We always do after a resident has received a visitor for the first time."

Visitor. That was the woman called Iris Kastelein who said she was my sister. The woman who had brought me the photos of my fish. In the end I'd been glad that she'd come after all. But I wasn't so sure anymore. People had gone into my room and touched my things because of her.

"Who went in my room?"

"I did," said Jeannie. "And one of the guards."

Jeannie being in my room wasn't that bad; I could bear it. She smelled nice and had small hands. But the guard, with his big stinky hands, I couldn't stand it.

"To my dismay, we found this." She held up a bag of white powder. Cocaine. I'd seen it often enough on television, and in prison I'd seen it, too. Only, I'd never seen such a big bag. Eddie once showed me his stash. The bag was so small he could roll it up and hide it up his nostril. I thought it must hurt quite a bit, though.

"The good thing is," he'd said, "the more you use, the bigger your nostrils get. Your septum gradually rots away, so there's more room in there to hide your stash." He'd started roaring with laughter and I stopped up my ears because his laugh made me crazy.

"Whose is it?" I asked. "That would never fit inside someone's nose."

"Not all at once, certainly not," said Jeannie.

"How did it get into my cell?" I asked.

"That's what I'm asking *you*." She leaned back, her arms crossed.

"I don't know. It isn't mine." It was getting wild inside my head. I tried to think. The right words. I tried to find them, but they wouldn't come. So I just said over and over, "I don't know. I don't know. I don't know. I don't *know*."

"We cannot assume those drugs just wandered into your suite by themselves," said Jeannie. "I'm really disappointed in you, Ray. I expected more of you." She stared at me, unsmiling. Meanwhile both my brain and my hands were flailing in all directions.

I didn't know what to do. My mother—she would know what to do. But she said I couldn't contact her anymore.

"We're going to have to revoke some of your privileges until we can trust you again. You will be confined to your suite at communal hours for the next month, and you'll no longer be able to work in the garden."

What she said slowly started to set in. The hedges. I wouldn't be allowed to trim the hedges. *God!* Always the same story. They accused me of something terrible and then they took away the only things I'd ever loved. Rosita and Anna. My fish. The bakery. I couldn't even keep the hedges.

"Not the hedges," I said. "Communal hours, fine—I couldn't care less about those. But not the hedges! I haven't done anything wrong. The drugs don't belong to me. I swear."

"The drugs were found in your suite, so there's no point denying it. You know it will only count against you," said Jeannie. "Your first review is nineteen months from now. The patients that have shown signs of recuperation may be given a chance to return to society. But those who persist in lying and who refuse to learn will not."

Learn? What I'd learned was that it didn't make any difference *what* you said or did. They'd always find some way to get you. *Always*. I didn't want to cave in.

"I *don't* keep drugs in my room. Someone else did it. While they were making me pee in the cup in front of the woman not wearing a white coat, and I didn't want to do that, either. It was someone else who did it. It wasn't me."

"I'm sorry," said Jeannie. "I wish this hadn't happened."

I had given her the recipe for La Souche and she was taking my hedges away from me. I was getting mad. Very mad. "*Not* the yard work!" I said, my voice breaking. "Can't you see they've already taken everything from me?"

"Calm down, Ray." But that made me even angrier. I wanted to grab Jeannie and shake her the way my mother used to do to me when I was little, a little boy who wouldn't listen.

"Not the yard work!" Now I was yelling. Not even so much at Jeannie and the guard—more at the whole entire world. Or maybe at the statue with the loincloth in the yard, or at my mother, or at Iris Kastelein who said she was my sister. Somebody come help me! Anybody! "Not the garden!"

"That's enough," said Jeannie. "We're done here. Return to your suite."

If I went back to my cell, it would all be over. The guard put his hand on my shoulder. "Get up."

I had to say something. I had to explain. But they wouldn't listen. No one ever listened. The pathetic little potted plant on the desk caught my eye. In prison workshop one of my jobs had been sticking labels on plants that gave the name and care instructions. This plant was a dracaena, and it needed a lot of light. I'd read that sticker at least six hundred times.

I grabbed the plant and hurled it against the wall. A flash of green flew right by Jeannie's head. Shards flew in all directions, one hit me in the forehead, and the soil left a dark spot on the white wall.

Jeannie dived sideways, even though the pot had already sailed past her head, and besides, I never meant to hit her.

The guard twisted both my arms back and handcuffed me. I started bellowing. Like an animal. Maybe I *was* an animal, and that was why things were always being taken away from me. But my fish were animals, too, and *they* had everything they needed.

The door flew open and the small room was suddenly crammed with guards. I can't remember moving my legs myself. They dragged me out of the unit, down corridors, across courtyards, and through other doors. I kept bellowing and tried to wrench myself free. I wanted to get out of there. I didn't belong in here. I'd done nothing wrong.

We reached a cell furnished with only a bed covered in paper sheets. Solitary. It had to be the solitary cell. "Let go of me! Let me out!" I yelled. No one was listening. I was surrounded by at least five people, and yet no one was listening. "I've done nothing wrong!"

They threw me on my stomach onto the bed. They pulled down my pants. I resisted as best I could, but they were too many for me. "We're going to give you a shot," the nurse without the white coat said. I felt a vicious stab in my buttock and then almost immediately felt woozy. They undressed me calmly and efficiently.

Which made me think of Rosita.

CHAPTER 24

IRIS

I was scheduled to have a meeting with Rence from eleven to eleven thirty. I could guess what it was about. I resolved to stay calm; I wouldn't apologize, but graciously acknowledge that I had lost my cool with Van Benschop, and promise it wouldn't happen again. Even though Rence could be unreasonable, even harsh sometimes, he usually came around fairly quickly. I hoped that would be the case again . . .

Stepping into Rence's office, I saw Martha Peters standing by the window. She nodded curtly.

During my first few months at Bartels & Peters I'd tried to forge a bond with her. Since there were nine people in the firm, and Martha was the only other woman besides the receptionist, I was sure the two of us would hit it off.

I'd suggested having lunch when I started working, so that we could get better acquainted, but her only response had been a scowl, as if she had a pesky fly buzzing around her head. I'd be lying if I said I hadn't taken it personally. I felt insulted and asked myself what I'd done wrong. Finally, though, it hit me. Just as there are some grade-school teachers who can make any child feel she's the teacher's pet, Martha Peters had the dubious gift of making people feel as if whatever they did, they were doing it wrong.

"I've brought in Martha," said Rence. "I think it's important that she also hears what happened yesterday."

I wondered what her presence meant, and cleared my throat. "Fine. I'm not going to offer an apology, but I do realize I was a bit harsh yesterday."

Rence was seated behind his imposing desk. His desk chair was set a few inches higher than the facing chair so that he always towered over you.

"Harsh is an understatement. I'd say 'aggressive' instead."

"Lawrence . . ." Martha tut-tutted, but I didn't suppose it was because she was coming to my aid.

"Your behavior was quite unacceptable," Rence went on. "Out of all proportion. Had the Van Benschops not been long-standing clients of this firm, I would call it catastrophic."

I waited for the official warning.

He sat back in his chair, his hands stretched out before him on the desk. "I am wondering if you're sufficiently able to keep your business and private life separate."

I felt frustration bubbling up in me. My voice came out sounding shriller than I meant it to. "It's not as if I *enjoy* being called away on account of my son. If you have a problem with it . . ."

"I'm not saying this for my own sake," he interrupted me. "I'm saying it for *yours.* You are still young, the world should be your oyster. Instead, I see you floundering. You have big bags under your eyes, do you know that?"

"What are you trying to say? That I can put in for my Touche Éclat on my expense account?"

"Touche what?"

"Touche Éclat," said Martha by the window. "By Yves Saint Laurent."

"Come again?"

"Never mind," I said.

"It's a concealer," said Martha. "For the bags under your eyes. You may want to try it."

Rence gave her an irritated look and turned back to me. "I'm considering giving you an official warning."

The dreaded word was out. "Just . . . 'considering'?"

"That's what I like about her," Rence said to Martha, as if I weren't even there. "Sharp as a tack, this one. Reminds me of you, when you were young."

I could have been wrong, but it seemed to me that the look on Martha's face was one of female solidarity.

"Well anyway, Iris. You did hear me correctly. I said 'considering,' and now it's up to you to move that consideration in the right direction."

I nodded. I wasn't being fired just yet.

"And now that I have you both here anyway—could we discuss the appeal?"

"The psychiatric inmate," said Martha.

"It's an interesting case," I said, happy to change the subject—but not yet ready to reveal my connection to the case. "The guy was convicted of murdering his neighbor and her little girl. And since he was determined to have developmental issues, he was sent to a psychiatric institution. But he swears he's innocent."

"Ever since convictions started getting overturned by DNA evidence, we have come to assume that everyone who's in prison is innocent, naturally," said Rence. "So we can bill even more hours."

"Exactly," I said, although I didn't mean it.

"Excellent, my girl. Bringing new business to the firm is a fine thing to do and one of the reasons you haven't received an official warning *yet.* How far are you on this case?"

"Not very far. I don't have the official court record yet, but I do have all the clippings."

"Don't get sidetracked by the media," said Martha, who had once more turned her back to us.

"I'm not."

"Why haven't you obtained the court record yet? And has the board of appeals given it a docket?" asked Rence.

"Not yet. But it's just a matter of days."

"Keep on top of it. Do what you have to do. Remember, once a good lawyer sinks his teeth in, he never lets go."

I nodded, like a good girl.

I called the Hopper Institute and asked to be put through to Mo, to plan a follow-up visit. But Mo told me Ray was in solitary and unable to receive visitors.

"What for?" I asked.

There was a brief silence. "After your visit, drugs were found in his room."

"What?"

"You don't even want to know how much drug smuggling goes on in here. Which is why we have a policy of searching our residents' quarters after their first visit from someone on the outside."

"*I* certainly didn't smuggle in any drugs," I said.

"I want to believe you, and in all honesty, it doesn't really add up. You see, Ray was clean: negative drug test. Most drug users don't have the patience to wait for the drug test to be over. They'll usually smoke or snort the stuff as soon as they get their hands on it. And Ray's never given me any reason to suspect he's using."

"And I can tell you that I'm one hundred percent positive those drugs did not come from me," I said again, chagrined.

"In view of the quantity of cocaine that was found in his suite, it's assumed that Ray was dealing."

"Surely no one can believe that. Just *look* at the guy."

"Doesn't seem the type. But don't be fooled. You can't go by the way someone looks. We've started an investigation—but no matter what the outcome, there's a chance you'll be blacklisted."

"But that's absurd! I've got nothing to do with it."

"You could send a letter to the administration, I guess."

"If I became his lawyer, would that change things?"

"As his lawyer you are allowed to visit him as often as you like. You'd need to fill out an official application to represent him. I can mail you the forms if you want."

"Yes, please. You do believe me, don't you? That I didn't bring in those drugs?"

Silence. "I believe you," he finally said. "Besides, there's been a problem with drugs before Ray arrived. Kind of feels like an inside job."

"I'm glad you believe me."

"Fill in the forms and send them back to me. I'll let you know when the permission comes through. It usually takes three days or so. Maybe we can meet the next time you come? I can fill you in a bit more about Ray's time here."

"I'd appreciate that."

CHAPTER 25

RAY

A few days after I slashed Anna's father's tires, Rosita stood at my door. I'd seen her approach, but I'd quickly ducked behind the double pleats of my curtains—my mother thought the pleats were "richer looking."

"I know you're in there!" she yelled through the letterbox after ringing the doorbell three times. "Open up—I want to talk to you."

It was quiet awhile. Then she cried, "I'm not mad. Promise."

Another silence. Finally she called, "I'm not leaving until you open the door, you hear me?"

I got up and went into the hallway. It was too cold outside to have her stay out there until early the next morning, when I'd leave for work.

She stood in a miniskirt and the kind of boots people wear for motorbiking. So I asked her, "Are you going motorbiking?"

She burst out laughing. "Of course not, silly, it's the fashion."

I forgave her for calling me silly because I was so happy to see her smiling at me.

"May I come in?" she asked.

"Where's Anna?"

"My stepdad is taking her to the toy store. Can I come in?"

"Uh, yeah, I guess." I walked hurriedly ahead of her, to straighten the sofa cushions.

"Heavens, it's tidy in here! Why do we always hang out at my place? It's much nicer here. You even have candles on the table! But you never light them, I see. What's the point of having them?"

"My mother thinks they make it look cozy."

"They make it look cozy if you *light* them. Come, let's close the curtains and make the room a bit darker. Do you have a light?"

Before I could answer she took out her own lighter. "Go on, close them."

As I closed the curtains that matched the sofa cushions, which were also chosen for me by my mother, she lit the candles. Then she sat down on the sofa.

"See how nice it is in here, Ray?" In the candlelight her face looked even prettier than usual. "Come sit next to me."

I did what she said. How could I not?

She sighed. "Ray, what you did to Victor's Jaguar was very bad."

I kept my mouth shut.

"Very bad, but also very sweet." She began to laugh. "And funny, too."

I laughed along with her. It was impossible not to.

She took my hand and squeezed it. Her hand was warm. It was a warm, soft hand. My penis immediately jumped; I couldn't help it. I wanted her to touch it with her soft, warm hand. But at the same time I was afraid.

"But the thing I really wanted you to know is that I regret what I said about . . . well, you remember. I didn't mean to make fun of you or call you an idiot. I think you're great. You do know that, don't you?"

My penis was pointing straight up. I didn't want her to make fun of me again. I folded one leg over the other.

"Why are you squirming like that? Oh, God, don't tell me." She got up and pulled her miniskirt straight. "So your mother has done all this nice decorating but will not tell you who your father is."

It always worried me when she started talking about my mother. I tried to think of a way to change the subject.

"Turns out your impeccable mother hasn't been a very good girl, either. Did you know your father is a married man? Married to somebody other than your mother, that is. I guess his poor wife won't be too happy when she finds out." She started laughing.

I cleared my throat. "Let's go buy the fish for Anna tomorrow."

Rosita gave me a peck on the cheek.

"You don't want to talk about it? Fine." She blew out the candles. "Anyway, what I wanted to tell you was, don't worry about Victor going to the police for what you did to his poor car. He can't explain, see, why his car was parked on this street in the first place." She giggled and flounced out of the room, hips swaying, leaving me sitting on the sofa. I heard the door slam shut and stared at the smoke curling up from the blown-out candles.

Rosita and Anna were already waiting for me when I returned from the bakery the next day. They were both looking very smart. Rosita wore a dress and the navy raincoat that we had recently bought together.

"I feel like a princess," she'd said when she'd tried it on. I had paid for it, though my savings were almost all gone.

"Ray!" Anna stretched her arms up and came running toward me.

For an instant I wondered if she really meant me. But she stopped right in front of me, her arms still outstretched.

"Hey," I said. "How you doing?" I handed her the paper bag with the madeleine. But instead of tearing it open, she just stood there gazing up at me.

"Pick her up," said Rosita. "Can't you see that's what she wants?"

I bent down and placed my hands under her armpits. Carefully, I picked her up. It was the first time I'd ever done that. Anna flung her arms around my neck and gave me a kiss on the cheek. It felt nice. But awkward, too.

"You're blushing," said Rosita. "How cute."

The three of us walked to the bus stop. Anna wouldn't stop talking about the fish I was going to buy for her.

"Do you know what kind you want yet?" I asked. "A clownfish, a blenny, an angelfish, a doctorfish . . ."

"I want blue," she said.

We came home with a magnificent angelfish. Van de Akker had just received it in a shipment from the Caribbean. It was a prize specimen. Anna named it King Kong.

Together we recorded the purchase in the logbook. I put my hand over hers and helped her make the letters. The words *King Kong* wound up smudged across at least four lines. Even so, I didn't mind.

At the door, when they were leaving, Rosita said to me, "It almost feels as if we're a family. You, me, and Anna."

I stared at the floor.

"Thanks for everything you do for us. You're really a very sweet man."

She grabbed my chin, tilted my head up, and kissed me on the mouth. Her lips were soft, and sticky with red lipstick. What did this mean? Did the kiss mean she loved me? Did she want to marry me? Or was it normal to kiss someone you think is "a very sweet man"? And what about Anna's father? And was it right for us to kiss in front of Anna?

She peeled her lips off mine and gazed at me, smiling. I hardly dared look back at her.

"See you tomorrow, Ray."

Rosita and Anna walked down my front path, turned right, walked ten steps, and then turned up their own front path. I kept on waving at them. Even after they stepped through the front door and disappeared inside. *Family.* She had said it herself. We were almost a family, the three of us. I think that evening I was happy.

I opened my eyes and saw I was lying in a solitary cell. It smelled of disinfectant. It wasn't an unpleasant scent. It reminded me of the cleaning stuff we used in the bakery.

I was dressed in an unfamiliar outfit made of something halfway between paper and cardboard. I shivered. I felt cold. Not because the temperature in the cell was cold; I was chilled from the inside out.

There was nothing to do, nothing to look at. The only distraction provided was a blackboard and a piece of chalk. I picked up the chalk and began to write. *Dear Mother.* I erased it. *Sweet Rosita.* Erased it. *Dear Iris.*

I never had a sister before, but I supposed siblings shared their secrets with each other. Hadn't she said she'd help me? I wrote and wrote until I'd filled the blackboard, and rubbed it all out and started over again. I just kept writing and erasing. Until I'd told her everything there was to tell. Even the things that must never be told.

CHAPTER 26

IRIS

She spotted me as soon as she stepped through the sliding doors into Arrivals Hall 1. I don't know if she was surprised; if so, she didn't let on. Our eyes met coolly. One of my mother's bridge friends, Lina, who shared her passion for spa treatments was with her. They had been friends for years.

When Lina caught sight of me she elbowed my mother and began waving enthusiastically. "Isn't *this* nice! You're so lucky, Agatha. It would take a serious bribe for my Carla to come meet me at the airport." Lina threw her arms around me and planted a big kiss on my cheek. "Hello, darling! How nice to see you again. Where's that dear little boy of yours?"

"Day care."

"Come, Agatha, give your daughter a hug!"

Stiffly my mother air-kissed me three times, in the Dutch manner.

"What a surprise, huh, Mother?" I said deliberately.

She shot me a sour look.

"Let's walk to the car. I'll drive you home."

"Wonderful," said Lina. "The taxi drivers these days barely speak Dutch. Let alone of knowing the way. This is nice, isn't it, dear?" She poked my mother in the ribs again. "You don't know how lucky you are, having such a thoughtful daughter."

"I certainly do," said my mother sarcastically.

After Lina had said an effusive good-bye, making me promise I'd come over with Aaron, my mother asked, "So what was this supposed to be all about, Iris?"

I started the car again. "Did you enjoy your vacation, Mother?" I asked sweetly.

"Of course not. How can I relax if you're nosing around?"

"Actually, I wonder how *you* can relax knowing your son is in an institution for the criminally insane."

"So you know."

"It wasn't all that hard to figure out."

My mother stared out the window. I didn't have to see her face to know she was fuming.

"Did you really think you could keep the fact that you had a son a secret forever?"

"Until you started sticking your nose in my business I managed to pretty well, actually."

"How *could* you, of all people? You are always harping on and on about responsibility."

"I don't owe you an explanation, Iris. You have no idea what it was like. What I had to go through."

I parked in front of my mother's house and turned off the engine. "Can I help you with your suitcase?"

"I can manage," she said icily. She got out, wrested the trunk open, and hauled her suitcase out with some difficulty.

I followed her to the front door.

She turned all three locks and went inside. The suitcase wobbled dangerously as she pulled it over the threshold. "Did I invite you to come in?"

"I don't need an invitation, Mother. I'm your daughter and you're not getting out of this conversation."

She sighed. Outwardly cool and collected. As always.

"There's a reason I have chosen not to tell anyone. I'm sorry you've found out about Ray, but I would like to leave it alone."

"Why? I already know the worst parts, so what's there to hide?"

"Just leave me alone. And leave Ray alone, too." She walked into the living room and pulled the throw off the couch. Then she started folding it in the neatest possible way.

"I won't. On the contrary, I'm going to have a look at his case, to see if there are grounds for appeal."

"What?!" My mother looked at me in disgust.

"Ray asked me to help him. And since he's my brother, I am going to do just that. It's bad enough you've washed your hands of him all these years. At least there's one member of the family who's interested in what happens to him. Besides, as his attorney I can visit him as often as he wants. And we must have quite some catching up to do, wouldn't you think?"

"I don't know what you *think* you're doing, but let me tell you this: Ray isn't the nice cuddly brother of your dreams. I mean—I assume you know *why* he's locked up."

"It remains to be seen if he is guilty."

"You don't know him, Iris. Ray can seem very sweet and cute, but he's dangerous. As a child he was quite irrational."

"Was that before or after you dumped him in the institution?"

"Don't forget I was very young when I had him. He was just impossible. You think Aaron's difficult? You should have seen Ray. I couldn't handle him at all."

I had a hard time believing there was anything my mother couldn't handle. But I did feel sympathy for her, for things to get so bad that she had to send her child away. I gazed at her face.

The hard lines around her mouth. Why couldn't she show me any emotion?

"Still, you should have told me. Didn't I have the right to know I have an older brother?"

"Funny, isn't it—it's always got to be about *you*. Don't you think it hurt *me,* to have to give up my son? Because I do love Ray. I have always loved him and will always love him. Having to part from him, do you hear that, Iris, *having* to, was very painful for me. But no, instead of trying to understand my feelings, you immediately turn it around to yourself. You're acting as if I've done something terrible to you."

"Won't you just tell me a little more? Maybe then I can understand where you are coming from."

"It's a chapter I've chosen to close and you will just have to respect that." She turned around and rolled her suitcase into her bedroom without a backward glance.

I wasn't willing to give it up, and followed her. "Have you ever visited Ray? In prison or at the institution?"

"I've been to the prison, yes," she said stiffly. Her suitcase lay open on the bed. Her clothing, in the gaudy shades women in their sixties tend to be partial to, was arranged in neatly folded piles. Off to the side I spotted a flesh-toned bra and lace-trimmed hip briefs. Apparently she'd had everything laundered while still at the hotel. It didn't surprise me.

My mother must have seen me stare. She snatched up her underwear with a catty gesture and stuffed it in her underwear drawer.

"But do you visit him still? He's terribly lonely, did you know that?"

My mother walked over to the closet with a stack of T-shirts in her arms. Standing with her back to me she said, "Let me refresh your memory. He *murdered* someone—what am I saying?—*two* people, a mother and child. You needn't feel sorry for him." She turned back to the bed, rummaged around in her suitcase, extracted a wrapped gift from the bottom, and tossed it in my direction. It landed at the foot of the bed. "Here, I got you something."

It was clearly a bottle of booze. I peeled off the thin giftwrap and read the label of some obscure Slovenian concoction. "Well, thanks."

"Local specialty, they told me. I also have something for Aaron, but I'd rather give that to him in person. If he's still allowed to come here, that is, now that you know what a horrible creature I am."

"Feel free to use Aaron to compensate for Ray as much as you like. He doesn't seem to have any objections."

"Nor do you, actually."

"You're right."

We were both silent.

"There's a chance that your son, your own flesh and blood, is in a mental institution after being wrongly convicted. Doesn't that bother you?"

She shook her head. "You don't know Ray. You have no idea what you're saying."

"Maybe not knowing him means I can be more objective." That wasn't true, of course. I wanted to believe in Ray's innocence just as fervently as my mother wanted to believe he was guilty.

"You have no idea, Iris. No idea."

"I'd still like to find out."

My mother walked into the adjoining bathroom to throw what little laundry there was in the hamper. When she returned, she said, "Please leave him alone. Just stay out of it—and out of my past."

CHAPTER 27

RAY

"Is anyone out there?" I banged on the cell door. "Hello?"

No answer.

I looked around hoping to find a way out. All I saw was four white walls and a small barred window that looked out on a strip of grass. Apart from that, the small space had a door with two little shutters—closed. I banged on the door again. Nothing.

I thought about what would happen if I used up all the air in the cramped space. It was already happening; with each breath I felt my lungs getting less oxygen. Breathing would keep getting more difficult, and in the end I knew I would suffocate.

My aquarium's air pump had stopped working once. I discovered it at three in the morning, when I was about to leave for work. I always checked the aquarium and recorded the levels at that time.

The first thing I'd noticed was the silence. The water wasn't bubbling, and I couldn't hear the pump's constant buzz. I peered into the aquarium to find the fish. They weren't darting through the anemones and weren't grazing on the coral. That's when I saw them. They were floating at the surface. Their mouths open wide.

I had to save my fish. What was my own life worth, if they

perished? Luckily I still had an old pump lying around, which I was able to use as a stopgap measure. "Hang on a little longer!" I remember saying that to them, even though fish can't hear, all they can sense, at most, is the vibration. Maybe I was saying it more to myself than to the fish. "Hang on a little longer." I installed the old pump and soon the water began bubbling again and the fish went about their business again as if nothing had happened.

My fish never lacked for anything. I made sure of that.

In the solitary cell there was no backup pump, no escape route. Nothing.

"Is anyone there?" I called again. "Please, is anybody there? I have to get out of here. I'm suffocating!"

I heard footsteps in the corridor. The little shutter slid open and I saw an unfamiliar face. "Everything all right in there?"

"No," I panted. "I can't breathe. I . . ." I clutched at my throat. "Please open the door. The oxygen is almost all used up."

"Impossible," said the face. "Look up at the ceiling. Do you see those white vents? Fresh air comes out of there. So you *can't* suffocate."

"It's not working," I said. "I can feel it isn't working. I'm suffocating. You want me to die."

"You're having a panic attack," said the face. "Try breathing in and out, nice and calm. And if after that you're still not feeling better, I'll ask the doctor to give you something to relax you, okay?"

"You planted drugs in my room so you could lock me in here. And now you're going to let me die. It's a trap. I've been lured into a trap."

"Calm down. Remember what I said. Look at the vents in the ceiling."

"It's not working. It isn't working."

"Do you want me to leave the hatch open? Then you can breathe through the opening if that'll make you feel better."

The face disappeared again and I stood on tiptoe so that my mouth could reach the hatch. I was like François, Maria, Hannibal, Peanut, Raisin, King Kong, and the others. I sucked in the scanty oxygen with my mouth wide open. Waiting for the backup pump.

After a few hours I had a cramp in my legs and a stiff neck. I sat down on the floor; I no longer cared that much about dying. It seemed a perfectly acceptable option.

They brought me a meal. The bigger shutter was pushed aside and a plastic plate of spaghetti was set down on a ledge with some plastic utensils and a cup of water.

I jumped to my feet. "Hey!" I yelled. "Hey, is anyone out there?"

Nobody replied. The hatch rammed shut.

I sank to the floor holding the plate of spaghetti. Tomato sauce dripped onto my white pants. It left a nasty red stain. Red on white.

Just like Rosita, when she was dead. She was wearing her white top, the top with the thin straps, that let you see her boobs—nipples and all. She always dressed too lightly for the weather. It wasn't very hot the day Rosita died. But Rosita would rather turn up the heat than put more clothes on. She'd have preferred walking around naked all day, she said.

The white top was torn and covered in red spots. Her miniskirt was smeared with blood, too. There was so much blood. Blood everywhere. I got dizzy looking at it and kept having to close my eyes because it was so hard to look at.

Anna was wearing a little pink dress. It had been on sale at H&M. Only, there was a big wet stain right across her tummy. Her eyes were open. They had an expression I couldn't place. Fear?

Surprise? I saw the blue irises with the pretty darker edge all around. But her eyes weren't shiny anymore.

Rosita's eyes were half-closed. Her mouth was slightly open, as if she were laughing. Even when she was dead she was still laughing. I had no idea why. Was she making fun of me? Was she *still* making fun of me?

There was blood on the ground all around them, like fried eggs with broken yolks. The blood wasn't very liquid; it was gluey, and it stuck to my shoes. My shoes left tracks on the beige carpet.

"Do you really want such a light color with a young child in the home?" the man in the store had asked us. He assumed we all lived together, maybe even thought I was Anna's father. I liked him for that reason. "We also have some lovely brown-flecked shades."

But Rosita didn't want any dark colors in her house. "Beige is chic," she said. "All the rich folks that live in the big houses have it. And if it gets dirty, we'll just buy a new one."

The carpet had cost almost six thousand euro, including installation. It took half of my savings.

And the carpet was ruined.

There was a smell of rusty iron in the air. It wasn't very pungent or strong, but it made my stomach turn. I never knew blood had an odor before.

I stared at the plate of spaghetti in my lap and couldn't think of what else to do but just start eating.

CHAPTER 28

IRIS

Martha Peters had the build of an Eastern European swimming champion. A broad back, sturdy thighs, no breasts to speak of, and a hard set to her mouth. She took up almost the entire corridor.

"Good afternoon, Martha."

Martha turned around. "Ah, just the person I wanted to see."

"Oh?"

"Walk with me. I have a surprise for you."

Without waiting for a reply, Martha turned and marched to the stairs. I decided I'd better follow her, although I couldn't think what the "surprise" could be. It reminded me of going to the dentist when I was little; if you kept your mouth open long enough without complaining, you'd get a "surprise." A toothbrush. Yippee.

Martha's office was on the top floor of the building, away from the noise and the fuss. In the three years I'd been working at Bartels & Peters I'd gone up there maybe twice. I followed Martha's robust backside up the stairs.

The room was bright, light, and remarkably elegant, in contrast to Martha's imposing form.

"Sit down, have a seat," she said, in a friendly voice, which immediately roused my suspicion.

"Don't look as if I'm going to bite you! Did you know I have a son, too?"

"I didn't." It was the last thing I'd have expected of her.

"Sam. He's twenty-two and moved out just recently. So I was a working mother, like you."

I nodded.

"I've always managed to keep my work and my private life separate. But in my case it was easier. The higher up you are on the corporate ladder, the more latitude and advantages you have. Take this room, for instance. Who's going to notice whether I'm in the office or not?"

"But don't you have to put in your quota of billable hours, like everyone else?"

"But *I'm* the one who decides when and where I work those hours. Nobody would dream of questioning it." She looked at me with a self-satisfied smirk.

"Fine; you're right. Why don't I just get rid of this kid? I can always have another one once I make partner."

She shook her head. "No need to be so touchy. That's one of your problems, Iris. You take everything so personally."

"It was a joke."

"Of course. Well, anyway, I think you're lucky that we had little choice but to take you on when we did."

Aha. There you had it. "What do you mean?"

"Nothing." Martha waved her enormous hands as if hoping to erase her last remark. "And I won't deny that you actually turned out better than I'd expected."

"Is that supposed to be a compliment? Am I wrong in assuming it wasn't the surprise you had in mind?"

"Oh, right." Martha rummaged in her desk and took out a stack of papers. "Here you are."

"What is it?"

"You've brought in a new client, didn't you? I just wanted to give you a little head start on your case."

I stared at the cardboard cover. *R. Boelens, 17th of May 2003—3rd of March 2005,* it said.

"How did you get this?"

"Connections. The only reason I go to all those cocktail parties, which you never attend. Connections, connections, connections. Interesting case, by the way. I don't know if it'll lead to anything, but it's definitely a juicy one."

Aaron was in bed and I was stretched out on the couch with the file, a cup of Sleepytime tea, and a bar of hazelnut milk chocolate. I was tired, and having a hard time focusing. The file was surprisingly meager. It contained the forensic report and some police interviews with local residents. Ray had made three different statements, each time incriminating himself a little more. That was enough to nail him as far as the police were concerned. Where were Rosita's friends and acquaintances, relatives, lovers—the mailman, even?

According to his first statement, Ray had gone home earlier than usual because he wasn't feeling well. On his way home he had seen Rosita and Anna's front door slightly open. He had walked over to investigate. The first thing he'd noticed was the red stain on the beige carpet. He had pushed the door open a bit more and then he had seen the two bodies bathed in blood. He'd stayed with the corpses a little while "to see what would happen." I felt a shudder go up my spine.

After that he had gone home. There he sat down to watch his fish, in order to make himself calm down. "I didn't call the police because I didn't think of it."

His next statements contained a number of incriminating remarks. "It was obvious Rosita and Anna had been stabbed with a sharp object. I'm thinking of a carving knife, like the kind I have at home." And: "I was mad at Rosita because she rejected me. When I get mad, I lose control. Sometimes I get so mad I start breaking things."

There was no explicit admission, but you didn't need a law degree to know where this was going. The deposition ended with: "I hereby swear that no words were put in my mouth and that I make this statement of my own free will and without any threats or promises extended."

I shuffled to the bottom of the pile and came upon a photo of the crime scene.

The dead girl especially broke my heart. An innocent child, her little face twisted with fear. The accompanying report from the crime scene investigator stated that the mother was killed first, then the child. She had left footprints in her mother's blood. The conclusion was that she had come running from the living room before being stabbed to death as well. I thought about Aaron, sleeping peacefully in his cot with his stuffed panda bear.

The murder weapon was not found at the crime scene. But the Netherlands Forensic Institute had established that it was, in all probability, a carving knife belonging to the kitchen starter set from Ikea, bluntly called "Börja," Swedish for "start." Some 130,000 of these sets had been sold from 1990 to 2009 in the Netherlands alone. In 2009 it had been redesigned; the carving knife's handle was no longer brown but black.

Ray owned one of those Börja starter sets. It had been a present from his mother, the statement read.

I remembered when I'd first left home. My mother thought it was ridiculous that I didn't want to live at home, when we lived so close to the city. "I let you come and go as you please, don't I?" But I longed for my own chaotic student digs, where I could drink Lambrusco with my friends until the early hours of the morning before passing out on a worn mattress on the floor.

The first time my mother came to look at my nine-by-twelve-foot room in the Jordaan quarter, she'd had little to say. But the disapproving look in her eyes said it all. Pushing a large box into my hands she'd said, "Don't you even have a proper chair to sit on?"

I'd torn off the blue-striped wrapping paper to reveal the Börja starter set. I'd completely forgotten its name, even though the empty box had served as the hall wastepaper basket for months.

"Thank you, Mother." She had offered her cheek, a sign that I was allowed to give her a kiss.

The thought that my mother had driven to Ikea to buy both of us a Börja set was almost laughable. For herself she bought only top quality, but for others she liked to see what was on sale that week. Ikea must have been having a two-for-one sale.

Ray's carving knife, the alleged murder weapon, had been found in his kitchen drawer. Not a trace of blood was detected on it, but it did have Ray's fingerprints as well as a number of residues with chemical-sounding names that meant nothing to me. Also, the knife was in pretty bad shape. Bent and chipped, well used.

Notwithstanding the puzzling fact that none of Rosita's or Anna's DNA was found on the blade, the Ikea knife was considered a very damning piece of evidence.

I stuck another piece of chocolate in my mouth. I told myself I would stock up on carrots and celery tomorrow.

Then there were the statements from the neighbors. One woman claimed that on another occasion Ray had slashed Rosita's boyfriend's tires with a knife. So Rosita had had a boyfriend. *Why was there no mention of him?*

CHAPTER 29

RAY

The day after Rosita kissed me, she acted as if nothing had happened. She let me in to give Anna the madeleine, but then she said, "If you don't mind, Ray . . . I'm expecting someone."

I had been hoping Anna's father wouldn't ever return. But there he was again.

Rosita was wearing a see-through dress. Her boobs were clearly visible, hard nipples and all. It was difficult not to look. I tried imagining how I'd touch her boobs, take them in my hands and knead them. The thought hurt my penis.

"Victor's going on a trip tomorrow with his family. Imagine, Ray, they're off to Crete—*just a little prelude for the summer.* In July they're spending three weeks in Italy. And last Christmas they were in the mountains skiing. But he doesn't care that Anna has never been anywhere except for Zandvoort-by-the-Sea. 'My family is my first priority,' he says. But what are we, then? What do we mean to him? Aren't we his family, too? Doesn't Anna have just as much right to a father as his other kids?"

"I don't know."

"You don't know? Well, I do. Don't you ever go on vacation?"

"No."

"Never?"

I shrugged.

"We should go to Crete, too. You, me, and Anna. That would make him sit up and take notice, wouldn't it?"

I felt a shudder of happiness. "I don't know if I dare to get on a plane."

"Of course you dare," said Rosita. "But anyway, he's coming over, and I was just wondering if you could take Anna for a while."

I didn't get it at all. Rosita wanted to go to Crete with *me*, but *I* had to take Anna back to my place because she wanted to take her clothes off for *him*?

Rosita crouched down in front of Anna. "Sweetie pie? You want to go with Uncle Ray? Maybe he'll even take you to the bakery. Or the playground."

"I wanna see King Kong," said Anna.

"Will you put on your jacket, please? It's cold out. And Ray?" She straightened up. "When you come back, I have a surprise for you. I want to tell you something about your mother."

Anna stepped outside holding my hand. Her hand felt fragile, just a few little bones packaged in soft, delicate skin. Rosita waved at us as we left. She did it by sticking just her hand out, hiding the rest of her skimpily dressed body behind the door.

Across the street the woman with the unkempt garden was peering out her window at us. She waved at us, too, but Anna didn't notice her.

"What do you want to do?" I asked in the high-pitched voice I had adopted specially for Anna.

"Look at fish."

"Not the playground? Or do you want to go shopping, like Mommy?"

"King Kong," she said firmly.

"Fine, fine." As I was sticking the key in the lock I heard a car screeching to a halt right in front of my house. I turned around and saw Victor driving up in his flashy car without even a dent or a scratch on it. He walked up to Rosita's door and I saw her open it even before he'd rung the bell. I had to gulp down some stomach acid that came up into my mouth.

Anna and I went inside and sat down in front of the aquarium. "King Kong, Hannibal, Maria, Peanut . . ."

Through the wall I thought I heard footsteps climbing Rosita's staircase. She was taking Anna's father upstairs with her. I had never been upstairs at Rosita's. Never. When would Rosita finally get it, that *I* would always be there for her? She'd said we were almost a family, but how long would I have to wait?

Anna and I had said the fishes' names I don't know how many times when she asked me to take her to feed the ducks. I realized I'd been concentrating so hard on the sound of footsteps on the stairs and Rosita's bed creaking that I'd completely forgotten where I was.

Anna looked up at me with eyes that were nearly as blue as King Kong.

"Of course," I said. "On the way we can stop at the bakery for some day-old bread. Even though my bread keeps for a lot longer; after three days it's still fresh and delicious. But you can't sell bread that's more than a day old, because then they call it *stale*. Ridiculous."

I helped her into her jacket. It was a pretty red jacket. It had cost 130 euros, but Rosita said it was excellent quality, and Anna could easily still wear it next year. Which was just as well, because the money in my savings account was getting dangerously low.

Anna skipped along next to me holding my hand as we walked to the bakery. I was getting used to the idea that she liked being with me. Victor's car was still parked in front of Rosita's door. I felt myself get mad but thought, *Not now.* Not while Anna was with me.

It was quiet in the bakery. The people usually came in the morning to buy their bread. That's why the store closed at four thirty in the afternoon. It was four fifteen when Anna and I got there. We had to wait for a lady to pay for her *pain de campagne* first before we could walk through to the back. The lady took her bread and turned around. "Ah, the baker," she said. "Aren't you on the wrong side of the counter?"

"I've come to get some stale bread. For the ducks," I said.

"Is that your daughter?"

"We're almost a family," I said. "Almost."

I think the lady looked surprised. "I have long wanted to tell you I think your bread is delicious. Truly remarkable."

"Thank you." Rosita would like to hear that. She always asked me if I'd had any compliments and then she'd say, "See what a great baker you are, Ray?"

The light was still on in the kitchen area on the other side of the glass wall. Every surface was sparkling and there wasn't a crumb on the floor. There was nothing to show that early that morning I'd prepared four hundred croissants, twelve kinds of bread, and a complete batch of pastries in there. All by myself. My boss had asked me if I wanted an assistant, but I liked the safety and comfort of my own thoughts and of doing it by myself.

"Would you like me to show you La Souche?" I asked Anna. "Of course you don't understand what that means, but it doesn't matter. Come with me."

She followed me to the back of the bakery, to the warming cupboard where La Souche was kept alive at a constant temperature of sixty degrees Fahrenheit and eighty percent humidity.

I opened the door and crouched before the earthenware pot.

"Shh, she's sleeping," said Anna next to me.

"That's right," I said, glad that she got it. "She's sleeping. Sleeping makes you grow, did you know that?" I carefully lifted a corner of the moist cotton cloth covering the mother dough. "Can you smell her? Go on, try. Take a big sniff."

Anna sniffed. "Yuck," she said.

"You just don't *get* it," I snapped at her, quickly covering La Souche back up.

Anna stared at me for a few seconds, dazed, and then burst into tears.

"Don't do that—stop!" I tried to remember what Rosita had said about what you were supposed to do if someone was crying. It took a little while before I remembered. You had to show you were interested. "What's the matter with you?"

"My God!" The girl who helped behind the counter on Wednesdays had come up to us; I hadn't heard her approach. "What on earth's going on here?" She picked Anna up. "What's wrong, my love?"

"Ray's a bad boy," said Anna.

"Not true," I said. "Not true at all."

"What are you two doing in the warming cupboard, for heaven's sake? What's this nonsense? What did Ray do?" she asked Anna.

"Bad boy," she said.

"Does her mommy know she's here?" The girl was scowling at me.

"Yes. Not that she's here, but that she's with me."

"Ray's angry," said Anna. She had stopped crying and was stretching her arms out at me.

I took her from the girl and turned my back so that she couldn't touch Anna.

"Well, I think there's something funny going on. Taking a little girl into the warming cupboard. It isn't normal." The girl put her hands on her hips. I didn't like her being there.

"We've got to shut the door, or the temperature will go haywire. And in case you didn't know, the kitchen is only for bakers. You're supposed to stay in the store."

"Never let outsiders set foot in your bakery," Pierre used to say. "They have no idea how delicate these processes are. They'll just make a mess of everything."

CHAPTER 30

IRIS

It was clear that Renzo de Winter, the detective who had led the homicide team in Ray's case, wasn't interested in meeting with me.

"I assure you every avenue was pursued in our investigation," he said. "All the facts point to your client's guilt. I don't know what you're hoping to dig up. Besides, I don't have to tell you I am not permitted to disclose any information about the case without the attorney general's approval."

"I completely understand that you can't say anything on the record. I'm just here for an informal chat." I looked out the window to take the pressure off the conversation. A young couple was cycling down the street holding hands. They looked happy.

Renzo de Winter gave a deep sigh.

"Please?"

"Off the record. It was a pretty straightforward case as far as we were concerned. Boelens had a history of violence, he had a motive, he was present at the scene of the crime, and he made a number of incriminating statements. That's four important grounds for indictment. In general it takes no more than two to bring it to the judge." Renzo de Winter gazed at me with a weary look. I suspected he was younger than he looked.

"What do you mean by 'history of violence'? My client didn't have a rap sheet."

"Your client spent his adolescence in an institution for troubled youth. His school records state he killed a dog when he was nine."

I tried to keep my face expressionless. *What kind of kid would kill an innocent animal?* Maybe my mother was right: I had no idea what kind of man Ray was.

"The neighbors also told us he'd slashed up the victim's boyfriend's car. Let me see . . ." De Winter rummaged through an impressive stack of papers on his desk. "Here it is: Boelens stormed outside with a kitchen knife and began slashing Mr. Asscher's tires. Next he broke the jaguar ornament off the hood and used it to smash the windshield. Never seemed to show remorse."

I tried not to think about the dead dog and concentrated on Asscher's Jag instead. "Did Asscher file a complaint?"

De Winter sighed, irritated. "No."

"Strange."

"What difference does it make? I'm sure the Jaguar repair shop could dig up a damage report for you. Mr. Asscher must have had his reasons."

"He must have. But can you explain to me why the police never took a statement from Asscher regarding the murder?"

"Unnecessary."

"Why?"

"Because Mr. Asscher was away on vacation when the murder occurred."

"Right. Well, then, could you explain the circumstances in which Mr. Boelens's statements were taken?"

"How do you mean?"

I took out my own stack of papers. "Let's see. Here: 'It was clear that Rosita and Anna were stabbed with a sharp object. I'm thinking of a carving knife, such as the one I have at home.' Are those literally Mr. Boelens's own words?"

"Yes."

"It reads a bit forced to me. Especially this: 'I hereby swear that no words were put in my mouth and that I make this statement of my own free will and without any threats or promises extended.' That sounds like a rather formal way for a baker to speak, don't you think? Knowing Mr. Boelens as I do, I can't imagine him using these words. Nor can I see Mr. Boelens being so enamored with the strong arm of the law that he would go out of his way to protect the officer who took the statement."

"Ms. Kastelein, I am sure you have a fine legal mind, but really, this case couldn't be more straightforward. Policemen are human, naturally, and if you kept digging you'd be bound to come across a typo or two, or some unfortunate wording. But what of it? As far as we are concerned, the culprit was caught and is paying for his crimes. Justice prevailed."

"How did Boelens strike you? Did he seem confused?"

De Winter glanced at his watch. "I'm running late."

"Was Boelens responsive? Did he understand what was happening?"

"He was panic-stricken. Because he knew what he'd done and knew *we* knew it, too."

"Panic-stricken?"

"He just went on and on about his fish. He kept raging and yelling about them."

"Ah, yes, he did . . ." I remembered the logbook Ray had kept so meticulously for all those years. The prizes he'd won. The way he'd tenderly touched the photos of his fish with his fingertips after I'd handed them to him. "He was in a panic about his beloved fish. And yet you claim that he managed to dictate a statement in elegant, well-turned prose."

"We did our best, naturally, to calm him down, and promised him we'd make sure the fish were looked after. We aren't ogres, you know."

"Or did you promise to look after the fish in exchange for his statement?"

"Now you're going too far." Again De Winter looked at his watch. "Time's up."

"Is there a recording of the interrogation?"

De Winter looked at me, irked. "I know what you're getting at. You think I have closed my mind, that I have tunnel vision. But I can assure you that this happens to be one of those cases in which I am absolutely convinced we got the right guy. I know you are just trying to do your job, but this one is a total waste of time. Not that I suppose you care. How many billable hours are you getting out of this little visit? Three? Four?"

I tried to keep my cool. Mentally I was hurling the contents of the entire police station at De Winter's head.

"I'm sure your boss is delighted," said De Winter.

"Now *you're* the one going too far."

CHAPTER 31

RAY

Iris Kastelein who said she was my sister was also going to be my lawyer.

"What's she going to do, then?" I asked Mo. We were sitting in the same office where I'd smashed the dracaena against the wall. Mo was one of the only ones I was still willing to talk to. All the others had tricked me. Jeannie and her too-sour, too-sticky bread; Hank and his lightning bolt; Eddie who called me Raynus; Rembrandt who called me Rainman. They were the ones who'd left the drugs in my room.

I wasn't completely sure if I could trust Mo, either, but I had to have *someone*. That's what the Mason Home principal used to say. "I know you have trouble trusting people, but if you're willing to risk it, then take a gamble on me. Because you've got to have *someone*." The principal had never let me down. Never. He'd made the others stop teasing me, and he'd signed me up for baking school. He had taken me to the planetarium and was always nice to me. And he often told me, "You're going to be okay, Ray." But I hadn't been okay.

"Iris wants to find out if the murder investigation and the trial were handled properly." Mo spoke very slowly. "The trial that led to your incarceration. You yourself asked her to help you, don't you remember?"

I did remember. Even though I was tired of it all. "And then?"

"I don't know. It depends on what emerges from her investigation, I think. Anyway, it does mean that, as your attorney, your sister can visit you more often. Would you like that?"

I stared at the wall, at the spot where the plant had hit the white plaster. It no longer showed. Iris Kastelein who said she was my sister wanted to visit more often. Which meant she'd bring me more pictures of the fish and tell me about them. But it also meant I'd have to pee in the cup in front of the nurse without the white coat again. And then they'd find drugs in my cell and then they'd put me in solitary again.

"I know you keep telling Dr. Römerman you didn't do it. If that's true, then here's your chance to prove your innocence."

"And then?"

"They'll let you go home."

I looked at Mo's face, which always seemed kind to me. I thought about the pictures of all the faces they'd shown me in therapy. The way you could tell from the mouth or the eyes if someone was happy or not.

"What's bothering you, Ray? What are you afraid of?"

"I don't want to go back to solitary," I said. "Never again."

"That's completely up to you," said Mo. "If you abide by the rules, there's no reason for you to be put into solitary."

"Oh no? Oh no? So what happened last time? Why was I thrown into solitary when I'd done nothing wrong? Nothing!"

"You threw a plant at Jeannie's head."

"She told me I wouldn't be allowed to do the gardening anymore. Don't you know I'm the one who trims the hedges? It's the only thing that makes me feel good. Because I still don't have my fish. Even though I'm always being told 'we'll discuss it' and 'we'll think about it.' Meanwhile weeks go by and I'm *still* waiting for an answer."

Mo was no longer smiling. He looked serious. His eyebrows were wrinkled; the corners of his mouth went straight across. "Ray, did those drugs belong to you?"

I banged my hand on the table. "Don't I keep telling you? I don't have any drugs! I don't use drugs! And I don't smoke, either and how the hell am I ever going to get out of here if nobody ever believes me?" I kept talking without stopping for breath. My head was spinning.

"Easy. Relax, nothing to get so upset about." Mo showed me how to breathe. "That's it. That's better. Feeling better? Listen, it's quite possible those drugs were hidden in your suite by someone else. It wouldn't be the first time. In fact, an investigation has been set up to find out what happened."

"Really?"

"Of course. But back to Iris. Let's arrange another meeting?"

"Will I have to pee into a cup?"

"There *is* that possibility."

I hesitated. I never again wanted to have to show my naked penis to the woman who didn't wear a white coat, but I also had to think of my fish. Of how I longed for Iris Kastelein who said she was my sister to tell me about them.

"But no matter what, you will have to go and have your urine tested from time to time. Whether you have visitors or not. Everyone is supposed to get tested every once in a while."

I stared at Mo. I wished I could read him, the way most folks know how to read other people. "*Normal* people," according to my mother. Though Rosita had decided my mother was far from normal herself, and my mother didn't think Rosita was normal either.

Maybe Iris Kastelein who said she was my sister was someone who was normal.

"Anyway, your sister is a very nice lady. She's got your best interests at heart."

"That's what they all say. Everybody always has my best interests at heart, and look where that got me."

Mo laughed. "Trust me."

I could say no, and then I'd never get out of here. I could say yes and never get out of here, either, and make things even harder for myself. But there *was* a chance Iris Kastelein could help me, and that could happen only if I said yes. It was a risk. I hated taking risks.

Then I remembered my fish. "Fine, let Iris Kastelein who says she's my sister come."

That afternoon they let me return to the workshop for the first time since I'd been in solitary. The plants had all been labeled, it seemed, because our job was to insert blank CDs into see-through cases.

I liked the plants better than the CDs. I liked finding out what the plants needed: a lot of light or just a little, to be watered daily or once a week, and whether they could stay outside in winter. The CDs didn't provide much useful information. The brand name was TDK and all it said on them was *CD-RW,* and *4x–12x high-speed, 80 minutes/700 MB.*

I sat at a round table with a box of CDs in front of me and a box of plastic cases. You were supposed to fill at least a hundred cases an hour; the pay was two euro. After the first hundred, you got two cents extra per case. If you filled less than a hundred, you got nothing.

Hank was there, and a bunch of other guys I didn't know. Hank never sat next to me anymore since I'd gotten out of solitary. I had no idea why. He used to say we were "mates." You wouldn't have guessed it.

Hank was furiously at work, filling cases like a maniac. I saw sweat patches under his armpits. I thought about the smell of tobacco always coming off him, and about the sweat patches. I ought to go up to him and tell him he was a traitor. A filthy, stinking, double-crossing traitor.

There was a clock on the wall. I'd been working for half an hour and had only done twenty cases.

"What up, little Rainman?" Rembrandt came and sat down next to me. I put another CD into a case, but my hands wouldn't do what I wanted. First the CD wouldn't slip into the groove, and then I couldn't close the sleeve properly. I tried forcing it, but then one of the hinges snapped. I quickly added the broken case to the pile, hoping no one would notice.

"Had fun in the hole? Do any nice doodling on the blackboard?"

I took another CD from the box. This time I did manage to get it into the case without damaging either it or the case. I felt myself starting to sweat. If I wasn't careful the sweat would show right through my shirt, like Hank's.

"You don't talk much, do you, dog? I like that. Can't never trust people that talk too much. The more shit they talk, the more they trying to hide, that's what I say." He inserted a CD in a case and deposited it on my pile with a big wink. "Must be burning a hole in that little brain of yours trying to figure out who done you in."

"Huh?"

Rembrandt leaned in closer. He smelled of aftershave. It smelled like the stuff in the blue bottle Rosita once bought me for Christmas. It was sexy, she said. She'd pressed her nose into my neck and inhaled the smell. "Mm, smells delicious on you, Ray." With Rembrandt sitting so close to me, I was getting almost as light-headed as I got then.

"I know, Ray. I know who's been fucking with you."

One of the CD cases cracked again.

"I could tell you, Ray Baby. But I could also *not* tell you. It all depends." He casually filled another case and put it on my pile.

I didn't know what to say.

"Go on, ask me. Nice and sweet, just like your momma taught you."

My hands were shaking and I felt the sweat rolling down my back. If only I knew what he wanted.

He reached out and touched my shoulder. It gave me goose bumps.

"You know where to find me. And take it easy with those cases." He walked over to Hank's table and sat down. The two of them started talking and laughing.

I tried to concentrate on the CDs. I managed not to break any more, and to fill ninety-one.

"Ah, too bad," said the workshop supervisor. "Do you want to try again for another hour, to see if you can make a hundred?"

"I want to go back to my cell."

"Your *suite.* In that case I'll see you tomorrow. Then you can try again. And the day after tomorrow we're assembling TV remotes. Maybe you'll do better at that."

CHAPTER 32

IRIS

I parked my car in front of Ray's old house. The curtains were drawn. There was no sign there'd been any activity since the last time I'd been there.

The sun was shining, but the wind was unpleasantly cold. I walked to number 11, Rosita and Anna's house. I thought it would be a good idea to survey the scene of the crime. The front yard was much neater than over at Ray's house. A neatly trimmed evergreen hedge, a climbing rose, pansies. Someone lived here who paid attention to detail.

The flower-festooned nameplate read *Hugo and Phyllis.* I rang. It was an electronic bell but had an old-fashioned ring.

Through the frosted glass I saw a red blur topped with a shock of blond hair approaching.

"Good morning," a woman I guessed was Phyllis said cheerfully. "What can I do for you?"

"Yes, good morning. I'm sorry to disturb you on such a lovely day, but I'd like to ask you a few questions."

"Are you one of those market researchers? Because if you are, I . . ."

"No," I said quickly. "It's about something else."

"Oh?" asked the woman. "Is it the children, is something wrong?"

"No, not at all. I just want to ask you about something that happened here a long time ago."

"Because our children are camping in the Dordogne with our grandson, Noah. Only nine months old—just think—a baby in a tent! I don't get it. Still, it could be fun, right?"

I didn't want to get involved in a debate about the dangers of camping with babies, so I said, "It's about the previous inhabitants. Rosita and Anna Angeli."

Phyllis looked upset.

"I'm sorry to bring this up. But I'm working on a possible appeal, which requires me to talk to some of the neighbors."

"I don't know."

I took out a business card. Heavy stock, ornate lettering. It was Lawrence's taste, but it made an impression. Phyllis's eyes scanned the card.

"You might as well come in, then." She flung the door open all the way for me.

I followed her down the corridor where eight years ago Rosita's and Anna's corpses had been discovered. The floor was oak parquet and the walls were painted an apricot shade probably called something like "Tuscan sunset." There was no sign of the grisly crime that had taken place here. But what did I expect? That I'd see the CSI team's chalk marks?

Phyllis pointed me to the sofa and dashed into the kitchen for a cup of coffee. I looked around. The living room wasn't very large; situated at the back of the house, it looked out on a lovely garden.

"Well, well, this *is* a coincidence," said Phyllis, coming in from the kitchen with two wobbly coffee cups and a cookie tin on a pretty serving tray. "Do you know that we received a letter addressed to Rosita just two weeks ago? A very grand envelope. I said to Hugo, 'What do you think we're supposed to do with this?' I thought of calling the police."

She put the cups down on the glass coffee table. Displayed under the glass top were books with titles like *The Birds in Our Garden.*

"That *is* a coincidence," I said.

She walked over to the sideboard in the corner of the room and picked up an envelope. "Here it is."

"Who's it from? Do you know?"

She handed me the letter. *Burley & Burley* it said in fancy script. *Solicitors.*

"Junk mail, probably. I'd just mark it *Return to sender,* if I were you," I said in a nonchalant way.

"You think?" Phyllis hesitated. I could see she was a woman who was determined to do the right thing. "I'm not sure."

"May I ask you a few questions?"

"Of course." She perched on the edge of the armchair.

"When did you move in here?"

"About seven years ago."

"So you were the first to live here after the murder."

"That's right. I did find the idea of it a bit creepy at first. But my Hugo said, 'You can't even tell it ever happened.' "

"And . . . *were* you able to tell?" A rather awkward question. What was I hoping to get out of this conversation, really, other than a look at the crime scene? Phyllis hadn't known Rosita and Anna, or Ray, either. What was there for her to tell me that I didn't already know from reading the police report?

"The police and the housing co-op had made sure the place was thoroughly cleaned. But you could still see the stains in the concrete. I had a wood floor installed right away." She leaned over toward me. "The blood's still there, underneath the wood. I try not to think about it."

"And the walls?"

"They were repainted."

I took a sip of my coffee. Phyllis hastened to offer me a cookie from the tin. "What about the neighbors? Did anyone ever talk to you about the murder?"

"I don't talk to the man next door. He's . . . different. I find him to be quite unpleasant. Although I have to say he does keep to himself. But you never hear him take a shower. Never seems to bother to air the place out, either." Phyllis shook her head disapprovingly. "You know who you should talk to? The lady across the street; she knew Rosita pretty well. She seems to think Rosita liked men *a lot.*"

"But she had a steady boyfriend, didn't she?"

"I believe she did. A classy guy in a fancy car. I remember him coming by from time to time after we'd just moved in. He'd park in front and peer inside. Gave me the creeps."

"Did you report it to the police?"

"Well, he wasn't really doing anything illegal, you know? He was just looking and lurking. But I didn't like it."

"Are you sure it was Rosita's boyfriend?"

"The lady across the street is sure. She . . . keeps an eye out."

"But you never talked to him."

She shook her head. "Hugo did step outside once. But he drove off in a hurry. Oh, you know, it was just when we first moved in. After a while he stopped coming."

"Could you explain what you mean when you say, 'She liked men'?"

Phyllis shrugged and took a bite of her cookie. "It's just what I heard, of course. She was a flirt, people say."

I got to my feet, for want of anything further to ask. I tried not to look too eagerly at the envelope on the sideboard. "I have to go to the post office anyway. Would you like me to mail that letter for you?"

She was hesitant.

"It seems to me you've had enough trouble with all this. I'll take care of it for you, it's the least I can do."

"Remind me, where are you from?"

"From the law firm." I said it categorically, leaving her no room to object.

"Oh, right." She handed the letter over.

"Thanks again for your time." I put the letter in my handbag. We shook hands. It wasn't until I'd reached my car that I heard the door close.

The lady in number 20 was already posted at the kitchen window, peering outside. One hand on her hip, the other holding a cigarette.

Putting on a friendly but professional face, I walked up to her door.

Before I had a chance to ring the bell, the door swung open. "I was wondering when you'd get to me." She had a strange, hoarse voice.

"Oh?"

"Yeah. If there's anyone in this street who knows what's going on, it's me."

"I'm Iris Kastelein." I put out my hand.

"Geraldine. You'd better come in." She led the way. We sat down at a little gingham-covered table by the kitchen window. The pungent mix of cigarette smoke and household cleaner made my eyes sting.

"I usually sit right here, except when I'm doing housework. I never sit in the living room, actually. What's there to look at in the backyard? At least here in the front there might be something going on."

Geraldine's house was right across the street from Rosita's. A stretch of about fifty feet. You didn't even need binoculars to spy on your neighbors.

"So you always know what goes on in this neighborhood?"

"Sure do. I see everything," she said proudly. "I also know you were here a week ago, with your kid. Little boy? Cute as a button. I could tell you hadn't come to view a house or to read the meter." She laughed.

"How clever of you to keep tabs on everything." I hoped I'd be able stick it out a bit longer in this stifling air. "I am representing Mr. Boelens, your former neighbor, as his attorney. I'm trying to learn more about the murder of Rosita and Anna Angeli."

"I'd gone to the market that morning. Just when something finally happens, there I am buying lettuce for fifty cents a head. So I didn't see it happen. But I *am* the one who called the police. I saw that her door was open and I thought, that isn't right; I walked over to the house and saw her lying there. Her and her kid. What a mess. You've never seen anything like it. I don't think I slept for a month."

She lit another cigarette. One of those extra-longs. From a black pack featuring a gold Playboy logo. An old man walked by. He lifted a hand to his Humphrey Bogart fedora by way of salute.

"That's old Col. He was Boelens's neighbor on the other side. You could try talking to him, too. Though he's not all there these days. He once told me that Ray could raise a mighty ruckus. He'd start roaring like an animal, he said."

"Did he do that a lot?"

"Depends. Sometimes. He was doing pretty well for a while. Before he began hanging out with that woman. But as soon as that started fizzling out—heaven help us."

"You weren't too fond of Rosita, were you?"

She rolled her eyes. "She was a piece of work, that one . . . Mustn't speak ill of the dead, but . . . How do I put it? She had a stick up her ass. Thought she was better than everyone else. But meanwhile she'd gotten herself knocked up by a married man, and she was on welfare. And always making eyes at men and leading them on. It's lucky my old man, Joe, wanted nothing to do with her. 'Give me a real woman,' he says, 'not one of those bimbos.' "

"But do you think Ray killed her?"

"He was crazy enough. Do you know he used to go around pruning the neighbors' hedges in the middle of the night? My husband once bumped into him wielding one of those"—she spread her arms wide—"huge hedge shears. With that crazed look in his eye, the way he'd look at you sometimes, you know. My old man almost had a heart attack. But apart from that he didn't really bother us. He was always at work, wasn't he? He'd set out for the bakery in the middle of the night. Then he'd be home for a couple of hours in the afternoon and you'd see the lights go out around eight o'clock. What kind of life is that? No wonder he went berserk."

She lit another cigarette. I was starting to get a headache, but I really wanted to hear what else she had to tell me.

"You know that rich prick, the father of that woman's kid? Ray once slashed the guy's tires. I saw the whole thing myself. He just went nuts, he did. Never seen anything like it. The way he went at it, hacking those tires with that knife! And then suddenly it was over. He calmed down and marched back to his house as if nothing was the matter. I said to Joe, I said, 'Mark my words, that's going to end badly.' And that's exactly what happened. But hey, everyone gets what they ask for, am I right?"

And what you're asking for is lung cancer, I thought.

She stared out the window. "I'm just sorry about the little girl. She was a dear little thing. She'd wave at me sometimes. But with a mother like that . . ."

"Do you think Ray and Rosita were lovers?"

"Who can say? Look, Ray lived here awhile before she came on the scene. He never saw anyone. Except for his mother. She sometimes came to see him."

I tried to wrap my head around the idea that my mother had been here, on this street. That she'd led a whole secret life neither my father nor I ever knew about.

"So when that woman moved in and started giving him the come-on, Ray naturally fell for her right away. But did they *do* it? Beats me. Never saw them holding hands or anything. They never spent the night together—at least, not as far as I know . . . I never understood it, the two of them. Never. What an unlikely pair."

I'd been back in the office for a while when I stumbled upon the forgotten envelope in my handbag. Rummaging for my keys, I saw it wedged between a pack of Wet Wipes and my notebook.

I wasn't expecting a miracle. Probably from an outfit that couldn't be bothered to shell out money for a current mailing list. But the letter did not trumpet *YOU are the LUCKY WINNER of a MILLION EURO if you invest NOW in some teakwood plantation somewhere!*

It was a carefully worded letter written in the kind of high-flown legalese favored by British solicitors. What it came down to was: Rosita was the sole heir of a great-uncle in England, recently deceased, and was requested to contact the solicitor's office.

It didn't have to mean anything. The great-uncle was just as likely to have left his niece nothing but debts as he was to have left her a fortune. I switched on my computer and Googled the great-uncle's name: *Richard Angeli.* No hits.

I glanced at my watch. I had fifteen minutes to get to the day care before it closed. And getting there would take at least ten. Shit. Burley & Burley would have to wait until tomorrow.

CHAPTER 33

RAY

Rosita opened the door dressed in sweatpants and a stained sweater. She was pale, with dark circles under her eyes I hadn't noticed before. She'd been looking much more presentable before Anna's father's visit. He could just come over whenever he liked, but as for taking care of her properly—don't hold your breath.

"How did it go with Anna? What did you guys do?"

"How come you let that Victor come in whenever he wants?"

"Ray, please. Not now." She took off Anna's jacket and hung it on the coatrack. "Hey, sweetie, did you feed the ducks?"

Anna said yes. Now she wanted to go watch TV.

"And you let him come upstairs, too. Why?" I asked when we were in the living room, after Rosita had turned on a cartoon for Anna. "Why? Did you let him touch you? Did he touch your privates? Is that it?"

Rosita lit a cigarette and inhaled deeply. "Stop it. Please, Ray. I'm too tired for this. Come, let's have a drink, and we'll order pizza. Pour me a glass of wine, will you?"

But I wasn't going to let her off that easy. "Why? Why do you let him come upstairs?"

"Why do I let *him* come upstairs and not *you,* is that what you mean?"

I didn't say anything; I lost my nerve.

She walked up to me, so close that I took a step back, even though I was a head taller than her. Smoke came blowing into my face. "Is that what you want, Ray? I thought you were different. I thought we were friends."

I was having trouble breathing.

Squinting, she puffed another cloud of smoke into my face. I didn't like it. "In that case, you'd better come upstairs with me, if that's what you so badly want. Come on. I'll show you my cunt. Because that's what it's called, Ray. 'Privates' is what little kids say."

She stubbed out her cigarette in the ashtray, grabbed my hand, and dragged me up the stairs. I followed her, not knowing what else I was supposed to do.

Her bedroom was mysterious, the bed hidden under a slick black coverlet. Quite a change from my own bedroom, which was all white, white, white. Nice and bright, said my mother.

"Okay, now lie down." Rosita pushed me roughly toward the bed. She was strong for a woman her size. I stumbled, lost my balance, and fell backward. I made the mattress bounce.

She pulled off her sweater. She wasn't wearing a bra. Her breasts weren't as round as you'd expect; they were kind of pointy, with big brown nipples. Still, I couldn't keep my eyes off them. I hoped she'd let me touch them. And I hoped she would touch me and take my penis in her mouth, just like on TV.

"Do you think I'm pretty, Ray? Is this what you wanted to see?" She cupped her hands around her boobs and squeezed.

I couldn't speak. My throat was all closed up. Her fingers started rubbing her nipples so that they grew hard.

"And this, Ray? My 'privates'? Do you want to see them, too?"

I nodded, my head moving like a thick pudding.

She yanked her pants down. They were down around her ankles; she didn't even bother stepping out of them.

I looked at her lovely round hips, which weren't very different from the photo in the living room, and at the narrow line of dark hair starting underneath her tummy and ending between her legs. I saw the two flaps down there with the little knob sticking out in between. I saw everything I'd never seen in real life.

It was as if a huge weight was pressing me down on the bed. It was giving me goose bumps and making my penis throb. I couldn't move. I could only stare.

"What would you like, Ray? Would you like a little show? Do you want to watch me jack off with my vibrator? Do you want me to sit on your face? Just say it." She sounded angry, angrier than I'd ever heard her.

My throat was thick and my jaw felt uncomfortably clenched.

"Do you want to touch me, Ray? Is that what you want?" She shuffled to the side of the bed, hobbled by the pants at her ankles. "Here, stick out your hand. Go on, touch my cunt. You want to, don't you?" She spread her legs as far apart as the pants let her.

I stretched my arm. My hand was shaking.

"It's just a cunt. Every woman has one. Even your mother has one. How do you think you got here?"

She grabbed my hand and pressed it to her privates. I shut my eyes. It felt warm, and as soft as the inside of a *canelé*. My fingers lay there motionless as I felt, just felt the sensation of the blood throbbing inside her.

"You have no idea how to turn a woman on, do you, Ray?" She laughed a short, hard laugh. "I bet you don't."

I opened my eyes. I had no idea what she wanted of me.

"Caress me. Start by stroking my cunt, but gently."

Cautiously I started stroking the flaps, the knob, and the

area around the little hole, which I knew could grow bigger. Big enough so a penis could fit inside. The flesh felt soft, like dolphin skin.

Rosita closed her eyes. "That's nice, Ray. That feels good. Now I want you to stick your finger inside my cunt. Feel how wet I'm getting?"

My hand was shaking again. I found the hole and gently inserted one finger. It was sticky in there, and tight. Rosita gasped. I quickly pulled my finger out. "Did I hurt you?" My voice sounded different. Hoarse, almost whispery.

"No, silly boy. Keep going."

It was wet inside the hole, Rosita's cunt, and even warmer than on the outside. "Move your finger up and down, and then back to my clit."

I let my finger slip inside her, up and down over the rough landscape of warm flesh. When I pulled my finger out again, she grabbed my hand and put it where she wanted it to go. "This is the clitoris, Ray. Maybe you remember it from biology class. You have to rub it."

I started rubbing my finger over the knob. It was easier when my fingers were wet. I heard her breathing heavily and groaning. The ache in my penis grew unbearable.

"Now circle your finger around my clit. Harder. Come on, Ray. Make me come."

I looked at her face. At the half-closed eyes and the gaping mouth making sounds I'd never heard her make before.

She pressed my hand even harder against her. "Don't stop, Ray. Keep it going." I went on rubbing the knob back and forth, the way she wanted. Then she gave a scream, squeezing my hand hard against her privates. She thrust her hips violently forward and screamed again.

All sorts of stuff was happening between her legs. I felt muscles contract, and it got even warmer and wetter than before.

Then it was over. She stopped screaming and pushed my hand off. It was quiet for a moment, except for some heavy breathing. Then, clearing her throat, she grunted, "Not bad for a beginner." She started pulling up her pants again, with me still lying on that bed, my penis about to explode.

She walked around the bed and picked up her sweater, the one with the stains, and pulled it on. "Okay. I'm going downstairs now. You can jerk off if you like. There's Kleenex on the bedside table."

She turned without another glance at me. I heard her walk downstairs and had no choice but to unzip my pants and relieve myself.

CHAPTER 34

IRIS

"He wasn't particularly outgoing before, but since his stay in solitary he's been completely uncommunicative," Mo told me. "The only time he seems even remotely present is in a one-on-one situation."

"How did *that* happen?" We were sitting in one of the consulting rooms. Mo had suggested giving me a rundown before my visit.

"It's probably a self-defense mechanism developed at an early age. Whenever the world around him doesn't feel safe, he retreats into his own little world."

"But shouldn't he feel safe in here? Isn't he getting therapy and counseling and everything?"

"Believe me, I'm not happy about it, either."

You could tell he meant it. Actually, he seemed like the sort of person who meant everything he said. It occurred to me how few of the people I knew were genuinely kind. And also how often I wasn't exactly kind myself.

"Let me explain to you how this treatment facility works so you'll have a clearer idea of what to expect. There are inmates for whom therapy of any sort is pointless. Take the psychopaths, for instance. They are quite incapable of changing, although one does notice that they tend to mellow a bit as they grow older, thanks to a decrease in the testosterone levels." He put his hand on mine for a second. "Not that Ray's a psychopath—far from it. Don't worry."

I nodded. Was this normal, for him to touch me? Did he do that to all the other patients' relatives? Or was it just me? Was there some special thing between us?

"If a psychopath has a miraculous 'turnaround,' you can bet it's to get out of his punishment; he doesn't actually understand it's wrong to hurt others. If you release him from prison, he'll just be even more careful to cover his tracks next time. Fortunately there *are* inmates who do profit from therapy. They're the ones we can see going back to their normal lives at some point."

"I take it Ray belongs in that category."

He was silent for a moment. It was clear the news he had to tell me was not good. "I'm not sure he's capable of dealing. There's nothing official to back this up, but from my own observation I've seen that some—not many—in here don't make it. When they arrive they're still fairly functional, but a few months later they're practically basket cases. There are units that offer more safety and structure, but it's always a while before we're able to place them there. Sometimes it's too late, I'm sorry to say."

The last thing I wanted to hear was that Ray wouldn't make it. "So what you're saying is, this isn't the right place for him."

"That's not what I'm saying. The problem is that there aren't many alternatives. An inmate may reach the point where he's served out his time, yet it would be irresponsible to release him. So what then?" He looked at me so intently with those lovely calm eyes of his that it got me all flustered. "Sorry, I haven't given you a chance to speak. What was your initial reaction?"

"It's hard. I feel bonded with him somehow. Maybe because my son looks so much like him . . ."

"How old is your son?"

"Three. His father and I don't live together." Why was I telling him that?

"That's great," said Mo. "Not that you don't live together, that's not what I mean, but I think it's great you have a little boy."

I felt myself getting red and tried to go on as normally as possible. "I've been hearing and reading the most terrible things about Ray. But when I saw him during my visit, I couldn't imagine him being capable of such violence. He seemed so naive and innocent."

"I do think he's basically a nice guy."

"I think so, too. And you'll probably laugh to hear me say this, but . . . isn't it possible he's innocent?"

"You're sweet to keep asking that question."

"See? You're not taking me seriously."

He laughed. Nice teeth. "I take you seriously."

I was sure my face had gone scarlet. I hoped he hadn't noticed.

"Much as I'd like, for your sake, to think Ray is innocent, you don't get placed in this kind of institution for nothing. Ray has been thoroughly evaluated by the nation's top forensic psychiatrists. If they've decided he needs to be confined in a mental institution, then you can take it there's definitely something wrong with him."

"We know there's something wrong with Ray. I'm not saying he's completely normal. But suppose there's a miscarriage of justice, and someone is wrongly convicted. In Ray's case, that would mean he's not only sent to prison an innocent man, but lands in a mental institution later on as well."

An amused smile hovered at the corners of Mo's mouth.

"It's possible, isn't it?" My boiling face was set to explode.

"Fine. In theory." He glanced at his watch. "If you'll excuse me a moment, I'll go get Ray."

Maybe I was chasing a total fantasy. A childish pipe dream in which families were reunited and everyone lived happily ever after. I already pictured myself sitting down at Christmas dinner with Ray, Aaron, and my mother. Why not?

I heard footsteps in the corridor, and sat up straight. My armpits felt clammy. I hoped I didn't smell of sweat.

Ray was the first to enter, closely followed by Mo and the guard.

I'd prepared myself for the worst, but Ray looked the same as the last time. I think he was even wearing the same outfit. He avoided my eyes, seeming more interested in the room's bare walls.

"Should we shake hands?" I asked.

"Better not," said Mo, standing in the corner. "If both the guard and I can confirm that there wasn't any physical contact between you two, it may help Ray avoid having to get drug tested again." His voice sounded neutral and professional. Of course.

"Okay." I sat down.

"Take a seat, Ray," said Mo.

Ray sat down, robotlike.

Silence.

"How are you?" I asked.

"Not great." He still wouldn't look at me, but started playing with his hands.

I glanced over my shoulder at Mo, who was sitting behind me. He gave me an encouraging nod.

"What's the matter, then?"

"They're all against me. I don't know how long they're going to keep this up. Until I'm dead?"

"I'm not against you," I said. "Do you hear me? I'm on your side."

He nodded, although I didn't know if it was because he understood what I was saying or because he was just acknowledging the sound of my voice.

"I want to help you. Will you let me discuss your case with you, Ray? Is that all right with you?"

He did not react, but I decided to go ahead anyway. "I've read your file. And to be honest, it's hard to find any obvious leads to help prove your innocence."

Still no reaction. Worse, Ray no longer appeared to be aware of my presence.

"Ray? I need you to help me. I very much want to represent you as your lawyer, and to mount an appeal, but I do need your cooperation."

"What?"

Even if it was just a monosyllable, I was happy to have him respond. "An appeal. Asking the court to reopen your case. But for that we need new evidence. Because in an appeal, the burden of proof is reversed."

His face gave no indication that he understood any of this. *Just keep talking,* I thought. "At your first trial the prosecutor had to prove you were guilty. Now it's the other way around. Now it's up to you to prove you're *not* guilty. Only, we're not allowed to use any evidence that's in the existing court record. So we need a new argument, and that's what I want to start looking into. But I can't unless you help me find it."

"Oh." His hands started flailing all over the place again, the way I'd sometimes also see Aaron excitedly flapping his hands around. I had to stop myself from grabbing them to make them stop.

"If you really are innocent, I can help you get out of here. Do you understand?"

I couldn't stop myself from glancing at Mo. He was following our conversation intently.

"Yes."

"What do you say?"

He looked at me and again I saw the resemblance—my mother's eyes, and Aaron's. "I want my fish."

"I take it that's a yes."

He nodded.

"I've brought you some more pictures of your fish. I'll give them to you later. But first we have to discuss your case. Can you do that? Can you tell me what happened the day Rosita and Anna were killed?"

I caught a look of panic in his eyes.

"We can start with some other questions, if you like."

He nodded vehemently. Like a toddler.

"Who were Rosita's friends? Did she ever have visitors?"

"Did she *ever*." He sounded angry suddenly.

"Who, then?"

"Anna's father."

"Victor Asscher. It sounds to me as if you don't really like him."

"Like him? He didn't take care of Rosita properly." He was furious. His eyes were black with rage and he looked as though he might explode. I could just see him wielding the Börja carving knife. Hadn't Mo and I just agreed he was a softie at heart?

I took my notebook out of my handbag and wrote down the name Victor Asscher. "In what way didn't he take care of Rosita properly?"

"He wouldn't buy carpeting for her. And he wouldn't buy her a couch, either, or clothes." He was getting more and more incensed.

"You can have a time-out if you feel yourself getting too angry, Ray. Are you okay?" asked Mo behind me.

"Yes," he said.

I raised my eyebrows and gripped my pen, but then I realized there wasn't much for me to write. I turned to Mo. "Is it all right if I keep going?"

"I think so."

"Okay. Ray, were Victor and Rosita happy? Did they get along?"

He shrugged and repeated stubbornly, "He didn't take care of her properly."

"What about his car? Is it correct that you slashed his tires?"

"I did." He seemed proud of it, even.

"Why?"

"So he wouldn't come anymore."

"Did it help?"

He didn't respond. I felt I'd reached a dead end.

"And who else? Rosita's stepdad, for instance, did he ever visit her?"

"Sometimes. He fixed things around the house for her."

"What's he like?"

He shrugged again. "Old. And very gray. He wears his hair in a ponytail."

"Did Rosita ever tell you anything about him? That he was aggressive, maybe? Or that he had money problems?"

"Why?"

"Because Rosita inherited a lot of money from her great-uncle."

"So he finally died," said Ray. Strangely enough his voice sounded kind of happy. "Rosita would have liked that."

"I bet she would have," I said. "But now her stepfather is the one getting all the money."

Ray didn't seem to see the connection. In fact, he seemed very confused. I decided to let it slide.

"Did she have any friends?"

"No."

"Surely everyone has at least a friend or two?"

"Not me."

It occurred to me that, in fact, I didn't have many friends myself. Clearly, neither Ray nor I had inherited my mother's sociability gene. For us, there were no golf outings with friends, no clubs, no dinner parties or endless phone conversations. I had tried. I'd even joined a sorority as a student. I'd paraded around in the navy vest all my sorority sisters wore. Later, just the thought of it was enough to make me cringe. But at the time it made me look like I belonged. That should have made me feel good, but what I mainly remember is the inherent threat: one wrong step and you were out.

"Anyone else?"

"No."

"Well, that makes it easy."

"What do you mean?"

"It means I don't have to interview lots of people in order to get a sense of what kind of person Rosita was."

"Oh."

"And now what about you and her? Were you good friends?"

Ray's face darkened, and he pursed his lips.

After waiting a few seconds for him to say something, I decided to try again. "Did you ever go over to her house?"

"Yes."

"So? What did you do when you were over there?"

"Talk."

"What about?"

He shrugged. "All sorts of things."

I sighed and looked at my watch. "We're not getting anywhere, Ray. I realize it must be very hard for you to talk about Rosita. But if you want me to help you, you'll just have to open your mouth and say something once in a while." I stuck my notebook back into my bag and thought, okay, that's it. He can yell he's innocent all he likes, but if he refuses to give me anything that will let me build a case, we're done. Otherwise what would I tell Lawrence? "He *seems* such a sweet guy"?

"I really didn't do it," he said suddenly. "Only, I'm not good at talking about those things. About Rosita and A—" His voice broke. "Because it's about feelings. I'm not good at feelings."

I shut my eyes. He did know how to get to me. "Are you really sure you didn't kill them? Not even by accident?"

He shook his head. "They were already dead. I promise."

I stared at him and had the sense that he was doing his best to return my gaze. Maybe that's why I believed him. It was just a feeling, based on nothing; yet in that instant I believed he was telling the truth. "Fine," I said. "Let's leave it there for today. I'll be back the day after tomorrow and then we really must talk about the day Rosita died. All right?"

He said yes and asked to see the photos of the fish.

"Of course," I said, handing them to the guard. "The fish are in good shape, and Mother bought a new protein skimmer."

"Where are Hannibal and King Kong?"

I'd been afraid he'd ask that question.

"Aren't there any photos of them?" I asked, cowardly.

He shook his head.

"So sorry. I'll bring you a picture of them the next time. I promise, okay?" *How could I tell him they were dead?*

"Great job," said Mo. "Really, it went well."

We were threading our way through the institute's endless corridors. "You think so? There are cement gnomes that are easier to talk to than him."

"He doesn't tell the shrink very much, either. He just isn't very talkative."

"I wish I could ask my mother if he's always been this way. But she refuses to talk about him."

"It isn't that unusual, you know. Most of our patients have problematic relationships with their families. There's often too much shame involved. On both sides."

I thought about my mother. I could understand she might have been ashamed that she'd been unable to deal with her own son. But I couldn't understand the way she had so radically turned her life around after dumping Ray at the Mason Home. She had simply erased him and started over again.

"You're quiet," Mo remarked. We were nearly at the exit.

"I've got a lot to think about."

"I know. Not only do you suddenly have a brother you'd like to get to know, but I imagine you're now not sure who your mother is, either."

I looked at him, startled. "You're right."

"If you want to talk about it, you know where to find me."

CHAPTER 35

RAY

I walked down the stairs and into the living room. Rosita was sitting on the couch watching TV with her arm around Anna. They were watching this yellow rabbity creature that couldn't even talk normal. I couldn't stand it, this *Pick-hatchoo* thing or whatever it was called, and his annoying buddies with the big buggy eyes. They gave me a headache.

When I got to the bottom of the stairs I just stood there, not knowing what to do next. What Rosita had done wasn't normal. I was sure of that. She could call me "silly" all she liked, but what *she* had done was completely cuckoo. Should I say something to her? Was I supposed to ask her how she was? Or should I act angry? I didn't know what to do.

I thought about what Margaret used to tell me in the bakery. "You should go by your gut feelings," she'd say. "Your own gut knows best." What my gut was telling me right then was that my penis hurt. What on earth did that tell me?

I caught sight of the picture of Rosita in the nude. It made me even more worried and confused than before, now that I knew what lurked between her legs.

"Ray?" said Rosita without turning to look at me. Her head

didn't move even a fraction. "I think you should go home." On the television the spiky yellow thing and his white, rosy-cheeked buddies were fighting a dragon. They were firing lightning bolts out of their fingertips.

I'd opened my mouth, my lips moved, but the voice coming out of me was my mother's. "Look at me when you're talking to me!"

"Excuse me?"

You were supposed to look people in the eye. That was the right thing to do. I'd had it hammered into me ever since I was little, when I'd still lived at home. The shrink at school kept telling me the same thing. Even Rosita said it.

"You heard me."

"Hey, cool it!" Now she did turn and look at me. It struck me that she was even paler than before she'd started pulling down her pants . . . Even her lips were white.

"You tilt my chin up when I forget to look at you. And now you just sit there watching that stupid *Pokémon* while you're talking to me."

"I tilt your chin up to make you stop staring at my tits." Nobody spoke for a moment. Then she sighed. "Ray, I'm sorry, I shouldn't have let that happen. Please, just go home. Tomorrow we'll see each other for a cup of coffee, and everything will be back to normal again."

"I won't leave."

Rosita turned her entire body toward me, so that Anna almost toppled over. Her eyes drilled into mine. "Eyes are the mirrors of the soul." That's another thing Margaret used to say. But I didn't see any soul. All I saw was a dull sort of brown.

Making eye contact had always been a big problem for me, but that day I could have kept it up for hours. Or maybe it *was* hours that we sat staring at each other.

In the end I won.

"Go ahead, stay there if you like, see if I care." Rosita turned back to the television and turned up the volume.

I covered my ears. The squeaky voices of Piki-doodooheadhatchoo and his pals were driving me crazy—like music, which I couldn't bear, either.

I stared out the window to make myself think of something else. It was already dark outside, but the backyard was lit by the street lamps. I could see the waterfall in the back corner. It splashed into a tiny pond that was shallow enough for birds to bathe in and for Anna not to drown in.

I thought about the past summer. I'd worked in her garden every day after work, ignoring my aching back. I wanted it to be perfect for Rosita. I wanted her to look outside and not feel so sad. And I wanted to be with her. That, especially. She stayed inside mostly, but when the weather was nice she'd come out and take in the sun on a lounge chair in her bikini. Those were the best days.

One day I looked up to see my mother standing there, right in Rosita's yard. I'd been planting shrubs when I heard her voice. "Ray! What are you doing out here?" She gave me such a turn that the spade clattered to the ground.

"You didn't tell me you were coming over."

"Is that necessary? Why aren't you in your own house?"

"Because he's helping me in the garden," said Rosita, who had stepped outside. "Maybe he'd do the gardening for you, too, if he had your address." She was wearing short shorts and a sun hat. One of those big floppy hats. She'd said the hat was "totally J. Lo," whatever that meant.

"Do you mind if I speak to my son in private?"

Rosita put her hands on her hips. "He's busy right now. And this is *my* backyard, so . . ."

"Come, we're going," my mother said to me. "I don't have time for this."

"I *do* have time for this," said Rosita. "I've always wanted to ask you about your—how shall I say—unorthodox parenting."

"Well! I don't think a child of four who's parked in front of the TV all day and still gets to sit in a stroller is an example of good parenting, actually."

"You seem to be well informed," said Rosita. "Great. Ray tells you everything, I see. Still, I *would* like to know why you hardly ever bother to see him. The poor kid doesn't even know who his father is. What's *that* all about?"

"I have absolutely no interest in this conversation. Perhaps you should go find yourself a job instead of meddling in other people's business. Come on, Ray, we're going."

I was going to put the spade back in the shed and go with my mother, but Rosita stopped me. "Are you out of your mind? I want your mother to answer me. Why doesn't he have your address or phone number? Why?"

"Ray." I knew that voice. It was the Last Warning voice. If I didn't listen to her she'd give me a spanking. She'd often had to spank me, even though I did try my best. "You're driving me nuts, Ray!" my mother would yell. "What am I supposed to *do* with you?"

At boarding school I'd learned to get better at controlling myself. We'd practiced with a stopwatch. I was allowed to draw pictures, and when the stopwatch beeped, I was supposed to stop. Then I was allowed to start again. Stop. Start again. Stop. And again and again and again.

"You're not going," said Rosita. "You're not going with her until she gives you an answer. Do you hear me?"

I looked at my mother and then at Rosita and then at my

mother again. They were both angry. Eyebrows down, mouth straight across. What was I supposed to do? The stopwatch technique was useless. How was I supposed to choose?

I could think of only one thing to do. I ran. I dashed into the living room, where Anna greeted me with a happy "Ray!" down the corridor, out the front door, up the street. I ran all the way to the bakery, where I plopped down on the ground next to the Dumpster, and sat there until it was three A.M. and I could start my work shift.

It wasn't until I got home the next afternoon that I realized I'd forgotten to take care of the fish. It was the first and only time that had ever happened to me. I called out their names until I got calmer. Then I went over and brought Anna her madeleine.

I didn't hear from my mother for several weeks. When she finally came again, the gardening was done and she found me at my usual spot by the kitchen window, behind the red curtain. I didn't know if I was happy to see her or not.

My mother walked in, spread a new tablecloth on the table, rearranged the sofa cushions, and moved one of the plants. Then she said she wanted a cup of tea. If I'd known she was coming, I'd have brought home some *tartelettes.* All I had to offer her was a day-old brioche. I spread some butter on it and waited for her reaction.

She took a bite and chewed without changing her expression even one little bit. "That woman's no good," my mother said with a mouthful of brioche. "She's just using you. Don't you see she's driving you crazy? Next she'll bleed you dry and then she'll dump you. Then you'll have a complete meltdown and end up in another institution. You don't want that, do you?"

"Well, if you really want to know, we're almost a family."

"*I'm* your family. Do you hear that, Ray? I'm your family, and nobody else."

"But you turned your back on me." It was the very first time I'd ever said anything like it to my mother.

"*Excuse me?*" She didn't say anything for a moment and her face went all red. "Don't you *dare* say that again! Why do you think I'm here? I *am* still here, aren't I?" A tear rolled down her cheek. "I love you, Ray. Don't you ever forget that I'm the only one who really loves you."

Standing with my hands over my ears on the bottom step of Rosita's staircase without really knowing why, I wondered if my mother had been right after all. I stared at the back of Rosita's head—she was watching something else, some dumb talk show—and was overcome with the urge to hurt her. Again I remembered what Margaret used to say. Go by your gut feelings. But I knew it wasn't right to hurt someone. I may not be normal, but I'm not crazy.

I removed my hands from my ears and said, "I've got to go take care of the fish."

No one replied, so I just left. I didn't even shut the door behind me. Let *her* have to do it.

CHAPTER 36

IRIS

"Did you know that if Rosita were alive she'd have been a millionairess?" I asked my mother.

She was standing in the kitchen preparing a casserole. Aaron was sitting on the sofa (protected with a quilt again, naturally) watching the fish. The news out of Utrecht was that the demise of King Kong and Hannibal was being attributed to some unknown organism. They were sending out a crew to take samples of the water and to observe the other fish. Apparently the deaths were a rather singular occurrence in the world of fish diseases.

My mother was in the process of fanatically slicing boiled potatoes into precise slivers and arranging these in a glass baking dish, alternating with layers of eggplant and tomato. It was a dish she often made. It was a bit like moussaka, although my mother denied any resemblance.

"Apparently Rosita's mother had an uncle in England who made a killing in the poultry business. He left Rosita two million pounds."

"Now *that's* what you'd call dumb luck," my mother said testily. "Can't we please talk about something else?"

"*No,* why?"

My mother scattered grated cheese over the casserole with short, irritable gestures.

"We're not done talking about it," I went on. "I've only just taken on this case, and already all these intriguing facts have started coming out. Want to know who's inheriting Rosita's two million pounds? You have three guesses."

My mother slid the casserole in the oven and slammed the oven door shut. "I'm not in the mood for guessing games, and I'm not in the mood for having this conversation."

"Her stepfather. Normally, her daughter, Anna, would have inherited all of it. But she isn't alive, either. The next legal heir would have been Rosita's mother. Also deceased. So who's left? Rosita's stepfather. He and her mother were legally married, therefore all her assets go to him. *Ka-ching*!"

"So then marry the guy."

"He's closer to your age than mine, Mother. All I'm trying to tell you is that someone stood to profit from Rosita's death. And even though I admit it's pretty unlikely that Ray wasn't the one to kill her, I still think we owe it to him to look into it."

My mother went into the living room. She suddenly got very busy tidying Aaron's toys.

"I just want to know what really happened. Can you blame me?"

My mother gave me an exasperated look and began tossing handfuls of Legos into the designated bin.

I kneeled down next to her to help. "What do you know about that Rosita, anyway?"

"Iris . . . I've had enough. For the last time, change the subject."

"Come on, help me out here. Please. Did you ever meet her? According to the woman across the street, you used to show up at Ray's place every so often."

"I saw her a few times."

"And?"

"What do you want me to say? A cunning little bitch. That's what she was. She knew exactly how to get whatever she wanted out of Ray."

"Like what?"

My mother got to her feet, sighing with annoyance. "I just told you, I'm not in the mood for this line of questioning. If all you want to do is whine about Ray, then don't come here anymore." She opened the cupboard to get the dishes out.

"I understand it upsets you that I keep harping on it. But can't you at least explain to me why you never told me about Ray? And why you no longer want to have anything to do with him? After all, he still is your son . . ."

My mother whipped around to face me. "I don't owe you an explanation, Iris. You have no idea what I went through with Ray. No idea."

"Then *give* me an idea. Because believe me, I'll keep bugging you until you give me an answer."

My mother sighed demonstratively.

"*What* did you go through, then? What was Ray like as a child?"

My mother put her hands on her hips. "Ray was a runaway train that couldn't be stopped, not even with the best will in the world. I just couldn't manage him. He was impossible. He was always breaking things, pooped all over the house, even when he was eight, and could spend hours on end banging his head against the wall." She rattled off the facts as if she'd learned them by heart.

"That must have been awful for you, Mother." I really meant it.

She went on in a quieter voice. "I could never predict what would set him off. He'd come out with this ear-splitting scream and keep it up for so long that it drove me up the wall. It was like living with some wild animal. Although he could also be very sweet. He'd sit and play with his Legos for hours, and he loved to draw. Beautiful drawings of birds or spaceships, extremely detailed. But then if I told him it was time to put the crayons away, he'd have a tantrum."

I looked at Aaron, who was still staring at the aquarium with empty, faraway eyes. I could picture him tumbling through space, way out beyond the Milky Way, among the millions of distant suns and their orbiting moons.

"And then all the problems with the other kids. The daily fights. Because teasing Ray always produced great results. You can't imagine how aggressive he could be. You don't even want to know how many times I had to humble myself and say I was sorry. 'You've got to be stricter with him,' I'd hear from Grandpa. 'Discipline him, give him a good spanking if he refuses to listen.' And from the neighbors: 'Single mother, no idea how to cope.' I kept punishing him, I yelled, begged, wept, bribed, ignored, smacked him, beat him, hit him hard, too hard, even . . . It was a nightmare."

There was something uncomfortably familiar about my mother's story. I, too, was often made to feel I was a failure at child rearing, in spite of all the well-intentioned advice.

"When it all got too much for me, I sent him to the Mason Home, a boarding institution for difficult children. That was"—my mother swallowed painfully—"after he killed a dog."

Hearing it from my mother felt different than hearing it from Detective De Winter. I could sense the horror, the shame and frustration lurking beneath my mother's words. How would I feel if Aaron did such a thing?

"The neighbors' dog," my mother went on. "It was scary. That he was capable of killing was bad enough. But even more worrying was the fact that he didn't seem at all aware that he'd done something wrong. It was then that I realized Ray was a threat to society. And that I no longer could be responsible for him." She gave me a tremulous smile. "There, now I've told you."

My mother and I rarely touched. But on an impulse I threw my arms around her and we hugged for a while. It was an awkward moment, but we somehow managed to get through it.

"What you doing?" asked Aaron from his perch on the sofa.

My mother and I quickly let go, as if we'd been caught in some perverted act.

"We're having dinner soon, my darling," said my mother, walking over to him and running a hand through his hair. It always astonished me how easy it was for her to show affection to Aaron, as opposed to the obvious difficulty she had being affectionate with me. "How are the fishes doing?"

"Venus is acting funny," said Aaron.

Venus was a Brazilian basslet: fuchsia in front and bright yellow in back. She and Peanut, her mate, spent most of their time in the grotto, a plastic contraption encrusted with coral and anemones. In spite of her bright coloring, Venus was a small fish that was easy to overlook.

Now she was floating at the surface, her mouth wide open. The same pose in which I had found King Kong. She was still alive, but the question was for how much longer.

"God, those wretched fish," said my mother. "What do we do now?"

"Add antibiotics to the water?"

My mother shook her head and walked over to the sideboard. "I'll just make a note to call Utrecht tomorrow, or I'll forget. If my head weren't attached to my body, I'd forget to take it along one of these days. It's taking me such effort to focus lately."

"Well, Ray would love to take care of them again."

"Can't you just see it? This enormous tank in a cell?" My mother put her pen down, a garish gold fountain pen.

"It's possible he'll get out in the near future."

"Are you still insisting on going on with that ridiculous non-sense?"

"I am."

"You *know* it's pointless."

"Most of the cases I deal with are pointless, Mother."

We heard a *ping* from the kitchen. The not-quite-moussaka casserole was done.

CHAPTER 37

RAY

"Is it okay if I come sit next to you?" Jeannie was looking at me. She was trying to be friendly, because the corners of her mouth went up and her eyes were slightly crinkled.

Everyone stared at us. Jeannie ought to leave me alone. Didn't she get it, that I didn't want to talk to her? I didn't want to talk to anyone anymore, except Iris Kastelein who said she was my sister, and maybe Mo, who I trusted because you have to trust *someone*. But Mo was sitting next to Jamal.

Maybe my mother was another one I wouldn't mind talking to. It had been a very long time since I'd seen her. The last time she'd come to see me was when I was in prison. She'd said, "Don't kid yourself, Ray. You're better off in here. At least now I don't need to worry about you anymore."

Since I didn't say anything, Jeannie seemed to take it for granted that she could sit down next to me. I made myself a bread and liverwurst sandwich. At mealtimes I still ended up eating whatever wound up at my end of the table, even though the only thing I considered palatable was the chocolate spread.

"You're mad at me, aren't you?"

I nodded with a mouth full of bread.

"I know it isn't any consolation, but I was really upset to have to send you to solitary. You got so violent that I didn't have a choice."

I looked out the window, hoping she'd take the hint and stop talking. There was a small robin sitting on the wall. You didn't see those very often in here. You didn't see any birds very often, as a matter of fact, not even in the yard. Birds didn't want to be here, apparently.

I thought about my own backyard, which was always teeming with sparrows, chickadees, and robins. Then I thought about my fish. I really, *really* wanted my fish back.

"Are you listening to me?"

In my head I saw Venus, Saturn, King Kong, and François swimming up to the glass. Every time their heads hit the transparent wall, I'd hear a soft *bonk*.

"Ray?"

The bonking grew louder and louder and the fish kept reeling through my head. They wanted to get out. *Out.*

I couldn't help yelling. Or was I howling? All I knew was that there was a horrible sound coming from my throat.

"Calm down," I heard Jeannie say from somewhere far away. She put her hand on my arm, but I slapped it away. I didn't want to be touched, especially not by her.

The buzzer went off—the buzzer that sounded whenever there was a fight on, or if Ricky started throwing things at the television. A couple of seconds later the doors swung open and two guards rushed inside.

They twisted my hands behind my back, making me bend over. Big drops started plopping down on the table. They were coming from my eyes. I was crying. That was it. That's what you do when you're sad. That realization, strangely enough, made me feel calmer. I was no longer bawling, just sniffing.

"Get up." One of the guards yanked at my arms. It hurt. A lot. I was forced to do what he said.

"Wait." Mo came up to us and started waving something in front of my face. It was a white napkin. "Do you want to blow your nose, Ray?"

I nodded.

"Let him go a second, let him dry his face."

The guards did what Mo told them.

I took the hanky, dabbed at my eyes, and then blew my nose. I felt light-headed, but I'd stopped crying.

"I think he's already calmed down," Mo told the guards. "You can leave him here. I don't think there's any point taking him to the solitary unit. But thanks for your help."

"Mo," said Jeannie in a voice I couldn't interpret. "What are you doing?"

"Tell you later."

The guards left the floor and nobody spoke. Then Rembrandt said, "Let's give Mo a big hand." And everyone began to clap.

It felt a bit as if they were also clapping for me.

Mo let me stay in my cell the rest of the day, to recover. The door wasn't locked; I could leave if I wanted to. I studied the photos of my fish for a while and tacked them up on the wall next to the others. I'd first sorted them alphabetically by name, and then by color.

Thinking of different ways to sort the photos of my fish took so much time that I decided to skip dinner. Mo offered to have them bring me food in my cell, but I wasn't hungry.

"Tomorrow you're going back to having regular meals again, though," said Mo, and then he left me alone.

Over an hour later there was a knock on the door. It was André.

"Good evening, Ray."

I quickly took the photos down off the wall. You never knew what André was going to do.

"I just wanted you to know I've taken over Mo's shift."

"Okay." I waited for him to leave. But he stepped into my cell and shut the door. I clenched my hands around the edge of my bed to stop them from thrashing around.

André sat down next to me.

I shifted away from him a little, still clutching the bedframe, the way I'd clung to my mother's hand when she'd brought me to the Mason Home when I was nine. *Look, Ray, a Ping-Pong table. You're going to have a great time in here.*

"So," he said.

"So," I echoed.

"Everything okay?"

I nodded.

"Have you recovered from your stay in solitary?"

I nodded again.

"Strange, isn't it, that they found drugs in your suite?" The social worker scratched his chin. "Do you have any idea how they got here?"

I shook my head no.

"You don't?"

"No."

"Are you quite sure?"

I nodded.

"Great." He got to his feet, opened the door, but then seemed to change his mind. "And nobody's ever talked about it to you?"

I shook my head, but at the same time realized it wasn't true. Someone *had* talked to me about it. Rembrandt.

André shut the door again. "You don't seem very sure about it. Think again."

I let go of the bedframe; my hands immediately shot out wildly. "Leave me alone!" I said.

The buzzer went off, the signal that the cell doors would be locked for the night.

André's eyes blinked behind his glasses. "I'm keeping an eye on you, Boelens. Don't try anything funny, you hear?" Then he left the cell.

Unlike every other night, this time lockdown felt like a reprieve.

CHAPTER 38

IRIS

Oskar Kool's name did not come up in the record. Yet he must have known Rosita very well, and the man did have a motive, even if it came years and years after the fact.

Ray's description of him was pretty accurate. Despite being in his late sixties, Kool wore his hair long in the back, short in the front. His skin had the parchment cast of someone who's smoked roll-ups all his life. When I found him, he was outside chopping wood.

"So? Have you heard the news?"

The old man didn't react. He didn't say yes or no, but just stared back at me dourly, clutching his ax.

"I understand you've come into a nice inheritance. Haven't you?"

"What you want from me? If you're looking for a handout, I can tell you right now that you've come to the wrong place." He swung the ax high in the air and split a log with a mighty crash, spraying wood chips all over the front of my coat. I took a step back.

"I've come to talk to you about Rosita and Anna. I am Ray Boelens's attorney."

"Ray Boelens."

"You know him, don't you?"

"A nice boy."

I felt my face brighten. "A nice boy?" I repeated. I'd been hoping all this time to hear someone say something positive about Ray, the way a rejected lover sits waiting by the phone even though she ought to know better. And here it was—the phone was ringing at last.

"That's right. Until he went and hacked them to death."

"Right." Wrong number. Foiled again.

Kool lived in a small farmhouse, though "dump" might be a more accurate description. There were holes in the thatched roof and the woodwork was begging for a coat of paint. The farmyard was littered with machinery that looked as if it hadn't been touched since the sixties.

He put another log on the chopping block and brought the ax down. It struck me how shiny and clean this piece of equipment was compared to everything else, including Kool's dirty overalls. The log split into two.

"You're one of the first to say anything positive about him."

Again he didn't respond.

"Funny, though. I mean—you just called Ray Boelens a 'nice boy,'" I tried again.

"He shouldn't have done what he done. That goes without saying. But she did make him nuts. Just like her mom. Both of them knew exactly how to suck a man dry."

I didn't know what to say. But Kool's tongue had suddenly come loose. "Don't get me wrong—they was good women, both of 'em. But you had to know how to handle 'em, like a stray dog. You never knew what you were going to get. Are they going to love you, are they going to leave you, bite you or lick your hand? It's looking to be a cold winter," he went on without pausing. "They can say all they like the earth's getting warmer, but my bones are telling me something else."

"Do you have a fireplace?"

"Wood stove."

"Cozy."

"It helps with the heating costs. I couldn't care less about the coziness," said the new millionaire.

"Have you lived alone since Rosita's mother passed?"

"Yeah. Not all the time. But grief ain't sexy, now, is it? Well, at first, maybe. Especially after Rosita and Anna died. Women want to take care of you and take away your pain. They want to bake you apple pies and pour you a drink. They want to talk to you for hours at a time. So you keep rehashing the same old story, and you get to know exactly at what point they'll start sobbing. But after a month or so, they decide you should get over it. Time for the weeping and whining to stop. They wanna start having some fun. Fun? Who's in the mood for fun?" He spat for emphasis. A brownish gob of spit landed less than a foot from my suede boots.

"So why do you think Ray killed Rosita and Anna?"

Oskar Kool put down his ax on the chopping block. "I already told you. She drove him crazy. She was a looker and she could wind that boy around her little finger. She knew how to wangle a new couch out of him and then a new TV. 'Prezzie from my next-door neighbor,' she'd tell me, beaming. 'You don't get something for nothing,' I told her. 'You're making the guy horny as a tomcat.' That made her laugh. She claimed Ray gave her those things because he didn't have anything better to do with his money. 'I give him a pat on the head once in a while," she said. 'He'll just have to be satisfied with that.' " Kool shook his head. "Just like her old lady. Always take, take, take. But return the favor? Don't hold your breath."

"It doesn't sound very romantic."

"There's no such thing as romance. You'll find out yourself someday."

"Did you know your late wife had an uncle, Richard Angeli?"

"I met him once. At our wedding. Elisa didn't have much to do with him. Except they did exchange Christmas cards."

"And Rosita? Did she know him?"

"She was at our wedding, so she must have seen him there. But the family wasn't particularly close. To tell you the truth, my wife didn't have much to do with Rosita, either. Though maybe it would have been different if she'd been around to know the little kid. I bet she'd have loved to show off a little granddaughter."

"Did your wife know Richard was rich?"

"She did tell me once her uncle had plenty of money. But that's all," he said, nonchalant. *Too* nonchalant? I wondered.

"He certainly had plenty of money."

Oskar Kool picked up his ax again. He had a tattoo of three dots between his thumb and forefinger. "He sure did."

"The money should come in handy for fixing up the farm."

"I guess so." He put another log on the chopping block. It was clear that as far as he was concerned the conversation was over. Wood chips started flying in all directions; I could see the sweat breaking out on the old man's forehead. He acted as if I was no longer there. I realized that if I wanted to get him to keep talking, I'd have to find another subject.

"Did Rosita have any enemies that you know of?"

"Hmm." He scratched his chin. I noticed those three dots on his hand again. "I don't think folks were particularly crazy about her. But enemies, that's a big word."

"What about friends? Did she have any friends?"

"I guess. But—not really. Take the day she moved into her new house on Queen Wilhelmina Street. Do you think anyone came to help her? No, old Oskar was the one to come to the rescue. Whenever something in the house needed fixing, she'd know where to find me, too."

"So she had no friends, and no enemies, either, and you were her handyman. Did anyone else ever visit her, then?"

"Ray, of course. And that shithead. Asscher."

"Anna's father."

"*Father*'s a big a word for someone who gets a woman pregnant and then leaves her holding the bag."

"But he did take care of her, didn't he? Didn't he come over sometimes?"

Kool sniffed loudly. "What a prick. Rolling in dough, but doing the right thing? Don't hold your breath. Things were different in my time."

"Isn't it possible someone else killed them?"

He smiled scornfully. "Yeah, in your dreams. Boelens done it. No doubt." He picked up his ax and started hacking away like a madman again. It wasn't difficult to picture him wielding a carving knife. Was he capable of committing murder? Of committing cold, calculated murder on the vague expectation of a fortune somewhere down the road—unless he'd also given Rosita's biological father a helping hand, which was quite possible, too. In which case he'd been remarkably patient. Eight years! And he was far from being a spring chicken himself.

I stared at the three dots on his hand. I'd noticed the same kind of tattoo on a good number of our criminal cases. There were varied explanations for it. It was commonly thought to mean "Fuck the police."

Inmates gave it to each other in jail.

CHAPTER 39

RAY

After spending hours waiting at the bottom of Rosita's staircase, I finally walked back to my house. As soon as I got there I went and looked at my fish. At the way they swam round and round and always seemed to be in good spirits, although I could never really be sure. But I did think they were happy, since they always had somebody to take care of them. And that somebody was me.

To be on the safe side I checked all the levels, even though I'd done it that morning and would do it again before leaving for work later. Everything was A-OK. Knowing it calmed me down. I took a shower and went to bed.

Usually I got up at three A.M., but that night I woke up after midnight because I heard people shouting in Rosita's house. The noise was coming from her bedroom. I took a glass and held it against the wall to hear what they were yelling about.

"Are you out of your mind? How *dare* you get in touch with her! How dare you! Do you have any idea what kind of position you're putting me in?" I thought it was Anna's father's voice. It wasn't the first time I'd seen his car parked outside in the middle of the night. According to Rosita, his wife sometimes took the kids to sleep over at her mother's house. And then Victor would spend the night with Rosita.

I heard Rosita say something back. She wasn't yelling; she was talking softly. I couldn't understand what she was saying, no matter how hard I pressed my ear to the glass.

"Don't give me that crap!" Victor yelled back. "Know what you can do? You can go to hell. I've had it up to here with you! I'm going on vacation tomorrow, and then it's over. Do you hear me?"

Then Rosita's voice again. She was crying, I did hear that. But what she said wasn't clear. Victor was talking more quietly, too.

I stayed there awhile longer with my ear glued to the glass, listening hard. But I couldn't catch anything else they said. Then I heard footsteps on the stairs and the front door slamming shut. Looking out the window I saw Victor Asscher's silly car driving down the street. I heard Rosita crying.

It occurred to me that this fight was good news. Very good news.

There was nothing keeping Rosita, Anna, and me from being a family anymore. We already were almost a family—Rosita had said so herself. Besides, there were plenty of other signs: I was over there every day, and I'd touched Rosita's privates, and Anna was fond of me. Now we were really going to be inseparable.

I was so excited I couldn't get back to sleep. I got up and went to the bakery much earlier than usual and baked far too many croissants.

"Did you think it was Saturday?" my boss asked.

After work I picked out a madeleine for Anna. This time I tied the paper bag with a red ribbon. There was something to celebrate, after all. I couldn't seem to walk normally. I ended up skipping all the way to our street. I pressed Anna and Rosita's doorbell.

It took a long time. Maybe Rosita was in the bathroom. After a while I pressed the bell again. And again. Nobody came to answer. I hung the bag with the madeleine from the doorknob and walked over to my own house. Why wasn't she home? I kicked a door and smashed a vase my mother had given me on the floor. It didn't help at all. I forced myself to calm down. I recited all the fishes' names a few times. That did help. My heart stopped racing and my head stopped reeling. I decided to make myself something good to eat.

The day before, I'd brought home a *pain de figues,* which was delicious to eat with sheep's-milk cheese. As I was slicing the cheese, I thought I heard something through the wall. It was vague and sounded far away, but it was unmistakable: *"Tinky Winky . . . Dipsy . . . Laa-Laa . . . Po . . ."*

I knew that song. I took a bite of the delicious *pain de figues* and realized that if the TV was on, Rosita and Anna must be home. Which meant Rosita hadn't opened the door on purpose.

I climbed over the little gate leading to her backyard and peered through her window. Rosita was sitting next to Anna on the couch. She was wearing sweatpants and a tank top, and her feet were bare. She was smoking a cigarette. As if she'd been sitting there the whole time. But she'd refused to open the door. Anna was munching on the madeleine. The red ribbon was at her feet.

Then Rosita saw me. She stared at me. I must have given her a fright, because her shoulders went up and she dropped the cigarette on the couch. The couch *I'd* bought her. She snatched up the burning cigarette and started rubbing at the spot where it had fallen. Anna saw me, too. Her mouth formed the word *Ray!* She even waved at me.

I just stood there outside the window; I didn't know what else to do. Rosita got up off the couch. I thought she was going to let me in, because she walked over to the back door. She opened it a crack and stuck her head out. "What are you doing here, Ray? Can't you just leave me alone a *single* day?"

I took a deep breath and decided to just come out with it. The thing I'd been waiting to say for so long. I'd hoped it and dreamed about it, and the moment had come. "I've come to be a family. With you and with Anna."

For a moment she didn't say anything. Then she burst out laughing.

But what I'd said wasn't funny.

When she'd recovered a bit, she said, "Come on, Ray! You don't really think we can be a family, do you? Really, whatever gave you that idea? I think you're sweet and very nice, although I didn't think you were very nice yesterday, when you just stood there at the bottom of the stairs and wouldn't leave, but okay, maybe it was my fault. But now you're going too far. We are *neighbors*, Ray. Friends, even. But *family*? Come on, that's never going to happen."

"But you said so yourself." I went to the door to take her in my arms. To hug her and kiss her, the way people do who belong together.

But she jumped back. "Over my dead body!" She slammed the door in my face, turned the lock, and savagely drew the curtains shut.

I stared at the yellow drapes, her words tumbling through my head like raisins in the bread mixer. Suddenly I knew the awful truth. She had fooled me. She'd told me we were nearly a family. But *nearly* means "just a few more steps and you're there." But those few more steps didn't exist. Not then, not tomorrow, and not ever.

CHAPTER 40

IRIS

The next one on my list was Asscher. It hadn't been easy to get him to agree to a meeting. Only when I mentioned that I could also call him at home about this matter if he liked, he surrendered. We agreed to meet at a highway rest stop that I suspected was mainly frequented by traveling salesmen and people on Match.com dates. The tables had salmon-pink tablecloths and little vases with a couple of gerbera daisies wrapped in a caster bean leaf. An optimistic attempt at giving the dump some atmosphere.

I could understand what Rosita had seen in Victor. Not exactly handsome, he did radiate an unmistakable virility. Not bad for an accountant. Tall, sturdily built, and he wore his hair longer than you'd expect of someone wearing a gray tailored suit and striped silk tie.

"I already told you over the phone, I have nothing to add. I've told the police all I know. And I don't have much time."

"You spoke to the police? Strange . . ."

He didn't bother to hide his irritation. "What do you mean, strange?"

"Your statement isn't in the record."

"Right. So?" I stared at him quizzically for as long as it took for him to elaborate. "I was in Crete with my family at the time of the murder. I read about it in the newspaper." He swallowed.

"When you were still in Crete or after you got home?"

"In a café in one of those Greek fishing villages. I just happened to see a three-day-old Dutch newspaper. That's where I read it."

I pictured Asscher, surrounded by wife and kids, reading the terrible news about his mistress. "That must have been awful."

I saw that he was getting emotional. "Would you like a glass of water?"

He nodded.

When I returned with the water, Asscher was blowing his nose in a neatly pressed pale blue handkerchief. I was struck by how old-fashioned that was. I didn't know anyone who still used a linen handkerchief, let alone anyone who had the time or inclination to iron them.

"I'm sorry," said Asscher. "I'm not used to talking about it."

"I understand. It must feel very lonely, keeping a secret like that."

"Yes." His eyes were watery again. "Do we really need to dredge this all up?"

"I am so sorry. I will try to keep this as easy as possible. We were talking about why your statement wasn't in the official record, Mr. Asscher."

"You can call me Victor." He smiled through his tears. "I wasn't planning to go to the police at first. Not on my own account, but to spare my wife, Millie. It would break her heart if she ever knew I'd had a mistress and a child."

I gave a sympathetic murmur. Rence used to say, "Building trust is largely a matter of making the right reassuring noise at the right moment."

"After a few weeks I began to feel remorse," Asscher went on.

"I thought, what if I'm the one holding the missing piece of information? I went to the police, but they didn't seem too interested. They listened to my story and that was it. I asked if they wanted me to sign a statement or anything, but the case was already solved, they told me."

I raised my eyebrows. "I see."

"It was an open-and-shut case—Boelens did it. That guy isn't normal."

"Didn't he slash your tires once?"

"Yes. I did try to warn her about him. Especially after that slashing incident. The way he went at it like a maniac . . . terrifying. 'That man is dangerous,' I told Rosita. 'Stay away from him.' But no. She said he was a friend . . . A friend! 'He isn't like you or me,' she'd say, 'but he has a good heart.' Well, we sure have proof of that, don't we? Do you know how many times Rosita was stabbed? Fourteen."

"Do you have any idea why Rosita considered him a friend?"

He shrugged. "Mainly to make me jealous, I'd think. As if I could be jealous of someone like *that* guy. I can still see him coming home from work with one of those disgusting little cake offerings for Anna. Every day he'd bring her one. Can you imagine? He'd sometimes babysit Anna, too. I didn't think it was a great idea, but Rosita said it could do no harm. In hindsight . . ." He blew his nose again.

"Please, take your time."

"This is hard for me."

"I know."

"Shit. I'm not usually such an emotional wreck."

"As an accountant you're probably rarely in danger of getting your emotions involved."

He laughed.

"Did Rosita have any other enemies? Or any debts?"

Asscher took some time to think about it, then shook his head. "She was a spirited girl. I do have to say that. A ticking time bomb even, sometimes. But enemies? I don't think so."

"I don't quite get what you mean. In what sense was she a ticking time bomb?"

He hesitated. "*You* know. Hotheaded. Latin temperament."

"For a spirited girl like Rosita, wasn't it hard to play second fiddle all the time? To your wife, I mean?"

If I'd had Asscher's trust, it was over. The steel shutters came down with a mighty crash. "I don't see the relevance of this line of questioning. Where are you going with this?"

"I'm trying to get a better sense of the sort of people who knew Rosita Angeli. And you were one of them."

"I'd almost forgotten you were Boelens's attorney. Say hi to him for me. And tell him that once he's sprung from that institution he's going to get what's coming to him."

I tried to think of something to get Asscher talking again, but he was already on his feet. He stuck out his hand. "Good-bye."

I stayed behind, perplexed. I'd hit a raw nerve, obviously. I couldn't imagine Rosita being happy with her mistress status. She struck me as someone who liked to be number one. Why else would Asscher have said that she wanted to make him jealous?

As I picked up my purse, another thought occurred to me. *Had Rosita threatened to tell Asscher's wife about the relationship?*

CHAPTER 41

RAY

"Tell me," said Iris Kastelein. "When you were still living at home, what was Mother like?"

"Angry" was my answer. "She was almost always angry."

She laughed. I didn't know why. Was she making fun of me?

"What was she angry about, then?"

I shrugged my shoulders. "I'm no good at this."

"What do you mean?"

"You keep wanting to talk about feelings and stuff. I'm not good at feelings. Didn't you know that?"

She laughed again. "I don't mean to confuse you. Shall I tell you something about myself? I'm your sister, after all."

I was going to say no but remembered the shrink at school: You have to show you're interested in other people. So I nodded.

"Mother didn't get angry at me all that often. I'd say she was indifferent. As if I were a project yet to be finished. Luckily I had Dad. My father." She was silent awhile, and her forehead crinkled into a frown. "My father passed away ten years ago. Do you know who your father is?"

I started feeling warm. So warm I almost couldn't breathe. "Can I take off my sweater?" I asked Mo.

"Why?" he asked.

"I'm suffocating in here."

"Do you mind?" Mo asked Iris Kastelein.

"Of course not."

I pulled off my sweater so that I was sitting there across from her in my white undershirt. It helped a bit, but I was still hot.

"We were talking about your father," said Iris Kastelein. "Do you know who he is?"

I clenched my teeth, grinding them from side to side. It made a grating sound.

"Didn't Mother ever tell you anything about him?"

Why was everyone always asking me questions I couldn't answer? Who's your father, who's your father, your father's this, your father's that, when I had no idea. Did they all think I'd never asked her about it myself? Did they think I was a moron?

"Sorry," said Iris Kastelein. "I'll stop harping on it, all right? You know, I always had this feeling that something wasn't right. In hindsight, all of this explains a great deal. Why Mother would go off to garden shows every once in a while, for instance, and was adamant that Dad should stay home. And then there was her secret study. Did you know about that? There was this room in the house that was strictly off-limits to me. She was completely fanatic about it."

She looked over my shoulder at something in the room. I turned my head to follow her gaze and saw she was looking at Mo, who was sitting in the corner. What did she do that for?

"Another thing," said Iris Kastelein. "I've persuaded the warden here to try and find out how those drugs got into your cell."

"Suite," said Mo from the corner. "We call it a suite here."

"Oh, right." Iris Kastelein suddenly also seemed to be feeling the heat. But then she'd arrived wearing a classy pantsuit with a white blouse underneath. “Fancy-pants, la-di-da,” Rosita used to say. She didn't like Iris's sort. Rosita was pretty tolerant, even of the nosy neighbors, but she couldn't stand people who dressed up. “They always think they're better than everyone else. Why? Because they happen to have more money in the bank? Because the pearls they're wearing are *real*? You can't even tell the difference. You have to bite them to know. They can kiss my ass.”

I wondered if Iris Kastelein thought she was better than everyone else.

“Anyway,” she said, “I explained you couldn't possibly have had anything to do with the drugs that were found in your suite. You're neither a user nor a dealer. You've never had a positive urine test, and the social workers have never observed any behaviors that would indicate drug use. Isn't that so?”

“Yes.”

“Exactly. I'm demanding a thorough investigation into what really happened.”

She crossed her arms and looked at me with a funny expression. It was as if her mouth wanted to smile, but her eyes didn't. When people smile, they scrunch up their eyes a bit. Iris Kastelein's eyes were wide open.

“What are you now?” I asked.

“What do you mean?”

“What are you now? Angry? Sad? Scared? Happy?”

“Determined,” she replied.

“Oh.”

“Did you know I've spoken with Victor Asscher?” said Iris.

“He's a bad man.”

“He's still very emotional about Rosita's and Anna's deaths.”

“They'd been fighting,” I said. “Two days before Rosita died. He stormed out in the middle of the night and never came back.”

Iris leaned across the table toward me, her eyes narrowing a bit. "What was the fight about, do you think?"

"She told someone about something. I heard them shouting about it. In the middle of the night, right through the wall."

My words seemed to please Iris Kastelein greatly. She leaned in even closer. "You're sure?"

I nodded.

"And that's what they were arguing about?"

I nodded again.

"Interesting."

This time I didn't nod.

"I had the feeling something in his story didn't compute. Do you think Rosita might have threatened to tell Victor's wife about their relationship?"

"How should I know?" I started scanning the white wall looking for spiders. Maybe I could catch one and take it back to my cell. That way I'd have a pet.

Iris Kastelein sat back in her chair. "I know this is hard for you. But we *have* to talk about the day Rosita and Anna died. You were the one who found them, weren't you?"

I suddenly started feeling very hot again. I felt the sweat running down my back, even though all I was wearing was my undershirt. "Yes," I managed. "Yes."

"How did it happen?"

"I saw the door was open and went in. They were lying right there."

"And were they already dead?"

All that blood—I could see it again, in my mind. I tried shaking my head, but that didn't get rid of the blood.

"Ray?" asked Mo. "Did you hear the question?"

"Yes," I whispered. "They were already dead."

"Did you see anything else, before you went inside? Was there anyone else in the street? Neighbors? People you knew? Strangers?"

I tried to think, but it was hard to remember what happened on May 17, 2003. At night, in the darkness of my cell, it was all very clear-cut and real. But trying to talk about it with someone else was hard.

"No," I said, though I was far from sure. "I don't think so."

Iris Kastelein jotted something down in her notebook. This conversation was starting to tire me out. "I want to go back to my cell."

"Please, just a little longer."

I wanted to be strong, to answer all her questions. But the dough machine in my head was getting my thoughts all mixed up.

"I think it's time, actually," said Mo from his corner. "We don't want Ray's stress level to rise."

"Oh, okay. Of course."

I got up. "Bye, Iris."

As I was escorted out by the guard, I heard her say to Mo, "That was the first time I've heard him say my name."

CHAPTER 42

IRIS

"Iris! Yoo-hoo!"

I didn't know very many people who, in this day and age, still hollered *yoo-hoo*, so I guessed it had to be one of my mother's friends. It was lunchtime and I'd just run to the supermarket to buy the ingredients for a quick meal for me and Aaron. Spaghetti Bolognese. We had it for dinner at least twice a week.

I turned to see Lina. She was holding a bag of potatoes and waving like mad, even though she was standing only a dozen feet away from me.

"How lovely to see you, darling!"

"Hello, Lina. I didn't know you shopped here." Lina lived around the corner from my mother, in Buitenveldert. This inner-city market was a far cry from her natural habitat.

"I'm on my way to finger-paint with my sweet little Down-children," she said with a wink, whereby she had a hard time keeping the other, not-winking eye, open.

"Oh?"

"Didn't your mother tell you? I teach arts and crafts to the mentally handicapped. Every Wednesday afternoon."

"My mother never tells me anything, actually. Especially not the important stuff. How long have you and my mother known each other, anyway?"

Lina, frowning, looked up at the market's tiled ceiling. "Probably thirty-five years or so at least. Your mother had just moved to our neighborhood. I knew her neighbor—she's been dead for years, but I won't bother you by going into old wives' details. It was the neighbor's birthday, and that's how we met. Agatha knew practically no one back then. And I had just stopped work upon getting married; that's what we did in those days. So we'd look each other up. And after Carla and you left home, we started a bridge club, but that's a whole other story."

"Was she already seeing my dad?"

The frown-groove on Lina's forehead got even deeper, as if I'd asked her to multiply three hundred thirty-five by six thousand eight hundred ninety-three. "No, your father wasn't in the picture yet when I met Agatha. She only met him six months after she came to live here. I can still see her standing there blushing: 'Lina,' she said, 'I'm going to marry that man. That man's going to take good care of me.'"

I was afraid I'd taken over Lina's frown. "So she must have lived in another house at first."

"No . . . !" said Lina with a dramatic flourish. "No . . . she already owned the bungalow. That was quite something in those days. A woman owning her own home, with no husband in sight. We all secretly envied her a bit."

I wondered how my mother had managed to come up with the down payment on the bungalow. Nowadays homes like hers cost over a million. I knew she had gone to secretarial school, but I'd never heard her mention having had a job. I always blindly assumed my father was the one who'd bought the house. Who knew—perhaps my mother had a rich great-uncle stashed away somewhere who'd left her a nice little nest egg, like Rosita had. "How do you think she came up with the money?"

Lina shrugged. "She must have had savings."

"Savings from what?"

"Don't ask me. She'd had a good job, she said."

A good job, at the same time as looking after a young child? It sounded pretty far-fetched to me. "Strange, though," I said.

"It sounds strange. But that's the way the cookie crumbles. The older you get, the less you understand." She glanced at her watch. "Gee, is that the time? I have to go, kiddo. My special little friends are waiting for me."

She gave a whoop that sounded something like "*toodly-doo!*"—a farewell salutation of the over-sixty crowd, I had to presume—and briskly marched out of the vegetable section clutching her bag of potatoes.

As I hurriedly tossed a bunch of celery, a jar of spaghetti sauce, half a pound of organic ground beef, and a package of grated Parmesan into my basket, I wondered if Lina knew about Ray. I strongly suspected she didn't.

Back at the office I called the land registry. Within one minute I had an answer: the house was bought in 1983 for 150,000 guilders. In cash, no mortgage. It must have been an astronomic sum back then.

"My favorite girl!" I hadn't heard Rence come in. He wasn't in the habit of wandering into my room out of the blue in any case. Normally I was summoned to *his* office.

Rence sat down on the edge of my desk and crossed one leg over the other. He was wearing red socks.

"How are you getting on with the Boelens investigation?"

"Hmm," I said.

"Go on, tell. Who have you spoken with, what does the record say, first impressions?"

"The stories are all pretty consistent; everyone I've spoken to says the same thing. Ray Boelens is a disturbed individual, the woman next door was using him, then she dumped him, and he blew his top. He's never confessed, but has made some rather incriminating statements. Not only did he have a motive; he was also at the crime scene and he more or less admitted to owning the murder weapon. Not very helpful, any of it."

"Who have you talked to so far?"

"Neighbors. Friends and relatives of the victim . . ."

"And?"

"Well. The stepfather is a rather sleazy customer. Jailed for dealing drugs. With Rosita and Anna out of the picture, it turns out he's the sole heir to a fortune left by his late wife's uncle. Sounds like a motive, you might say. Were it not for the time gap—would you commit murder and then just sit around for years waiting for the uncle to die in his own sweet time? That's what I'd call *really* planning ahead."

"Hmm."

"Then there's the boyfriend. Boelens heard Asscher and Rosita having a fight not long before the murders. He heard Asscher shout something along the lines of 'You shouldn't have told her.' Maybe Rosita told the wife about their relationship. A plausible motive, you might think. Except that Asscher was vacationing in Crete at the time of the murder."

"A hit man?"

I shrugged. "It's possible."

Rence picked up the photo of Aaron and me at the zoo and glanced at it. "What do you think? Do you think Ray Boelens is innocent? Is there even a single indication to think that?"

"Except his own assertion?"

Rence nodded and put the photograph down.

"To be honest, nothing. Well, except for the fact that Ray doesn't smoke and the perpetrator stubbed out a cigarette on the little girl. Not that that's a very convincing argument."

"Clearly," said Rence. "And what's your hunch?"

"I can't say I have a very clear thought about it at this point."

He jumped up and shook his head vehemently. "No! I don't mean *thoughts*! I mean your intuition! Come on, Iris. What does your heart tell you when you look at Ray Boelens?"

"I feel confused," I answered wearily.

"We're at a place where we either get a whole team going on this or we give up. From what you're telling me, I guess it's going to be the latter."

I hesitated. If it came out that Ray was my brother, and that I'd spent an inordinate amount of time on his case, I'd be in big trouble. But I didn't want to leave Ray in the lurch. Not now that I knew Asscher and Rosita had quarreled right before her death. I could always give up later on. "I'd like to have another go at Asscher. He had a strong motive, and, as you just said, he needn't have carried out the murder himself. He could have hired someone."

"Would you like me to have a look at the dossier?"

"Please."

CHAPTER 43

RAY

The night after Rosita had drawn the curtains shut in my face, I couldn't sleep. Weirdly, though, I wasn't thinking about her—no, I was thinking about the day my mother brought me to the Mason Home.

We had a little suitcase with us, packed with some of my things. Enough underwear for a week, three pairs of pants, five T-shirts, and two sweaters. And the bird encyclopedia. "I can always bring you the rest later, Ray."

The size of the suitcase had given me hope that my stay at the Mason Home would be temporary. After all, my mother knew I couldn't live without my Lego Technic set, or my fossil collection.

But when I asked her how long I'd have to be there, she wouldn't look at me. Keeping her eyes on the road, she said, "No idea."

I was big for my age. Big enough to sit in the front seat. That's why it was extra difficult for people to understand that I was emotionally delayed. At least, that's what I'd heard my mother tell our neighbor. Later on she explained it to me as well. "People see a big kid, but they don't get that you're still very small inside," she'd said.

My mother and I were a family, and yet she told me I was going to love Mason, gushing about the homey dormitory, the varied menu, and the swing sets in the yard.

She'd left the little suitcase in the cubby I was supposed to keep my stuff in. It had once had a lock on it, but since boys kept losing their keys, the school had stopped giving them out.

"Later, when we say good-bye to your mother, you mustn't cry," said the nurse giving us the tour of the Mason Home. She put her arm around my shoulder, as if to show I belonged to her and not my mother. I promptly shrugged her arm off me.

"We're on our way to the exit. When we get there, give your mother a big hug and wave good-bye to her, like a big boy, all right? Don't disappoint your mother, Ray."

I waited for my mother to explain about the emotional delay, but she didn't. Instead she said, "Cute, aren't they, those little pots of watercress painted by the kids."

The nurse smiled. "We're always doing crafts projects with the children in here. Watercress is delicious and healthy, too."

"I think a nutritious diet is very important. Although Ray isn't too fond of his vegetables. I always make him eat the healthy stuff first, before I let him have any meat."

"I'll pass that along," said the nurse.

"It would also help if you allowed him to assist in the food preparation. Or if you'd let him grow vegetables in the garden." My mother's voice sounded different. I looked at her and saw that her mouth was a thin line and she was blinking her eyes a lot.

We had reached the exit.

I didn't really believe that my mother was just going to leave me there. I thought it was something like the Last Warning: "I'm letting you come home with me this time. But I'm warning you: The next time you're a bad boy, I'll leave you here for good."

"Now it's time to say good-bye."

My mother took my head in both her hands and pressed a kiss on my mouth. Then she wrapped her arms around me so tight that I was afraid I'd suffocate. My mother's chest was heaving, up and down.

"It's hard, isn't it," said the nurse. She patted my mother on the back.

My mother held me so tight and so long that I didn't think she'd ever let me go. But in the end she did. There was black on her cheeks and her eyes were red.

"You'd better go," said the nurse. "That would be best."

My mother opened her mouth to say something, but no sound came out. She turned and walked quickly down the path, her head lowered, to the parking lot.

I kept waving, though my mother never looked back. It wasn't until she was at the car that she turned to look at me and shouted, "Behave yourself, Ray, you hear? Be a good boy!"

I *was* a good boy. I didn't even cry, did I? Just as the nurse had said.

The tears came only in the night, when I was in bed.

I eventually got used to the Mason Home. Even the bad things, like the bullying or the other kids making fun of me. But worse were the days when nothing happened. The days I just sat around in the Mason Home common room, which my mother had told me was homey and fun. But what good were hominess and fun to me? As if a bunch of flowery cushions and a cup of tea and a cookie could make me happy.

CHAPTER 44

IRIS

In a sea of Volkswagens and the odd Saab, the Jaguar stood out. I assumed Victor Asscher had stayed faithful to his make of automobile. This one was a top-of-the-line model with beige leather seats. Aside from a crumpled-up windbreaker in the back, the car was spotless, as if it had just come from the dealer.

The man was neat, extremely neat. I thought of the Mars bar wrappers, empty juice boxes, and even banana peels littering the floor of my car. I was his polar opposite, but then again, I drove an old VW Golf.

The thought occurred to me that it was probably this neatness that made it possible for him to live a double life all those years. He was good at cleaning up the messes he left behind.

"I've already told you all there is to tell." Victor brushed past me coldly, his car key at the ready.

"I wonder."

"Let me put it another way. I've already told you more than I wanted to. And besides, I'm in no way obligated to cooperate with your investigation. If you have any further questions, I'd advise you to talk to my lawyer." He pushed the key's unlock button. The Jaguar's headlights lit up.

"I could ask your wife myself, if you'd rather not answer."

"You'd better not."

"Well, then?"

"Not a day went by when she didn't threaten me with something. Rosita liked to get her own way. But I knew she'd never actually go through with her threats."

"Really? So what was that huge fight you had with her about, just before she died? Wasn't it about that?"

"I don't remember."

"Strange. Most people wouldn't so quickly forget such a squabble if their mistress was murdered less than two days later. Rosita was threatening to tell Millie about your relationship, true or false? And that wasn't very convenient for you."

"And what about it? Are you going to accuse *me* of killing Rosita? Of killing my own kid? Now you've gone too far."

"I would imagine you'd be afraid Rosita would tell Millie no matter what. Not a very nice prospect, that. And you could also have asked someone else to do the dirty work for you, naturally."

"I am asking you one last time to step aside." He took his phone from his pants pocket and dialed a number. "Or would you rather find out what it's like to be escorted off the premises by security?"

"Fine, I'm going."

He put his phone away again. "Thank you."

An older man strolled past us in the parking lot. He had on a three-piece suit and walked with a cane. He was looking at us intently.

"Good evening, Mr. Van Benschop," said Asscher. *Van Benschop?* Was this Peter van Benschop's father? Studying the man's face, I realized I had seen him a couple of times before, at the office, when he'd come in for meetings with Martha Peters. Was Asscher his accountant?

"Now, now, that's no way to talk to a lady, Asscher." He glanced at me briefly. "Especially not such a charming specimen as this."

"Good evening, sir," I said.

He stopped and stared at me, frowning. "Do I know you?"

"I work at Bartels and Peters. You may have seen me there."

He put out his hand. "Antoine van Benschop."

"Iris Kastelein."

He immediately let go of my hand. Then he said, rather abruptly, "Well, have a nice day, Miss Kastelein. Victor." He nodded at Victor and continued on his way across the parking lot.

"You were just leaving," said Asscher threateningly.

The parking lot was completely deserted and it did seem the most sensible thing to do.

CHAPTER 45

RAY

Walking to work at three fifteen that morning, I was exhausted. Rosita's house was dark. The kitchen curtain was drawn, which only reminded me of the day before, when Rosita had yanked the curtain shut in my face so that she wouldn't have to look at me anymore.

I bit down hard on my lip. I had La Souche waiting for me, not to mention the four hundred croissants I had to bake, the twelve kinds of bread, and the *tartelettes.* I decided to forget about the madeleines. I was never going to bake a madeleine for anybody ever again.

First I switched on the lights and heated the ovens. Then I took La Souche out of her warming cupboard. Normally I'd do it while murmuring to her. "Did you sleep well, *ma chérie?* Are you still comfortable?" The way she smelled, and the sponginess of her structure, always gave me the answer. But I wasn't in any state to make conversation. I started mixing the ingredients for the twelve different kinds of bread: the *pain au céréales,* the *galette,* the *pain de seigle,* the *baguette,* and all the rest. Next came the proofing and the baking. All through the early hours of the morning, fresh loaves of bread went into the oven. Soon the heady, slightly sour and slightly sweet smell of fresh-baked bread came wafting through the kitchen. I realized the routine actions and familiar smell of my own bread were making me feel calmer.

At half past six, when the owner came in, I was right on schedule. The first hundred croissants were ready, and I'd spend a couple more hours baking the rest of the day's product. After that, I'd switch to preparing for the next day.

The owner and I didn't talk much. It wasn't like it used to be with Margaret, who hardly ever stopped talking even when nobody was listening. The owner and I said good morning to each other, and through the glass wall I could see him stocking the shelves and refilling the cash register with change.

The first customers came in for their fresh croissants and *pains au chocolat* and I wondered if Rosita would stop in at the bakery. I thought that maybe she'd come and have a coffee with me, and everything would be normal again. Even though I was angry, I was hopeful. As hopeful as I'd been all the days, months, and years I spent in the Mason Home, that my mother would show up and take me home. I should have known hoping was pointless.

Since I'd been watching the window from the minute the store was open, I was having a hard time concentrating on the bread baking. I left the next batch of croissants in the oven too long. When the buzzer went off, I did hear it somewhere in the back of my head, but it didn't register that I was supposed to take the croissants out.

It wasn't until the owner came running into the kitchen that I realized the place was blue with smoke. "Ray! What's going on in here?" He pulled the oven door open and exclaimed, "Shit! Didn't you set the timer?" What he pulled out was a tray of blackened croissants.

My legs began to shake.

"What's the matter with you? Are you ill or something? Do you need to go home?"

I splashed some cold water on my face and took a deep breath. Concentrate, I told myself. Concentrate on your daily routine. I thought about what Pierre used to say: "It's just like making wine. Time and temperature. Time and temperature."

I managed to bake another fifty croissants and twenty baguettes. They didn't look as perfect as usual. A bit too pale, not uniform in shape. The owner raised his eyebrows, but didn't say anything.

At around ten A.M. I was ready to start on the dough for the next day's croissants. I took La Souche out of the warming cupboard. She looked tired. I'd fed her earlier in the day, but it hadn't perked her up. She was pale and compact, and smelled sour. Not a nice sourdough smell, but an unpleasant one.

"What's the matter with you?" I whispered. "*Ma chérie,* what on earth's the matter with you?"

I closed my eyes and waited for the answer to come. Had I set the temperature of the warming cupboard wrong? Was she still hungry? Did I need to lower the pH? I opened my eyes and studied the dough intently. Sugar, I suddenly thought. She needs to be sweetened. I gave her two tablespoons of sugar and returned her to the warming cupboard.

For the next hour I couldn't do anything except hope she'd get better. I couldn't make the croissant dough with La Souche in this state. Meanwhile I was keeping a constant eye on the store, in case Rosita came in.

Rosita still hadn't appeared by eleven, and La Souche was worse off than before. She had shrunk even more and seemed to be having trouble breathing. I peered into the store, where my boss and one of the girls were busily serving the people from the fancy neighborhood. They didn't seem to have any inkling of the drama that was playing out in the kitchen.

"*Ma chérie,*" I pleaded. "Don't abandon me. Stay with me." A tear came rolling down my cheek. I felt it happen but didn't have the presence of mind to wipe it away. The mixture of water, protein, sodium, potassium, lysozyme, and all the rest dripped into the mother dough. She bravely resisted for a few seconds. "*No!*" I shouted. "No! No!" The tears kept falling, and as I looked on helplessly she collapsed, slowly but surely. I could neither stop crying nor try to save La Souche. I was paralyzed. I might have saved her if I'd come to my senses in time. But I just couldn't. I just let it happen.

I was calm by the time I took off my apron and threaded my way through the line of customers to the exit. I heard my boss shout, "Where do you think you're going?" I had nothing to say to him.

It was quiet on my street. Everyone was at the market, which came to town once a week. The sky was cloudy and the wind was cold, even though it was May. I realized I'd left my coat hanging in the bakery, but didn't feel like going back for it.

When I turned onto our street I saw that Rosita and Anna's front door had been left open. I tried to think of all the wise lessons I'd ever learned from the Mason Home shrink. For example: If you're not seeing eye to eye with someone, it's best to stay out of their way.

I shouldn't have walked up to Rosita's front door. I was still hoping it had all been a misunderstanding. That Rosita would take me back and we'd be almost a family once more. Walking up to her door, I snapped off a few dead twigs in her bushes. Now that La Souche was dead, I had all the time in the world to get her garden into shape.

"Rosita?" I called. She didn't answer. She was refusing to answer me again. My hope promptly turned back into anger. She'd lied to me, and she was acting as if I didn't even exist. But I did exist. I did very much exist. She wouldn't get rid of me that easily.

Slowly I pushed the door open.

CHAPTER 46

IRIS

The days my mother agreed to babysit Aaron had always been a welcome break for me. I'd walk in to find them sitting on the sofa reading a book together, or playing a game called Little Polar Bear Wants to Fly. My mother would have dinner ready, and all I had to do was hang up my coat and sit down to eat. Mealtimes were always a time for pleasant chitchat, and then at around seven o'clock, Aaron and I would get in the car and drive home. But ever since I had found out about Ray, small talk had gone out the window. I just couldn't talk about the weather when there was so much I needed to know.

"I had an interesting week," I said over the meal of roast pork, fries, carrots, and peas.

"Here we go again," said my mother, and started sawing furiously at her meat.

"Do you know Ray hasn't been doing well at all? The social worker is afraid he isn't cut out for life in the institution."

"And do *you* know I went to the doctor yesterday about that nail infection?" my mother responded in a loud voice. "He gave me a prescription for a salve I'm supposed to apply to it twice a day."

"He's being transferred to another ward soon. There he'll

finally be getting the structure he needs. Was he always like that, Mother?"

My mother just continued. "So I went to the pharmacy. With Aaron. The woman at the register says to me, 'You do know how you're supposed to treat that nail fungus, don't you?' I told her, 'Excuse me, Miss, this is an *infection.* And I should very much appreciate it if you would lower your voice, and not trumpet confidential information to the whole world.' "

"Mother, I was trying to tell you something."

"And *I* am trying to tell *you* something." If it weren't for the fact that she was my mother, I'd have sworn she was looking at me with contempt.

"I want more," said Aaron.

My mother put some more carrots and fries on his plate, and then mashed everything together.

"How come with you he's such a good eater?" I asked. "I have to talk him into taking every bite."

"So there you have it, the irony of being a mother in a nutshell. By the time you've mastered this child-rearing business, your children are grown up and out of the house, and you're left with all that knowledge and expertise and nothing to use it on."

"That's why in many cultures it's normal for the grandmothers to raise the kids. Just tell me when you want to start."

"Ha! In your dreams."

"But having a partner must make a difference, don't you think? Not always having to do everything by yourself, and having someone to talk things over with? Someone who'll let you sleep in once in a while, or watch the kid so you can get to the gym, so that you're not constantly stressed and can keep your figure, too. You're the perfect example, having tried it both ways. With me you had Daddy, and with Ray you were on your own, weren't you? Or weren't you? Who *was* Ray's father, anyway?"

My mother pursed her lips.

"Not a good subject?"

My mother picked up a napkin and started wiping Aaron's mouth. "What a good boy. You finished your plate, sweetie pie. You may leave the table."

Aaron clambered off his chair. "Can I sit on your lap, Grandma?"

"You may." She opened her arms and let Aaron climb onto her knees. She hugged him close.

I had mixed feelings watching them together. She had sent her first child away and pretended he didn't exist. She had raised her second child with icy perfection. But her grandchild was her everything. I had never seen her come up short with Aaron. I was glad, yet at the same time it was unfair.

"So who is Ray's father, and where is he?" I asked sharply.

Instead of answering me, she stroked Aaron's head and said, "You need a haircut, young man."

I started clearing the dishes, peeved.

"Will you please bring in the vanilla pudding?" my mother called after me.

"Bitch," I snarled at the refrigerator.

"What kind of job did you have before you met Dad?" I tried again as we were doing the dishes together in the kitchen.

"I worked as a secretary for a while." The answer was grudging.

"Do you know you've never told me that before? What kind of office were you working in then?"

"What *difference* does it make?" My mother started scrubbing fanatically at the tiles with a rag and green soap. "You know, I can't even remember the last time we had a normal conversation. Everything is an interrogation with you these days. I guess I should be grateful I don't have a spotlight shining in my face."

"You've got it all wrong, Mother. *This* is a normal conversation—what a normal conversation should be like, anyway—about us, you and me. About the stuff that matters. The ones we're always having about supermarket coupons and Lina's eyelid surgery, *that's* what isn't normal."

"Excuse me?"

"You're never willing to discuss anything. Not even now, now that I've been finding out all kinds of things about your life that are important to *me* as well. Who are you really, Mother? I haven't got the slightest idea."

My mother pushed the rag into my hands and walked away. "Right. You do the rest."

I looked around. The kitchen was already spotlessly clean.

CHAPTER 47

RAY

"I've got some good news for you."

I braced myself. What other people considered good news was often the worst news you could imagine. But Mo's eyes were so shiny that I figured it might actually be true this time.

"You're moving to a new ward very soon. One where you'll fit in better. Doctor Römerman wants you to come see him, to talk it over with you. I'll be there, too."

I nodded. You had to have someone you could trust, and I had Mo.

"Can I tell you a secret?" Mo leaned forward until his face was close to mine. It made me feel uncomfortable. "On the new ward you'll be given a bigger suite. And you have three guesses what you'll have room for in there."

I didn't dare guess the thing I wanted most in the whole wide world.

Mo started making swimming-fish movements with his hands. "But I haven't breathed a word to you, all right?"

He walked out of the common room on his way to the social workers' office, and I was left alone, standing by the window as usual. *My fish!* Did he really mean I was going to get my fish back?

I raised my hands over my head and started running through the common room like a soccer player who's just scored a goal. I kept cheering and running up and down. I kept it up until Richard put his hands to his ears and started moaning, "Stop it! Stop it!" Then Mo poked his head out of the office and said, "Ray, I know you're happy, but take it down a notch, okay?"

"I'm doing my best," I answered.

"You won't tell a soul yet, all right?"

"Okay."

Dr. Römerman explained to me what being placed in the new unit would mean. It was the "autism unit" and was meant for people who weren't good at feelings. Like me.

I would have to stick to a strict daily schedule and would have to keep going to therapy.

"Fine!" I wanted to shout. "Now tell me about my fish!" But Mo, sitting beside me, was watching me, so I tried to control myself.

"During the intake session, you made a request," said Dr. Römerman. "You asked if you could have your aquarium in your suite."

I leaned forward. "Yes? Yes?"

"We have decided to grant your request."

"That means you're getting your fish," said Mo, with a meaningful wink.

"But," said Dr. Römerman, "first we'll have to take the dimensions of the tank into account. If it's too large, we'll give you permission for a smaller one. Would that be a problem?"

I shook my head. "François! Maria! Hannibal! King Kong! Saturn! Venus! Peanut! Raisin! Margie!"

"I see," said Römerman. He put on his horn-rimmed glasses and started writing something on his notepad. "I think we'll move you next Tuesday. If you want, you may visit the new unit today with Mo. Would you like to do that?"

"Then we can take a look and decide where your aquarium would go in your new suite," Mo added.

Again I was overwhelmed with an indescribable sense of happiness. On an impulse I threw my arms around Mo and rested my head on his shoulder.

"Well, well," said Dr. Römerman, smiling.

Mo patted me on the back. "I'm delighted you're so happy, Ray."

The autism unit didn't look any different from the orientation unit. It had the same sofa and chairs upholstered in blue with thin red stripes, the blond oak coffee table, the yellow polyester carpet . . . even the plants were in the exact same places.

Most of the residents were out, at therapy or at work, the autism social worker told me. He was an older man with a beard and a deep, calm, and clear voice. There were only two of the residents in the common room. They were on a break between activities.

They didn't say hello. They didn't even seem aware of our presence. One of them sat on the couch reading a book about ferns. The other was working on a 1,500-piece puzzle.

I was going to like it there.

"You'll have more freedom here," the new therapist told me. "But we'll start you off slow. The first few weeks you'll remain under close observation. If all goes well, you'll be given increased independence. Such as being allowed to go to the library on your own, or the canteen."

"Can I see my cell?"

"Your suite. I must warn you, it isn't in the greatest shape. We're having it painted, and you'll be getting new furniture."

We walked into a corridor lined with steel doors fitted with little shutters. My cell was at the very end. The social worker tapped in a code and the door swung open.

I stepped into the bare room. There was a stench of sweat, and one wall had a huge damp spot on it. "It hasn't been cleaned yet," said the social worker. "But I warned you."

I started pacing. From one wall to the opposite wall I was able to take exactly eight steps. So I'd have three more feet than before, a definite improvement. The new cell was also wider, and it had a window that looked out on an empty wall.

"What do you think?" asked Mo.

"Very nice," I said.

"We're going to clean it up for you, naturally. *That* won't be there anymore, either." The social worker was pointing at the huge stain on the wall, as if it had escaped my notice.

"Great," said Mo. "If we place your bed here, you'll have room over there for your aquarium."

"Oh, yes, I'd heard about that," said the new social worker. "A saltwater aquarium, right? What kind of fish do you have?"

"All kinds. Angelfish, surgeonfish, clownfish, blennies . . ."

"We have another a resident here who also keeps fish. Only in his case it's just two goldfish in a bowl."

Mo glanced at his watch. "We have to get back, Ray. It's almost the end of my shift."

I looked around the empty space one last time.

Not too bad, I decided.

CHAPTER 48

IRIS

Lawrence asked me to go for a brisk walk with him around Vondel Park. "I'm feeling too restless today to sit in a chair. Besides, all my pants are getting too tight, and I don't believe in dieting."

On our way to the park I could tell by his face that he was upset. Once we were inside, he began, "What were you thinking going after Asscher like that? This guy has been the Van Benschop family's accountant forever—don't you see this makes us look very bad?"

"But how was I to know he was Van Benschop's accountant?"

"Research!" he snapped. "Isn't that what you were told to do?"

"I am sorry," I said. "I only just found out myself. But just so you know, he has a very strong motive."

"I don't want to hear about it. All I want to say is that you are not allowed to come near him or the Van Benschop family ever again! Now, about the things you *are* supposed to go after . . ." Huffing and puffing, he started telling me what conclusions he'd drawn from reading the report. I had trouble keeping up with him. "The number of eyewitnesses is very low, as you yourself already established, and Boelens was clearly coerced into making his statement. Tunnel vision," he said, with a grand sweep of the arm.

"That should be the mantra of every twenty-first-century criminal defender."

I nodded in agreement, just barely managing to avoid a big puddle.

"There is, however, a great deal of solid evidence pointing to Boelens's involvement in the Angeli double murder. To begin with, he was definitely present at the scene of the crime. That's forensically established, not a shadow of a doubt; we're talking about a trail of blood leading from their house to his." Suddenly Rence stopped short. He stood bent over forward, hands on his thighs, gasping for breath.

"Maybe we should slow down a bit. It's important when exercising to preserve your stamina," I said.

"No way." Rence hauled himself up again. His face was red and his hair was so windblown that his bald spot was unveiled. "Tomorrow I'm bringing my running shoes. Let's do this every day from now on."

"Super."

"Are you making fun of me?"

"Of course not."

Rence stepped up the pace again. The park was nearly deserted, even though the sun was out for the first time in ages.

"Anyway. Let's talk about the murder weapon. The Ikea knife. The forensic report isn't completely positive that the weapon used to kill the victims was Boelens's knife. The Netherlands Forensic Institute puts the likelihood at seventy-two percent. That's up there, but it's not a hundred percent. I should add that they found no trace of the victims' DNA on that knife. It's possible that Boelens did a thorough job scrubbing it clean. I myself always advise my clients to use Brillo." Rence paused to give me a chance to laugh at his joke.

"Now, everyone knows Ikea's stuff is complete junk. Why is the Höteknöte desk lamp so cheap? Because after spending an hour in line to purchase it, it'll last exactly a day and a half, two hours, three minutes, and fourteen seconds before crapping out. I'd wager that if that knife was used to stab someone fourteen times—granted that we humans are sixty percent water, but then there are also the extremely hard bones and tough sinews as well, so . . ." Rence was so out of breath that it was growing harder and harder to understand him.

"Let's walk a little slower," I suggested.

"Not going to happen. So anyway, I'd imagine the knife wouldn't come away from that kind of use without a scratch. Maybe the tip would be bent or the blade would have come loose. Maybe we should have it tested to determine the effect of that sort of violence on an Ikea knife. Although . . ." He looked at me with a frown. "Let's assume we can prove the knife can't have been the murder weapon. Then we're still left with the problem of Boelens being at the crime scene."

"There was some other residue on that knife. Some complicated chemical name, I haven't had the time to find out what it was," I said.

"Oh, that. I did ask someone I know in Forensic Services. It's vulcanized rubber."

"What?" I stopped dead in my tracks.

"Come on," said Rence, not slowing down even a mite. "Keep going."

I had to run a few steps to catch up with him. "As in car tires?" I asked.

"Car tires, rubber sheeting, wiring . . ."

Again I stood still. "You don't say."

This time Rence was kind enough to wait for me. His face was extremely red.

"Did you know that Boelens had slashed Rosita's boyfriend's tires not long before the murder? If the rubber on the knife came from that, it can't have been the murder weapon."

"Because . . . ?"

"Because if he had washed the knife carefully enough to erase all traces of the girls' DNA, why would there still be some rubber residue? Surely that, too, would have been cleaned off?"

"Interesting," said Rence. "But we don't know, naturally, how stubborn the rubber deposit is. Maybe it's impossible to get rid of no matter how hard you scrub. Besides, it won't count as new evidence."

"Why not?"

Annoyed, Rence shook his head and set off again, though fortunately at a more normal pace. "Iris . . . don't you get it? It's already in the court record. Except that the defense lawyer never bothered looking into it. That was dumb. And a great shame for Boelens. But no good to us. No, what I'm more interested in is Boelens's presence at the crime scene. What was the guy doing there?"

"I haven't yet figured that out either. He's a man of few words."

"Maybe I should pay him a visit."

"I'm not sure there's any point. He's exceptionally cagey. He won't even tell his psychiatrist what happened. He just keeps repeating he's innocent."

Rence studied my face closely. "Or is there another reason you don't want me to meet Mr. Boelens?"

I felt myself go red. "What do you mean?"

"Nothing."

I tried to think if it was wise to confess that Ray was my brother. Chances were, Rence already knew. But how could he? To be on the safe side I said airily, "Oh, I've got plenty of reasons. You know me."

"Don't worry. It's not as if I won't help you with your brother's appeal anyway," he said nonchalantly.

I gasped, though I should have guessed. "How did you know?"

Rence put a fatherly hand on my shoulder. "Come, let's get back to the office." After a few steps he took his hand away. "I knew as soon as I heard the last name."

"Boelens?"

"Right."

"You knew immediately?"

"Of course." He seemed very pleased with himself.

I tried to find the connection but didn't get very far. "But we don't even have the same surname. Do you know my mother, then?"

"I can't answer that question. Client confidentiality."

"Oh, come on. How do you know my mother's maiden name?"

"Don't forget I've been a lawyer for a long time, and so has Martha. Between us, we've come to know quite a few people."

"So you know my mother."

"I don't know her personally. I know people who know her, and so . . ."

I remembered the strange conversation I'd had with Martha a while back. What had she said? That she'd had little choice but to hire me? Had my mother had something to do with it? "Tell me. You can't leave me hanging on like this."

"Maybe you shouldn't have kept quiet about the fact that your new client was your half-brother. How did you put it again? 'It'll be prestigious for the firm' or something? All this time I was hoping you'd tell me yourself."

What could I say to that?

We walked back to the office in silence. Before going in, Rence said, "But you're forgiven, kid." He sighed. "Forgiven *again,*" as if my employment history at Bartels & Peters had been one endless stream of lies and deception.

"What now?" I said when we arrived at the place in the hall where I'd have to climb the stairs and he had to turn left to his office.

"Just push ahead, kid. I'll run your rubber theory by Forensic Services. And you'll have to try to get Boelens to open up to you about the day of the crime. What was he doing at the crime scene? Why did he leave his work early when he didn't usually get out of there before three P.M.? That's what we have to know."

"It's very hard to get any information out of him," I said. "Half the time it's as if he doesn't even follow what I'm saying."

"That's yet another obstacle we have to overcome. I do think I'd like to meet him myself before investing any more time and energy into this probe. Not because I think I'll be able to get through to him better than you, but because it's always good to have a second opinion. Especially since I think you may be getting too emotionally involved. There's a reason we have a rule never to take on a family member as a client."

"I'll arrange it so that you can come with me next time," I said.

"And stay away from Asscher. And the Van Benschop family." Rence parted from me with a lordly nod.

CHAPTER 49

RAY

We were sitting at breakfast. Normally, I hated having to sit through communal meals, but since I knew I'd be getting my fish back soon, anything was bearable.

"So I hear they hooking you up with the other Rainmen." Over the past several days Rembrandt kept coming and sitting down next to me. Usually I didn't respond when he talked to me, but this time I nodded.

"The big question is, where's our homie André"—he jerked his head at the social worker with the glasses—"going to keep his stash now? But hey, he'll find another sucker, know what I mean?"

André was looking in our direction. His eyes were narrowed behind the round frames.

Rembrandt went on in a whisper, "He can tell we talking about him. Just look at them sneaky-pig eyes. Trying to read our lips, man."

"No gossiping at the table," said André. "We're not running a boarding school for girls here."

"No shit! I'm so sick of all the hairy dudes in here. What about you, Rainman?" He elbowed me in the ribs. I froze and stared fixedly at my peanut butter sandwich on factory bread. "Speaking of bitches, when's our horny little social worker back on duty? With you leaving and all, I might be getting some of the action. Why don't you put in a word for me, Rainman?"

"You know that kind of talk will get you in trouble. I'm giving you your first warning," said André.

"What for? I done nothing wrong!" The black cowboy put his hands up in the air, as if to emphasize his innocence.

"You know perfectly well what I'm talking about."

"Chill, bro. I'm cool." Rembrandt waited for the social worker to turn and talk to Hank, sitting next to him, then leaned in close. "If I was you, I'd pay him back for what he done. Messed you up good, didn't he? Or maybe you like getting put in the hole. That it, Rainman? Give you a boner, does it, those paper pants rubbing your prick?" Rembrandt took a bite of his sandwich and chewed with his mouth open. I twisted my head the other way. "Soon you'll be put in another unit and then it'll be too late."

I hoped breakfast would be over soon. But I saw the social worker with the glasses taking another piece of bread from the basket. We had another five minutes at least.

"Know what you do?" Rembrandt's cheesy breath blew in my face. I leaned as far away from him as I could and tried to make myself think of my fish.

"Get in his grill, bro. Say that you know he did it. Then watch, and see what he does."

Venus. Saturn. Hannibal. King Kong. Peanut. Raisin.

"Rembrandt. Warning number two. No whispering at the breakfast table. The next warning means you'll be confined to your suite."

"Oh yeah?" Rembrandt stood up. Everyone stopped chewing. Except for Richard, who was cutting out shapes in his bread as usual. Today it was a butter-and-jelly Christmas tree.

Rembrandt suddenly pulled his pants down and whipped out his penis. "Know what you can do? You can suck my dick." He started waving the brown thing back and forth. "Suck my big black dick," he said again.

"Now you're asking for trouble," said the other social worker, the new one. I hadn't seen him around much.

"I know you want it. Look at the size of it. Nothing like that little thing you carry around in your panties." Rembrandt was swinging his penis around less than a foot from where I sat. The other guys started cheering, as if this was a good thing.

I dived under the table.

"I'm giving you *one* last chance to pull those pants up, and then I'll have to call in security and we all know how that ends."

"Fuck you, motherfucker," I heard Rembrandt say one more time. From my hiding place under the table I saw him hoisting his pants back up.

"Fine," said André. "But you're grounded for at least a week. Breakfast is over."

I stayed where I was. I only came out when everyone had left the table.

Since I had kitchen duty, I had to clear the dishes and take them to the little kitchen, and then I had to load the dishwasher and put the food away in the fridge or pantry cupboard. Suddenly I wasn't alone in the little kitchen: the social worker with the glasses had come in. I worried that maybe he'd overheard what Rembrandt had said about confronting the guy, before he'd started whipping out his penis. I hastily put the leftovers back in the bread bin, concentrating on my task.

"What the hell was that, at breakfast?"

Here it was again—trouble. I tried to think about my fish again, and hoped he'd go away.

"Are we playing deaf? As long as you understand that not a word Rembrandt says is true."

I opened the refrigerator and put the cheese and butter on the shelf.

"Well, anyway, that's not what I came in here for. What I wanted to tell you was that you're having a visitor today."

I hadn't been expecting Iris Kastelein, but it was good news. Now I could tell her I was getting my fish back. She'd be pleased. I knew she would.

"Your mother. It's her first visit, isn't it?"

I froze. The jam jar I was holding slipped out of my hands. It crashed onto the floor tiles. The red jam spattered everywhere.

"Does that alarm you? Why?"

I said nothing, but stared at the red mess, thinking about the last time my mother had visited me, in the prison. "It's over," she'd said. "I can't come and see you anymore. I just can't take it any longer." She hadn't cried or hugged me that time.

"Did you hear what I said?" André tapped me on the arm.

There was a long silence. I couldn't think of what I was supposed to do or say.

He cleared his throat. "I see. Fine. I'll come get you around eleven, then. You'll do a good job cleaning up this mess, won't you?"

CHAPTER 50

IRIS

My mother had a bridge game every Wednesday night from seven thirty to ten thirty at the senior center a couple of blocks from her house. The bridge club had a jolly-sounding name, "Gray Matters." The name referred not only to the color of the players' hair but also to the fact that bridge is supposed to keep your brain cells youthful. My mother still colored her hair. She always said she'd stay blond until the day she died. I'd even had to promise I'd touch up her roots before she was laid out for the final viewing.

At her house a light was on in the hall, and one little lamp in the living room. If you want to show there's nobody home, do by all means leave on a single lamp, like a lighthouse beacon guiding ships into port. I'd tried to point this out to her, but according to my mother, thieves wouldn't dare break in if they saw a light, even if it was just one brave little lamp in a corner of the room.

Binnie was babysitting Aaron, and I wasn't completely reassured that it would go well. The last time she'd watched him I'd found chewing gum in his hair the next morning. But Binnie had sworn she wouldn't give him any gum and my mother was the only other person I trusted to watch Aaron and I obviously couldn't ask her to watch him so I could break into her house.

I stuck the key in the lock and glanced over my shoulder. A man walking his dog strolled past, but didn't seem to be paying attention to me. I turned the key and stepped inside.

I was nervous. Even though it was unlikely my mother would come home early from her bridge game, it *was* possible. She would be unpleasantly surprised to find me here, to say the least.

Since my mother was refusing to tell me anything about Ray or his dad, I had decided to take it upon myself to do a little investigating. The last time I had gone hunting for clues in her study, Ray had been the focus of my search. This time I wanted to see if I could ferret out anything that might lead me to Ray's father.

I tiptoed through the living room—not that anyone could hear me—and shone my flashlight on my mother's little desk.

The aquarium looked spooky in the dark. It gave a greenish-blue cast to the room, as in an underwater cave. The fish were calmly swimming around, blissfully unaware.

I opened the drawers and examined their contents. My mother's bank statements; warranties; gas, water, and electric bills. A box of rubber bands and paper clips. A street map of Amstelveen, bus tickets, and a two-year-old postcard from Spain sent by one of my father's former colleagues. I leafed through her address book. It contained so many names of people I didn't know that it didn't make me any the wiser.

A gold fountain pen lying on the desk caught my eye. I had seen my mother write with it often, but suddenly I noticed its resemblance to the pen I'd seen Peter van Benschop use. I spun it around until my flashlight revealed the inscription: *Van Benschop Shipping Co.*

Where did my mother get this? A pen like this was too expensive to be handed out as a freebie. Someone must have given it to her. I picked up my mother's address book and redirected my focus. What was the name of the old man I'd met in Victor Asscher's parking lot again? I found him under the *A*'s. *Antoine*, without a surname.

"Aha," I said out loud. How many Antoines could there be? I took out my cell phone and dialed the number. After a couple of seconds, I heard an old man say "Hello?" I quickly hung up and thanked myself for having a restricted number.

My mother knew Antoine van Benschop. The Van Benschop family was one of Bartels & Peters's biggest clients, going way back. Had my mother asked Antoine van Benschop to get Bartels & Peters to take me on? The perfect job: practically around the corner from where I lived, and part-time to boot. In hindsight, the way I'd been hired was almost too good to be true. Before I'd had Aaron, it wasn't unusual for me to be approached by headhunters on behalf of competing firms. Once I got pregnant, the offers had dried up completely.

My mother had urged me to look for another job. I'd reluctantly put a few feelers out, but it seemed that no law firm in the land was just waiting for a young single mother wishing to work part-time. Just before I went on maternity leave, however, Lawrence had called. He just happened to be looking for a part-time associate. I was too delighted and relieved to be surprised. My colleagues were envious. "You're going to work part-time at a firm? Really? Unbelievable."

The more I thought about it, the more certain I grew. It couldn't have been a coincidence that I was offered this job. Martha had dropped hints about it, Rence was indirectly acquainted with my mother, and Van Benschop had reacted like a cornered dog when he'd heard my name. The question was: How did my mother know Antoine van Benschop, and what made her able to demand favors of him?

The two hours Aaron had been in Binnie's care had passed without calamity. He'd just woken up briefly, and she'd given him some juice. I was delighted.

"All I can do is guess," I said after filling Binnie in on my visit to my mother's house. "The question is, how well does my mother know him? I'm beginning to think . . ."

". . . that Antoine van Benschop is Ray's father."

"Hard to believe, but it's beginning to look that way. What do you know about this Antoine? Didn't you do some research on—what did you call them—your 'future in-laws'?"

Binnie put her hands to her temples—it helped her think, she said—and closed her eyes. "Antoine van Benschop . . ." she muttered a few times. "His name isn't originally Van Benschop, for starters."

"What?"

"He had a different name originally, something along the lines of Blumenveld, Parrotpiss or whatever, doesn't matter. He took his wife's name when they got married."

"Well! I assume he had a good reason?"

"What do you think? Pop van Benschop, Barbara's old man, insisted that his sons-in-law take the family name if they wanted to take over the family business."

"Okay . . ."

"It's coming back to me now," said Binnie, letting go of her temples. "I also remember that Antoine had been employed at Van Benschop, and was just about pushed into Barb's arms by Pops."

"True love."

"True love," Binnie agreed.

"Who would ever turn down the Van Benschop Shipping Co. as a dowry?"

"*I* wouldn't, anyway."

"My mother used to work as a secretary. Maybe she worked there. Maybe she met Antoine van Benschop that way."

"But what are you going to do? Confront your mother? Call Antoine?"

"I may do both."

"You know what's such a weird idea?" said Binnie. "If Antoine is Ray's father, then Ray is Pissing Peter's half-brother."

I grasped my head in both hands and groaned.

"Don't worry, at least *you're* not related to him by blood," Binnie added with a laugh.

At nine thirty the next morning I was put through to a secretary. "Mr. Van Benschop only comes in on Tuesdays and Wednesdays. I'm afraid you'll have to call back next week."

"I must speak to him urgently," I said. "Perhaps you'd be kind enough to tell him that Iris Kastelein of Bartels & Peters would like to speak with him about an important matter."

"I've made a note of it. But I can't promise anything. Mr. Van Benschop makes up his own mind."

"I'm sure he does."

Antoine van Benschop returned my call the same day. The exchange was brief. Before I had a chance to explain what I wanted with him, he said, "Stay out of it."

"What do you mean?"

"You know perfectly well what I mean. If you're a sensible girl, you'll leave well enough alone."

"Well! Going by the vehemence of your reaction, I almost *have* to conclude you are Ray Boelens's father."

"There is absolutely nothing *to conclude,*" he said, and hung up.

CHAPTER 51

RAY

On entering the visiting room, my mother didn't say anything. She gave me a curt nod and sat down in the chair across from me. The first thing I noticed was the huge gold bee pin on her red sweater. Then I saw that her hair was a bit shorter than the last time I'd seen her. It framed her face in tight little waves. I wished I could reach out and touch it.

She folded her hands together and parked her elbows on the table. "You must be wondering what I'm doing here."

I realized I was shaking, and pushed my hands under my thighs so they wouldn't flap and hover. Was she going to hug me? Was she going to tell me I was her son and she'd always be there for me, even if we did no longer live together?

"I understand you've met your sister." She gave a little laugh, but I didn't think it was a genuine laugh. "And that she's offered to help you with your case."

I nodded. Iris Kastelein. My little sister.

"That's what I've come to speak with you about." My mother was looking at me sternly through her blue eyes edged with black. She had never been fooled by my size. She knew exactly how small I was on the inside.

"But first, let's discuss something else. Am I to understand that you're allowed to keep your aquarium in your suite?"

"Yeah! Next week." I suddenly started feeling anxious. "I can, Mother, can't I?"

She smiled. "Of course, darling. You can have your aquarium. As long as you're good, and you're not breaking any rules."

"I am. I really am."

"Good. I know you're doing your best, Ray."

"Yes." I pulled my hands out from under my legs. They remained calm, resting in my lap.

"But there are some new rules you'll have to follow. Rules you don't know about yet."

"Okay."

"Would you mind getting us some coffees?" my mother asked André.

"Fine," he said. He left the room with the guard. It surprised me. Mo never got visitors anything to drink. And he would never leave the room, either.

"The new rule, Ray," said my mother slowly, "is that you've got to stop telling everyone you're innocent."

I wasn't sure I'd heard her right. "But I *am* innocent, Mother!"

"The new rule," my mother repeated, calmly and emphatically, "is that you say you *did* commit the murder. That's the condition for keeping the fish. Do you understand?"

I shook my head and shoved my hands under my legs again, just in case.

"Ray, you killed Rosita and Anna. You're going to write that down, in a note to your sister. You're going to tell her she has to stop her ridiculous snooping. And that it's best if you don't ever see each other again. Never." My mother took out a notepad and pen and slapped them down in front of me. "Write down what I said."

"No," I said. "I didn't do it. I *really* didn't do it! *You* know that. And I don't want to write a letter to Iris Kastelein, either. I want her to go on helping me."

She stared at me coolly. "Very well, then. I didn't want to have to do this, but you leave me no choice." She leaned down to take something else out of her bag. It was a cookie tin.

Where was the social worker with the glasses? Where was the guard?

My mother lifted off the lid and took out a frozen icepack. Underneath was something wrapped in a paper towel with pictures of little kittens. She unfolded it. "You asked for it."

A mutilated fish fell out. Even though it had been sliced open on both sides, I immediately recognized it. It was Hannibal, and I could see his intestines.

The next fish she rolled out of the paper towel was King Kong. He, too, had been cut open. I couldn't look. Not King Kong! Not my majestic King Kong, the one I'd bought for Anna!

"Now you will write down exactly what I tell you, or there won't be any fish left in your aquarium." I knew my mother meant it. This was the Last Warning.

As my mother dictated the letter and I started writing down the words without even thinking what they meant, I tried not to cry. King Kong! Hannibal! My best, my most beautiful fish. They'd always been there for me, swimming around calmly in their perfectly calibrated world where the pH levels were exactly right and they got fed every day the exact same amount of fish food at the exact same time.

"Here we are," I heard André say. He walked in, followed by the guard. My mother had just told me to sign the letter.

I wrote my name at the end of the note.

André coughed, staring with raised eyebrows at the dead fish on the table. My mother quickly rolled them up in the paper towel and stuffed them back in the tin.

"Are you done, Mrs. Boelens?" asked André.

"Yes, indeed." My mother's voice sounded completely normal. She picked up the notepad and tore off the top page. "There, that goes in the mail."

My mouth opened and a bellowing sound came out. I banged my fists on the table. *"No! No! No!"*

"You'd better give him something to calm him down," said my mother. She got up and put a hand on my shoulder. "It's best this way. Believe me, Ray. In a few days you'll have your aquarium and you'll have forgotten about this whole thing."

She strode out of the room with André close behind.

The guard let me bawl for a while longer. Finally he tapped me on the shoulder. "Time to pipe down."

I couldn't, not even when I tried following the steps I'd been taught in therapy at the Mason Home. First I took a deep breath in through my nose. Then I blew it out of my mouth. I breathed in and out a few times like that, trying to calm down. It worked for a few seconds, but then I started screaming again, banging my fists on the table.

"Stop it!" The guard started shaking me. "Stop it, damn you!"

I nodded and tried to stop, I really did, but I was just too upset.

The guard slapped me in the face. I hadn't seen it coming. My head snapped back and my hands went up to the spot where he'd hit me.

"There," he said. "Now we'll get you back to your suite."

CHAPTER 52

IRIS

"I just don't get it," I said to Mo. He moved up a little closer and touched my hand. It was sweet of him to come right over after I called. Though it was strange to see him sitting here on the stained couch in my living room. Aaron had already gone to bed. Luckily he'd fallen asleep with no problem this time. "Why would Ray not want to see me anymore?"

"Yeah, hard to understand."

"Did something happen? In the unit? In his session with the shrink?"

"Not that I know of. On the contrary, he seemed to be over the moon about getting transferred to another floor."

"Which floor?"

"The autism unit. You'll see, he'll be much happier there. The residents are much calmer there; they keep to themselves more. Besides, Ray can keep his aquarium in his room."

"That's great! But maybe that's why he wrote the letter. He doesn't feel the need to be a free man anymore now that he's finally getting his fish back."

"Possibly. But why would that make him want to stop communicating with you? I had the impression he was starting to enjoy your visits."

I felt myself blushing, even though it wasn't a real compliment. So I focused on rereading the letter Ray had sent me; it still didn't add up. After insisting all along that he was innocent, here, suddenly, was his confession to the murders in black and white, on a sheet of A4 paper, with the request never to contact him again. "Do you think I did something wrong?"

"Of course not. You were great. I thought the way you talked to him was just right. He was trying so hard to relate to you and answer your questions, even though it was very hard for him. In all these months, you're the only one who's come to see him. That's something he won't soon forget, believe me."

"But I failed." It came out sounding more dramatic than I'd intended, and to make matters worse I felt my eyes well up. Crying in Mo's presence was the last thing I wanted to do.

You could tell this was someone who was used to dealing with emotional people. He shook his head and patted my arm. "You haven't failed. Why would you even think that?"

I let out a tremulous sigh. "I guess I'm just tired." I hadn't realized how stressed out Ray's case had made me.

"Who wouldn't be? Look at what you're dealing with. It's a lot to take in. Can I make you a cup of tea or something?"

"That would be great!" I think my exclamation embarrassed us both. I felt the blood rush up to my cheeks again, and Mo suddenly wasn't looking my way. "Uh, I'm sorry,"

He cleared his throat. "No need to excuse yourself. I . . ."

I don't know *what* came over me. Whether it was because it was the first time I heard some uncertainty in his voice, or because it occurred to me this might be the last time I'd ever see him, I leaned forward and kissed him on the cheek.

For a moment we just stared at each other. Then he took me in his arms and kissed me back. It felt good. We kissed some more and for the first time in years I felt like I was someone different than a stressed-out, single, working mother.

"Mommy?" We both looked up to see Aaron standing in the room with a teddy bear in his arms. "What you doing?"

I didn't have a clue what to say. "I . . . uh" was all that came out of my mouth.

"You must be Aaron," said Mo. "My name is Mo. I was just going to make Mommy some tea. Would you like something to drink, too?"

Aaron didn't say anything. He just stared at him.

Mo stood up and went to the kitchen as if it was the most normal thing in the world. A little while later he returned with a pot of tea, two mugs, and a glass of apple juice on the hideous plastic tray my mother brought back for me from her last spa vacation.

"Here you go," he said to Aaron, handing over the juice.

Aaron accepted it, and seemed perfectly happy sipping his drink next to me on the couch, with my arm around his shoulder.

"The autism unit, huh? So Ray has a social disorder?" I asked, to get the conversation going again.

"That's one way of looking at it. Autism is a complicated thing. Recent studies show that people with autism aren't able to filter the way we are. Imagine what it would be like if you were constantly aware of the clock ticking, the neighbor's television blaring, the bright color of that pillow there, that that vase over there contains exactly twenty-three flowers, and . . ."

"Twenty-seven," said Aaron. "I want to go back to bed." He got up and started walking back to his bedroom, so I followed and tucked him in. I wondered if I should say something about Mo, but Aaron's eyes were already shut and his breathing was getting heavy and slow. I looked at his sweet face and realized that I really, really loved him, and whatever happened I would never let him go. I didn't care anymore if I would lose my job or what the girls at the day care thought. We belonged together. I touched his soft hair and hoped he was dreaming a happy dream.

When I came back, Mo was sitting on the couch again. I sat down next to him. "Sorry about that," I said.

"He seems like a great kid," Mo said.

"He really is."

Then he leaned over and stroked my cheek. "I'm not in the habit of making house calls, you know."

I felt myself blush. "I understand that. But you know what's so ironic? I never had any concrete evidence of Ray's innocence. No matter who I spoke to, no matter what I found out, everything still pointed to Ray as the likely culprit. But the moment I stumble on a lead, or, rather, my boss does, Ray changes his mind and I have to stop."

"You don't still think he's innocent, do you?"

"Yes. I still do. I just can't imagine he lied to me. I don't think he's even *capable* of lying. What do you think?"

"Maybe he wasn't lying; maybe he truly did believe he was innocent. But just think it through a sec, Iris. Of *course* he did it. It does all add up, doesn't it? A man who's developmentally delayed, a neighbor who drives him off his rocker, and a mean mother who keeps tormenting him, to this day."

"What do you mean? My mother hasn't had any contact with Ray in years."

"Actually, she did visit him just recently."

"What? Why wasn't I told about that?"

"Why, what's so strange about that?"

"Everything, believe me. But how did you hear she was such a terror? Who told you?"

He shrugged. "Stephen, my colleague, gave me that idea."

"What did he say exactly?"

"I just remember the general drift. Which was that Ray's mother—your mother, too—is an awful witch. Sorry."

"What makes him think that?"

"I believe he was there when she came to see Ray."

"But why would he say my mother's a witch? Wasn't she being nice?"

"We didn't discuss it, really; we're not that close, to tell you the truth. But Stephen made it pretty clear that your mother was bad news. In his eyes, anyway."

I wondered what my mother could have done to give him that impression. She was normally every inch the lady. It was what lay beneath the surface that was unsettling. "Could my mother have said something to Ray to make him not want to see me anymore?"

"It's possible. Why not?"

"Do you think the visit was recorded? There are security cameras everywhere, aren't there?"

"They get erased after twenty-four hours, I'm afraid."

I jumped off the couch. My mind was racing. Something had definitely happened between my mother and Ray—for sure. I grabbed my phone and pushed it into Mo's hand. "Can you please call security?"

"It's too late. Really, there's no point."

"Call them anyway. Maybe they still have the tapes."

The phone call took a few minutes. Mo explained the situation and then all I heard on my end were things like, "Ah, I see," "So . . . ," and "Okay."

When he hung up I could hardly contain myself. "What did they say?"

"You'd better come back to this couch," he said, "because you're an extraordinarily lucky lady."

"Really?" I sat down next to him.

"It seems that there's an ongoing investigation into Stephen's activities because of his possible involvement in drug smuggling, so they've been saving every tape he's in."

"Fantastic! When can we pick them up?"

"That's a problem. They can't release them. But they will let me 'drop in' tomorrow when they 'happen to be' reviewing the tapes."

"Great!" I cried.

"Why? To be honest, I don't really understand what you're after."

"I think my mother made Ray stop talking to me," I said. "And I hope the tapes will show that's what happened."

"There's no audio on the tapes, though."

"Then I'll hire a lip reader."

"Nothing's going to stop you, is it?"

CHAPTER 53

RAY

I was sitting in front of my aquarium looking at the fish. Watching Venus and Peanut sticking their heads out of their grotto every once in a while and then darting back inside. Watching Margie swimming around and around in her little circles. Watching François, who'd grown quite a bit bigger since the last time—nearly nine years—I'd seen him. It's lucky that fish live a long time when you take good care of them. We were going to have many more years together.

"You'll get used to it," I told them. "It's hard at first, but you'll see, you'll start liking it in here eventually."

I could stay here all day if I wanted, the autism unit's social worker had told me. This time they wouldn't come and take me away, the way they did the last time I saw my fish. I remembered being pushed into the police car still calling out their names.

It happened just after I had found Rosita and Anna. I tried not to think about what I saw when I pushed the door open and saw them lying in the hallway. So still. Dead.

"Hey, Anna. Hi, Rosita," I whispered anyway. "We were almost a family. Weren't we?" But Rosita didn't say anything back to me.

She just lay there staring at the ceiling. She'd finally found a way to shut me out for good. It made me very sad.

I touched Rosita. I put my fingers on the hollow of her collarbone, the *fossa supraclavicularis,* and the most beautiful spot in the whole entire world. Her skin was still warm. I don't know how long I sat there. I do know that at some point the smell of blood went up my nostrils and made me gag.

I ran back to my own house. When I stepped into the hallway, I saw a garbage bag that I hadn't left there. I heard the water running.

"*Ray!*" My mother was washing up. She was shocked to see me and I was shocked to see her. She let something fall into the sink and wiped her hands on a dishtowel. "What are you doing here?"

I stared at her and wanted to say something, but couldn't find my words.

"Why aren't you at your work?"

"I couldn't do it anymore," I said.

My mother looked at my feet. Her face turned pale. "There's *blood* all over the floor!" My mother ran into the hall and opened the front door. "Oh, Christ, you've left footprints all the way from their house to yours. Oh my God!" Back in the kitchen she started wrapping up whatever it was that she'd dropped into the sink in some newspaper.

"Why didn't you stay at work? You should have stayed at work today. Jesus Christ, Ray!" She had tears in her eyes. She took the newspaper-wrapped package from the sink and took it out into the hall. I followed her and saw her toss it in the garbage bag.

"I can't stay. I'm sorry. I . . ." My mother was hardly ever at a loss for words. "You just shouldn't have shown up here." She shook her head. "Now I won't be able to help you. Sorry, but you're on your own." She picked up the garbage bag and walked through the living room to the back door. "I've got to go. I'm sorry. I didn't want it to end like this."

Just before stepping outside, she turned and grabbed me by the shoulders. "You can't tell *anyone* you saw me today, you hear, Ray? No matter what they ask you." She was hurting my arms with her grip; she was very strong, my mother. "Look at me, Ray. Focus. They are going to come and get you, Ray. I wish they wouldn't, but you only have yourself to blame for it. You should never have come home this morning. But if you tell them I was here, I won't be able to take care of your fish, and then who knows what will happen to them. Do you understand? You have not seen me here. Don't even mention my name."

After she left I went back to my aquarium and sat there reciting the fishes' names until I was calm again. And then they came and took me away, just like my mother had told me.

Now that I had my fish with me in my cell, I no longer needed to say their names over and over again. I felt at peace. Nothing bad could happen to me. I was safe at last.

I shut my eyes and listened to the drone of the pump. At home the aquarium had been downstairs, so I couldn't hear it when I was in bed. I was glad that, in here, the aquarium was less than five feet from my bed, so we could see each other all the time, my fish and I. I loved the noise the aquarium's equipment made. I loved the gentle metallic glow it cast.

Daylight, Van de Akker once told me. The aquarium's lightbulbs mimic the daylight filtered through the water on a sunny day—fifteen feet under the surface of the ocean. I liked it so much better than ordinary light that I decided never to open the curtains again.

CHAPTER 54

IRIS

Not ringing the doorbell at my mother's house was starting to be a habit with me. The only difference between this visit and the last one was that it was broad daylight. I stuck my key in the lock and pushed the door open. No sooner had I done so than I heard my mother call out, "Who's there?" It pleased me to hear the uncertainty in her voice.

I walked down the hall to the living room, where I found my mother sitting on the sofa with a newspaper she must have been reading spread out beside her. She stared up at me, startled.

"It isn't very nice to have someone just come walking into your house, is it, Mother?" I said. "It must be pretty scary to hear a key turn in the lock when you're home alone and not expecting anybody. Or have you never had that feeling? Do you even *have* any feelings?"

"Jesus, Iris." My mother pressed her hand to her heart in a theatrical gesture. "You just gave me a heart attack! What were you thinking, waltzing in here right in the middle of the day? You know I want you to ring the doorbell before you come in."

"I do know that. Actually, there are lots of things I know about you."

"Excuse me? Are you starting that again? You've got to stop, do you hear me, Iris? I've had enough of this nonsense. I'd appreciate it if you'd leave. Now."

I heard a noise in the kitchen, as if something were being shoved aside. I froze, and listened. Silence. I must have been mistaken. The empty space where the aquarium had stood all those years caught my eye. You could still see the outline of it; the wall would have to be repainted. "Isn't it great, Mother, that Ray has his aquarium again?"

My mother didn't answer.

"So noble of you to let him have it. I know how fond you were of those fish. Especially the dead ones. I do wonder, though—how did you persuade the lab in Utrecht to send them back to you? What did you tell them? That you wanted to bury them in your backyard, with a nice little gravestone and flowers?"

"What are you talking about?" My mother picked up her newspaper and pretended to read. But I could see her eyes drifting emptily down the page.

"Or did you tell them the truth? That you needed those poor fish to trick your own son?"

She lowered the newspaper. "Now you're going too far. I've had enough of this nonsense. You may be my own flesh and blood, but don't think I'll hesitate to call the police if you don't leave my house."

"No, you wouldn't hesitate to turn in your own flesh and blood. We know that now."

"I'm calling the police." But she didn't move.

"You do that. You and I can have a nice little chat while waiting for them to show up. Because I've come to know some interesting things about you these past few months. I found out you have a son. And that that son has a father. And that the father's name is Antoine van Benschop. And that when you got pregnant, Antoine van Benschop paid you off with a nice nest egg. And that he also—and I must thank you, Mother—did me a favor when *I* got pregnant, by arranging a convenient little job for me. Have you two stayed in contact this whole time? Do you still see each other?"

"Stop it," said my mother. "Stop it, stop it, *stop* it."

"I won't, sorry. I've only begun to scratch the surface of the fascinating secret life of Agatha Antonia Boelens."

"Which is none of your business."

"You're wrong about that. *It is* my business. Not because I'm your daughter, but because Ray is my brother."

"Spare me the sentimental claptrap. You don't know the first thing about Ray."

"I think I do. And I've come to realize that you and Rosita are two of a kind. Just like her, you fell for the charms of a married man and got knocked up at a very young age. Was that why you despised her so?"

"Amateur psychology." My mother picked up the newspaper again, but I could see her hands shake.

"Why don't you tell me the truth for once in your life? What do you think you are doing? Bribing the staff at a criminal mental facility? Threatening a patient? Those are punishable offenses. We're talking prison, Mother. Are you still in touch with Antoine van Benschop?"

"Yes."

"Where, when, how often?"

"Not as often as before. But we're still in touch." She said it with palpable reluctance.

"Were you sleeping with him while you were married to Dad?"

"Yes." She stuck out her chin defiantly.

For a moment I was speechless, thinking of my kind-hearted father. He'd worshipped my mother, always did everything she asked of him, to the irritating extreme. "How did you manage it? How long has this been going on?"

"Forty-five years," said my mother, with a tinge of pride.

"You're mad! What were you thinking? Did you think he'd ever turn his back on the shipping business to be with you?"

"No. I always knew he never would."

"And yet you went on seeing him. *Why?*"

"Because I love him," she snapped.

I shook my head. "I find it hard to believe you're capable of loving anyone. You dumped Ray in a home, you never showed me any real affection, you cheated on your adoring husband all those years and . . . oh, I guess there *is* Aaron. You do love Aaron, don't you? If it weren't for that, I'd think you were a robot."

My mother didn't show any reaction. She didn't even blink. I had the urge to slap her in the face. Hard.

"Fine, don't say anything. I can fill in a great deal of what's missing myself." I took a deep breath, speaking slowly and stressing every word. "You don't want me looking into Ray's case because you are afraid certain things will come to light that are . . . *inconvenient.* Your affair with Antoine van Benschop, for one. But is that the only reason? You know, killing someone with a Börja knife isn't easy. Ikea quality—not so good, you know? After putting it to the test, the applied sciences research lab has established that it's impossible to stab someone in the chest fourteen times with that knife. By the seventh or eighth jab, the blade will usually snap off. And anyway, Ray's knife had already had its share of action, when he used it to slash the tires of Victor Asscher's Jag. No, Mother. The murder weapon used was probably a top-quality chef's knife similar in size and shape to the Början. Forensic Services thinks it would have been a Wüsthof, the twenty-three-centimeter Le Cordon Bleu Chef's Knife, to be precise. Forged from a single piece of steel. Indestructible. So when I read the report, I thought to myself, 'Shit, I *know* someone who owns one of those fancy German knives.' "

My mother sat on the sofa, motionless.

"Please talk to me. What am I supposed to think? I need your help, Mom. Please explain how this all happened. I know you know. Did you tell Ray to kill Rosita? Did you give him the knife? Or . . ." I could not imagine the alternative.

My mother was still sitting there not blinking an eye. Again, I felt the urge to slap her in her face, if only to make her react.

"We *are* done here. *You're* done." It wasn't my mother's voice. It was a male voice. I nearly fell backward on the glass coffee table.

Antoine van Benschop stepped out of the kitchen holding the twenty-three-centimeter chef's knife from Wüsthof's Cordon Bleu series. "Is this, perhaps, the knife you mean?"

I tried not to show how startled I was to see Antoine here, in my mother's house.

Antoine stepped closer. I wondered if I should make a run for it, but I couldn't believe the old man would actually attack me, especially with my mother present. I decided to try to stay calm. Cool. Collected. Panicking would only make the situation worse, I decided.

"Listen, Iris, your mother is not a murderer. She just did what she had to do," Antoine said with an authoritative voice that reminded me of his son Peter's.

"What have you done, Mother?" I asked. "Were you the one who stabbed Rosita? And her little girl, too? Little Anna with the angelic blond curls?"

"I had no choice," my mother finally said. "I wish it were

different. I wish I could change it all, but Rosita left me no choice."

My legs started shaking. "*You* killed her. You?"

"Rosita was blackmailing us. Asscher had told her everything about us. She was threatening to tell Antoine's wife *and* his father-in-law. Don't you see that everyone's life would have been ruined? My life, Antoine's life, the Van Benschop family's life. Even your life, Iris. And what about the shipyard? The whole goddamn company would have been ruined! So yes, she needed to be stopped. But what worried me the most . . ." My mother paused for a second, seemingly overcome with emotion. "What worried me the most was the way that dirty little whore was driving Ray up the wall. I could tell it was just a matter of time before he'd snap. And you think you know Ray, but you don't. You don't know what he can be like when he loses it. I just couldn't let that happen."

"So you did it all for Ray? You honestly expect me to believe that you had his best interests at heart? That's a little hard to believe since he's serving your time, locked up in a mental institution, and . . ." I could hear my voice tremble.

"Enough!" Antoine waved the knife at me. "Your mother warned you to stay out of it, but you just had to go on with your silly investigation, didn't you?"

It crossed my mind that Rosita had been staring at this very knifepoint just before she was killed. I needed to stay cool. Keep talking. I tried to appeal to my mother. "Why are you letting him threaten me? Why did you let Ray take the rap? We are your children!"

My mother shook her head. She looked sad, but it was hard to trust anything about her. "That was never the intention. I did my very best to keep him out of it. How was I to know he'd leave work early that day? He never came home early. *Never.* But it's too late now. Ray can live in the institution with his fish and be safe. And I know you won't agree, but I promise you that it's better this way."

"But what about the little girl?" I said. "How could you do that to her? Not only *stab* her, but to put out that cigarette on her . . ."

My mother was crying now. "She should have been at day care, like she always was in the mornings. How was I supposed to know that . . . She just came running out and Antoine . . ."

"Antoine?" I looked at the old man standing next to me. Again the resemblance with his son Peter was striking. "You were there, too? You killed the girl and made that cigarette mark on her?"

"He was trying to protect Ray!" my mother exclaimed. "Since Ray hates smoking, we . . ."

"Enough!" said Antoine. "You are leaving us no choice, Iris. Just as Rosita left us no choice." Then, suddenly, he pounced, putting me in a stranglehold. He was surprisingly strong for his age. I felt the bent tip of the knife graze my throat. Cold steel cutting my skin. It was sharp. It didn't take much pressure for it to cut. I tried to twist out of Antoine's grip, but I couldn't shake free. I looked at my mother. She wouldn't let this happen—would she? I was still her daughter. Her goddamn daughter.

But my mother was stoically staring straight ahead at the wall.

"Mother?" I was a bewildered fifteen-year-old again, back in the red-light district crack house. "Mom?" My voice was getting more and more panicked.

"I *begged* you. I begged you several times, Iris. You should have stayed out of this."

Only then did I realize I was in real danger. I had to try to escape. I jabbed both elbows back into Van Benschop's rib cage. He didn't budge. All it achieved was allowing the knife to dig deeper into my throat. I felt something warm trickling down my neck. My heart pulsing against the blade.

"*Move.* We're going into the kitchen. So we don't make a mess in your mother's living room. Start walking."

I looked at my mother. She *had* to intervene. I still could not believe she would let someone kill me. She would step in at the last minute. Just as she had that time in the crack house. But she looked frozen.

Antoine pushed me ahead of him. "Mother?" I pleaded, my voice sounding all choked and teary. "*Say* something! You can't let this happen!"

"Shut up." Van Benschop kicked me in the back of the knees. "You've got only yourself to blame."

I looked at my mother, convinced she would save me. Her mouth opened and then closed again.

I felt myself being pushed into the kitchen. I tried to push back, but somehow Antoine knew how to force me to walk ahead of him. I thought about how easy it would be just to slide the blade across my throat, slicing open the artery. I'd be dead in less than a minute.

Who would take care of Aaron? What would happen to Ray? I felt my whole body go into a spasm of shaking.

Finally, after what seemed a lifetime, my mother spoke up. "No, Antoine," she said. Her voice sounded weepy, barely convincing. But she did say it. "*Stop.*"

It was all I needed. Van Benschop's grip on me slackened for a second. I stomped hard on his foot and managed to slip from his grasp. Then I kicked him in the groin. He crumpled forward, crying like a wounded animal.

I raced out the front door and into the street.

The police arrived within minutes. Neither my mother nor Antoine tried to run.

I stood across the street and watched them being led to a police car by two officers.

My mother looked old and helpless in the bright sunlight. For a second our eyes met. Then she turned away, a final fierce gesture. And with that, the squad car door was closed.

"Are you okay?" asked the policeman who was standing next to me. "The ambulance will be here soon to fix you up. That's quite a nasty cut you've got on your neck there."

I couldn't answer, because I honestly didn't know.

CHAPTER 55

RAY

It almost looked like my aquarium down there, fifteen feet below the surface. Only, everything was much bigger and you could see much farther, you could see as far as you wanted to. As I swam around, I started naming the fish in my head. "Hey, you, little zebrafish, I see you darting away, but I see you! You I'll call Hank. Oh, and you, parrotfish, nibbling on the coral over there, your name is Rembrandt."

I had gone scuba diving every day since I'd been there. I'd stay under until the diving instructor ticked on his watch, telling me that our time was up and we had to swim back up to the surface.

Then I saw her. A beautiful queen angelfish colored the brightest of blues and the yellowest of yellows with a lovely crown-shaped spot on her forehead. "You, I will name Rosita." I thought about the letter Dr. Römerman had told me to write. I had never been able to, but sitting by the ocean I knew exactly what I wanted to say. It wasn't much. But I felt it was true.

I never meant for anything bad to happen to you and Anna. I will always love you.

I didn't mind having to go back to the shore. I knew Iris and Mo and Aaron were waiting for me at the dive shop. Then the four of us would walk to the beach, and Aaron and I would build castles together, just like I used to do with Anna, except that these were made of sand instead of Legos. Then I'd play paddleball with Mo or go for a swim with Iris Kastelein who was definitely my sister over to the raft out in the middle of the bay.

We'd sit there for a while, dangling our legs in the water, our faces turned to the setting sun. Soon the sun would disappear into the water. Iris said this time of day was called "the magic hour."

I had to ask. "So are we a family now?"

She looked at me with those clear blue eyes edged in black, just like Mother's, only much kinder.

"I think a family is more like—a father and a mother and their kids. So that's not really what we are. But we *are* related. We're kin."

I stared at my feet.

Then Iris said, "Hey, why am I making it so complicated? Of *course* we're a family. Maybe not your average family, but we definitely belong together. What do *you* think?"

I cleared my throat. "I always wanted to belong to a family."

"Me too," she said. "Me too."

ACKNOWLEDGMENTS

Thanks to all the beautiful people who made *Girl in the Dark* happen:

Patrizia Gelvatti
Sarah Miles
Michael Carlisle and Lauren Smythe at Inkwell
Hester Velmans
Emily Krump at William Morrow
Chris Herschdorfer and Dorien van Londen at Ambos|Anthos
Masie Cochran

ABOUT THE AUTHOR

Marion Pauw (b. 1973) is one of the bestselling writers of the Netherlands, whose books also have been published in Germany, Turkey, Italy, Hungary, and the United States. She made her debut with *Villa Serena* in 2005. Her big breakthrough to a wider readership and critics came with *Girl in the Dark* (2009), which won the Golden Noose Dutch Crime award. The Dutch film rights were sold to Eyeworks and successfully adapted into a movie. Next, she wrote the thrillers *Sinner Child, Jet-Set,* and *Kicking the Bucket. The Savages* is considered to be her debut as a novelist. She most recently published *Something We Need to Tell You.* Her books have sold half a million copies in the Netherlands. Marion lives in Amsterdam with her two children.